Monsters in the Mills

edited by Christa Carmen and L. E. Daniels

Glass House Books
Brisbane

Glass House Books
an imprint of IP (Interactive Publications Pty Ltd)
Treetop Studio • 9 Kuhler Court
Carindale, Queensland, Australia 4152
sales@ipoz.biz
http://ipoz.biz/

Printed in 12 pt Adobe Caslon Pro on 14 pt Avenir Book.

ISBN: 9781922830685 (PB); 9781922830692 (eBk)

Book design: David P Reiter

Cover design: Mr. Michael Squid, mrmichaelsquid.com

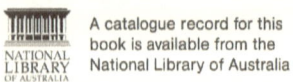

A catalogue record for this
book is available from the
National Library of Australia

Contents

Introduction *Faye Ringel*   iv

The Children at the Spindles *Mary Robles*   1

The Web *Joshua Rex*   4

Under the Frozen Sky *Brennan LaFaro*   15

Darkness Repeats *L. E. Daniels*   28

Mill Dues *Jason Parent*   44

The Cleaner *Victoria Dalpe*   56

The Circle *Christa Carmen*   68

In the Belly of the Mills *Elizabeth Devecchi*   89

The Gourmand *Mr. Michael Squid*   91

The Spinning Mule *Paul Magnan*   101

Gourd Guy *Rick Claypool*   112

Strike *Jessica P. Wick*   119

Blackstone *Steven Belanger*   134

The Medians of Providence *Erric Nunnally*   149

Cinched *Kristi Petersen Schoonover*   166

We Created a God Monster *Gage Greenwood & Kylee Jones*   178

Kiss of Death *Ricardo D. Rebelo*   187

The Devolution of Doyle *Aron Beauregard*   199

Introduction

Faye Ringel

I grew up in Norwich, Connecticut, once a thriving manufacturing center, now the site of brick and stone mills in various states of abandonment and adaptive reuse. In the late 1960s, some were still operating: a few friends had summer jobs at Thermos, when those vacuum bottles were made in the USA.

My friends reported that on their first day at work, an old hag approached the "new girls" and cackled at them, "See that machine over there? It'll EAT your FINGERS!"—and she waved her hands at them, each missing a digit or two. Amazingly, they didn't run screaming. It was business as usual: mutilated bodies and minds were horrors inherent in the system.

In New England, abandoned mills are common: derelict or converted to loft housing, they loom like the ruins of Gothic cathedrals or castles, relics of a feudal past. The haunted reputation of some abandoned mills attracts ghost-hunting urban explorers, but in their heyday and in their decline, they housed monsters. Serving these monsters sucked the life out of generations of children and young women workers. In these stories, the mill machinery may be monstrous; the grounds or ruins of the mills may be haunted; the workers themselves may be portrayed as less than human—but the system of industrial capitalism is itself the monstrosity. Karl Marx and Fredrich Engels's *Communist Manifesto* of 1848 may open with "A spectre is haunting Europe—the spectre of communism," but in his theory, the mill-owning capitalists were the vampires, exploiting their workers and draining their life force. The victims of the capitalist system, the mill workers, evoked the living dead, having lost their humanity to the monstrous machines. The machines create body horror: missing parts, white lung disease, and other mutilations of the human form. Though the mills may be dead, some of their victims remain, as Steven E. Belanger writes, suffering "pinched nerves and herniated disks, coughing up plaster-dust-colored phlegm."

Rhode Island holds the birthplace of the Industrial Revolution in America: Old Slater Mill in Pawtucket, where Samuel Slater brought the plans he had memorized for a water-powered textile mill, breaking the British monopoly on the technology. The mill required large supplies of cotton, grown cheaply by Southern slaves. Joshua Rex's story "The Web" draws on this history, in which "lords of the loom partnered with lords of the lash," and all were woven together with inextricable ties in the first "World Wide Web." Jessica P. Wick's "Strike" is another view of this symbiotic relationship of mill, machines, workers, and owners.

It wasn't only Marx who likened capitalists to vampires—how often have we heard Chambers of Commerce or politicians refer to manufacturing as "the lifeblood of our nation"? But when the capitalist vampires took themselves—and their jobs—out of state or offshore, they left behind towns drained of that lifeblood, along with empty husks of mills ripe for haunting. As Ricardo D. Rebelo writes, "If every person who died in a mill haunted it, we would be shoulder to shoulder with ghosts..."

Prior to the decline of manufacturing in New England, the region had seen the collapse of agriculture, as farmers left New England for more fertile, less stony fields to the West. By the late 19th century, decaying farmhouses were a regular feature of the landscape, along with stone fences that marked formerly cultivated fields. Today, mills and other industrial relics are highly visible, while those farmhouses have disappeared into cellar holes. Many authors in this anthology have family connections with the mills, their mothers or grandparents worked in them, and they've grown up with the ruined or repurposed buildings.

You are holding the first anthology devoted to Industrial Gothic Horror, though we are not the first to tread on this haunted ground. Some New England horror writers have transformed the metaphorical monstrosity of capitalism into actively monstrous beings. Stephen King's "Graveyard Shift" shows the influence of Lovecraft with monsters haunting the basement of the textile mill where King once worked. Another dreadful job inspired King's "The Mangler," with its possessed laundry machine. Paul Magnan introduces us to a different haunted machine, "The Spinning Mule," amidst the crime and punishment of present-day Fall River, Massachusetts. Also set in Fall River, in the "ruins of the past with little hope for a future," is Jason Parent's "Mill Dues." In both stories, lives on the margins are drawn to abandoned mills. And, like these stories, Ricardo D. Rebelo's "Kiss of Death" reminds us that the victims of the system cannot leave the place of their torment, their Hell on Earth.

The horror of child labor is particularly haunting: see Mary Robles's powerful poem, "The Children at the Spindles," in which she gives voice to the voiceless, supplying memories and bodies for those who left "no memory or trace of themselves." Elizabeth Devecchi's poem, "In the Belly of the Mills," merges present and past in what feels like a traditional playground rhyme. Other terrifying glimpses of this widely accepted system of child abuse can be found in the stories by Jessica P. Wick, Paul Magnan, Ricardo D. Rebelo, and Aron Beauregard. Steven E. Belanger's "Blackstone" takes us deep into a haunted mill's history of worker exploitation that continues to the present day: the horrors inherent in that system more frightening than the ghost of a child victim. Brennan LaFaro's "Under the Frozen Sky" provokes shivers as its child protagonist encounters that history.

Though H. P. Lovecraft despised the industrial development that brought immigrants into Rhode Island, his mother's family wealth came from entrepreneurship and a high-tech fringing machine—and was lost when his enterprising grandfather died. Errick Nunnally's "The Medians of Providence," haunted by the writer who claimed he was Providence, turns Lovecraft's worldview inside out, remaking weird fiction for the 2020s. Aron Beauregard's "The Devolution of Doyle" features a heartless cast of mill owners and an overseer more monstrous than the monsters they create.

When abandoned mills are repurposed, their history remains. Some mills in New England have become luxury residences: the oil-stained wood floors and exposed brick are selling points—the former workers and the deceased permanent residents, less so. Kristi Petersen Schoonover's generational haunting, "Cinched," warns us of what lies beneath the upscale condos.

Victoria Dalpe's Providence mills have not been transformed into expensive condos. In "A Creak in the Floor, A Slant of Light," from her collection *Les Femmes Grotesques*, they house artists, transients, victims of high rents—and monsters in the basement who prey upon them. Her story for this anthology, "The Cleaner," performs a necessary if horrific function in this economy. Punk musicians and artists fill a condemned Providence warehouse and provide similar prey in "The Gourmand," by Mr. Michael Squid, who is also our cover artist. Similarly, Gage Greenwood and Kylee Jones's "We Created a God Monster" features would-be rockstars who practice in an old mill, but these monsters come from the protagonist's id, from "a catharsis of guilt and fear." Rick Claypool's "The Gourd Guy" combines contemporary legends of an organic haunting with a repurposed mill that has again begun to decline.

L. E. Daniels's "Darkness Repeats" returns to the factory-floor horrors of her Stoker-Awards® nominated short story "Silk," from *Hush, Don't Wake the Monster: Stories Inspired by Stephen King*, combining them with the horrors of war. Based on family memories, her "Spectacle Cloak" factory reflects the brief revival that Northern textile mills experienced during World War II, supplying blankets and wool coats from buildings that were outdated firetraps.

Rhode Island has an officially recognized haunted mill, the Ramtail Factory in Foster, where a night watchman hanged himself from the bell rope. Thereafter the bell would ring by itself at midnight, and the millwheel would revolve backwards against the current. Christa Carmen's "The Circle" combines folklore from the Ramtail Factory with other tales of the notoriously isolated town, as well as characters inspired by modern-day demonologist ghost hunters Ed and Lorraine Warren, whose investigations in Burrillville, Rhode Island inspired *The Conjuring* franchise.

The essence of Gothic horror is abjection, that which we deny, regard as worthless, and throw away. Garbage, blood, excrement, the hated Other—that nevertheless returns to haunt us. Ending where I began, in Norwich, the castle-like Ponemah textile mill thrived during the Civil War with Irish labor, willing to do anything to avoid being sent to the front. After the War, however, they unionized—and were fired and replaced by workers recruited from French Canada. The same scenario repeated for several generations with successive waves of immigrants, until the mill owners moved the operation to North Carolina to avoid unions. Factory workers are the abjected material of industrial Gothic horror. Their bodies are disposable and interchangeable, used up and thrown away when no longer needed—or when they unionize. Small wonder they return to haunt us, no matter how we abject or repress the memories. The monsters in the basement, the haunted machines, the cannibals, and more are the outward signs of a system that first fed and then ate its own.

– FAYE RINGEL is Professor Emerita of Humanities, U.S. Coast Guard Academy, New London, Connecticut and the author of *New England's Gothic Literature: History and Folklore of the Supernatural* (E. Mellen, 1995) and *The Gothic Literature and History of New England: Secrets of the Restless Dead*, Anthem Press (2022), International Gothic series. She contributed chapters to *The Cambridge Companion to American Gothic* (Weinstock, ed. 2017) and to *A Companion to American Gothic* (Crow, ed. 2013); she has also given papers and published on (among other subjects) New England vampires, urban fantasy, Lovecraft, King, Shirley Jackson. She has been a program participant at conventions devoted to science fiction, fantasy, and horror for decades. Her PhD in Comparative Literature is from Brown University; she lived in Providence through the 70s and early 80s. She lives in Norwich, Connecticut in the house where she grew up, built over the Mohegan Royal Burial Ground.

The Children at the Spindles

Mary Robles

In the early mill villages
children powered the machinery
with their voices. They wore coarse cloth,
and denim bibs, and gutted light in their eyes
the color of wolf's clothing. At Blackstone River,
they ran along the mills and sang, past
dams and millponds, counting hours, chanting,
cotton fever, cotton fever as it overtook the Spinners.
Into this land he came, a small boy

with a crooked back. He sat alongside his mother
and his hair looked painted-black. Her long linen skirts
pale as oatmeal lay about her booted feet,
and she toiled her days away. Her little son stayed
near her ankles, changing spindles, changing spindles
(all the boys—overalls, girls—skirts and blouses, New Orleans
trampled cotton). The fabric they spun seemed to build,
and pile, and fill, and overwhelm the very room.
Deep into the Finishing Room he ran

with his mother at the sound of the bell,
where the hours fell around them like heavy garments
rank with damp, rust, insects, hair of the long-backed women
standing over the whirring machinery like gowned birds.
Cotton fever with soapstone on their hemlines, dreaming
of the banking fires of home. His wending voice
was black calligraphy on parchment. Where did his voice go,
if not out to the field where the farmers were haying,
stoking the golden burned hair of the land,

to play? This black-haired boy, stooping
to change spindles, a song in his throat for his mother.
He watched her work. He touched the thin rag of her skirts,
and she spoke of canals, then railroads, *cotton fever*,
fisher cats, and *unskilled workers*, and the child sat
with his back aching. For so long his eyes
had seen only spindles, spindles, thread and fabric,
carding machines, spinning machines,
and looms so that he crept around the mill

with not much in his heart, asking for money.
Asking the cold walls for money,
asking the black dolls in the foundation for money,
tugging at his mother's skirts,
wanting money for food, to be warm, to be away
from the thick air. The place stank and hung
with sour raw fabric. He thought he would go mad,
he crept and stooped. One day his mother had to carry him
to the spindles and guide his hand to change each one.

He wrang his raw fingers and rocked himself
in the pitiful damp room.
He closed his eyes, and a black bird
shining and wet touched his face. It stood
on his shoulder and spoke: *Do you grieve?* it asked.
Yes, I grieve, the boy said. The bird's voice sounded
like a bent violin. *What is yes?* the bird replied
and moved its head like a pendulum.
You will not grow straight, you will never be a man

in the grist or sawmill.

You touched the millionth spindle where I live.
My twin flies in the power looms, we eat the cotton cloth.
We cover the earth with threads that turn to bone.
The boy slept deeply and dreamed,
and his muscles and back relaxed.
When he awoke, his mother was holding him.
The whirring sounds of the looms had stopped.
His mother sang to him,

and her pale skirts all around her
looked like long wings.
From the torn fabric around her body
began to fall *sugar, wire, fish, shingles,*
endless cotton. Salt, molasses, bush corn, rye.
Lime, gypsum, coal. Hemp and oil.
Scythes, chairs, bricks, and twine.
Cords of tanner's bark, wood, soapstone, timber.
Spirits, boards and plank, wool. Coffins, iron, nails.

The boy held his mother's hem and they collected their tarnished belongings.

Leaving no memory or trace of themselves, they gathered their voices, and flew upward.

– MARY ROBLES is an MFA candidate in poetry at Bowling Green State University and Poetry Editor at *Mid-American Review*. Her work has been published in *AGNI* and *Salt Hill Journal*, among others, and is forthcoming in *Spoon River Poetry Review* and *Strange Horizons*.

The Web

Joshua Rex

George Hope departed home—a simple I-house, two rooms up, two down, attached kitchen on the back—and set out on foot along the river road north that led to his most recent successful business venture. It was a brisk, cinder-gray November morning, the road wet and clotted with mud and dung. Though he could afford a horse, nay a team of them, to draw him in his own carriage if he so desired, he was not his brother Richard. George did not go about in silk stockings and silver buttons and carry a golden-tipped walking stick, nor did he ride through the town's humble streets in an opulent, elevated vehicle clad with fringe and footmen like some haughty European prince. George's waistcoat was plain, brown, cut from broadcloth; it reflected more the thrift of a farmer than one of the town's most affluent merchants. It would be wrong to do otherwise—that is, to wear that which belied his faith. He had for these two decades since the death of his wife worn such clothing, and the hat of the Quaker, and so too did he subscribe to the axioms and teachings of that good faith. Yes, he would go on foot (like his Lord had done) to do his business—good, and honest in his work, relations, life. He had been blessed with success and prosperity as a result of his renunciation of the Great Evil that, sadly, continued, and would continue for another generation, to pervade the town.

Three miles on, George spotted the dam in the river, and beyond, the red mill building, two and one-half stories, forty-five feet long, thirty wide, five-ranked façade, small bell tower at the center of the roof. George could hear the whirring of the water wheel as he approached the door; the clacking, insect sound of the water frame; the clock-like mechanization that made measurable production as well as profit. Though modest in appearance, the mill was nonetheless a revolution on the old river, the combination of George's business savvy and the technological ingenuity of Ezekiel Truth, George's partner. It was the first of its kind not only to spin cotton fiber, but to do the spinning, drawing, and carding all in the same manufacturing center.

Inside, George was met by the cacophony of the machines, and the grim glances of the operators seated behind them. Entire families, men, women, and children all laboring together, monitoring and tending to the machinery and the thread they produced. They looked up only momentarily from their work, bound to the endless churning of the wheel that turned the shaft, moved the belts, ran the equipment. Twelve to fourteen hours daily, paid not in coin but in credit, and in the assurance of food and shelter. Assurance for them, yes, and thus a guarantee for the partners, the mutual agreement that made Truth's Mill the incomparable success that it was.

George was told by the foreman that his partner was "at home," and so he left the noise and monotony, a filament thin as the thread of the spider trailing from one foot, and crossed the yard to the red clapboard gambrel house set at the bottom of a slope beyond the mill. There he rapped upon the door. It was answered by a servant girl who led George into a large chamber where sat his partner before a fire, smoking a long pipe and perusing the day's *Gazette*. Ezekiel Truth was tall and gangling, with thick white-blonde hair, a complexion like yellowy alabaster, and crow-dark eyes. Unlike Hope, Truth wore his wealth in silk and brocade, gold buttons and buckles, his ostentation of appearance often causing him to be mistaken for an aristocratic Frenchman rather than a patrician English gentleman transplanted from the motherland to what Ezekiel shamelessly referred to as "this backwater republic."

After salutations, Ezekiel bade George sit across from him in one of the upholstered Queen Anne chairs placed before the hearth where a substantial blaze burned. They spoke of matters of business and the daily operations of the mill—the primary concern being for Truth the recent murmurs of a workers' revolt.

"They complain of the length of the workday," Ezekiel said. "Too many hours, they say. Naturally, they would prefer to labor under the put-out system."

"Working in their homes, making their own schedules? No, we have discussed this. That way yields indolence and less profit," George said.

"Of course," Ezekiel replied. "It is no matter, ultimately. Reliant on our stores with the winter coming, it would be self-destruction for them to abandon their duties now. Though the summer may prove another matter..."

Ezekiel paused, glanced back at the servant girl standing beside the door. "Hettie, see if Mr. Ring has the carriage ready." The girl curtsied, departed. Ezekiel turned to George. "A free girl," he said. "The niece of one of Richard's slaves."

"Yes, I recognize her."

"And how is your *dear* brother, George? Rumor goes about that despite his recent near imprisonment he still plans to send a ship to the forbidden coast."

"It has not been verified, though I suspect this to be true." George in fact knew it *to* be true, but he had planned on first issuing one last appeal to Richard before exposing his plan and condemning his brother to what would this time most likely result in a jail sentence.

Ezekiel sipped from his glass, his eyes never leaving his partner's. "And so the question must be asked: If this is in fact the case, what is to be done about him? Your fellow Friends in the Society urge you to consult your Inner Light on the matter, for the will of God is greater than the will of Man, and he who is a transgressor must be held accountable for violating Divine Law."

"My morals and my heart are in agreement with what is right—

make no mistake, and do not doubt that if the moment of judgment arrives, I shall not shrink from the duty of seeking prosecution for Richard's crimes. I have done so before, and so again will it be my policy."

"You have always been a man of great integrity and principle," Ezekiel said. "I know unequivocally that your pronouncements here are nothing less than those of an honest and pious man of God." Ezekiel paused, relit his pipe. "Now then, enough on this most unpleasant matter. We have much of our own business to discuss."

"I would welcome eagerly a change in subject," George said, then continued with: "I have just this morning received word from our planter colleagues in the South that the cotton crop has been a successful one this season, and that both the supply and cost of raw product will be to our liking..." Figures were then discussed— prices, rates, quantities, the latest on the great tariff debate, until at length the tall clock near the hearth struck four, and with the November daylight waning, George departed the warmth of his partner's hearth and his genial company and stepped into the bitter wind scented with wood smoke and the salt tide.

He drew down the wide brim of his hat and started east, the thread trailing from one leg, along the road that led to Hard Town. There, he stopped at the humble house of Prime and Desire, two individuals George once claimed as property, now with a home of their own (partly sustained by George's aid) which they occupied with their substantial family of eight children, all born free as a result of the Gradual Emancipation Act, which George was integral in seeing passed into law. The family welcomed their benefactor warmly into their tallow-lit rooms, George taking the youngest of their brood onto his lap and placing in the boy's palm a silver coin which caused his eyes to widen in a manner that delighted George. The boy passed the coin to his brothers, who passed it to their sisters, then their mother, and finally their father, the latter stowing it in

the breast pocket of his tattered overcoat. Then the family shared
a meal of bread crusts and small side of beef around their crude
table, the sacred supper blessed by the good Quaker himself before
they commenced eating. While they ate, the weather worsened,
rain mucking the road. The family offered George shelter for the
evening, but he declined; there was more business to discuss before
the day was through, business much less pleasant than this, to be
sure.

So, he left the ramshackle hovel occupied by his manumitted
charges, and walked south on the high road that led up one of
the city's seven hills. The way became soft and soupy, and George's
shoes saturated with mud and water. But Providence was with
him, for a carriage, as if delivered by the hand of God himself,
appeared on the road and the driver, arrested by a signal given by
the sole passenger and owner of the vehicle, stopped the horses
and George was beckoned inside the dry cab. George recognized
the man—Joseph Brunwell—a local merchant and architect who
had designed the First Church as well as the Market Building and
even Richard's magnificent Federal mansion atop the city's highest
hill, where George requested now to be delivered. Brunwell gave
the order to the coachman, and the carriage started off at once,
rollicking and rumbling along the cratered road, the thread caught
in the door unfurling as if from a spool behind them.

Brunwell inquired about the mill, and George in turn asked
about the progress of the arcade presently under construction on
the west bank where a new town center was emerging. As the two
eminent men of town congratulated each other on their mutual
successes the carriage climbed higher, leveled off near the new
University Building, and then proceeded along the cobbles of
Neighboring Lane and thence along Amity Street to the entrance
of Richard's imposing brick mansion. Three stories of seemingly
immovable brick constructed only five years earlier, the house was
one of the grandest on the entire continent, and Brunwell admired

his work as he bid George a good evening and the latter departed, the driver noting the taut strand clear like glass following the Quaker up the brown sandstone steps in the moment before he cracked the reins.

The brass knocker upon the door was incised with the block capitals *R. H.* George used it, and was at once admitted into the grandiose silence of Richard's foyer by a dour servant. It was dusky and high-ceilinged, the hall flanked by a pair of marble busts mounted upon classically expressed columns. The elegantly sculpted heads stared omnisciently down at George as he strode the low-lit silence and mounted the elegant mahogany staircase. At the top of the stairs he turned, mounted three more steps, and upon the second-floor landing paused to regard the commanding view through the Palladian window at the end of the hall. The moon hung like an ornament in the window's upper arch, its light lying like frozen breath upon the hill and the mouth of the river below. George entered the bedchamber on the left where sat his brother before a modest fire—still at his business despite the lateness of the hour. Richard Hope, a colossal figure of nearly six feet four inches and over twenty-one stone, did not look up, though the hardness of his expression belied the presumed tedium of his affairs.

"What charges have you come to place upon me now, dear brother?"

"None as such. That is the duty of your own conscience," replied George.

Richard put his papers aside, "You will be disappointed, I'm sure, to find no self-examination in progress here. I have no time for it, nor much patience for those who speak in such lofty platitudes."

"Be not hard on me in your judgments, Richard," George admonished, settling into the seat opposite his brother without invitation. "I did my duty only as my own conscience decreed—not to mention that of the law."

"The law of the Society of Friends, to be sure," Richard scoffed.

"And of the new nation," George added.

"The *nation* only exists because of men like us who willed it so. It was made to serve *us*, not the other way around."

"Nonetheless, we are now bound to its code and strictures."

"Of which you fancy yourself the enforcer."

"No, brother. I am only a servant of God, concerned for the plight of your soul."

"You have become more nearsighted than enlightened since your conversion, do you know that, George?" Richard said. He gestured to a corner of the room, where emerged from the shadows a black servant whom George knew to be called Phippa.

Born before 1784's Gradual Emancipation, and therefore a slave for life, Phippa had labored in Richard's household both here and in his more modest home down the hill on the river. She carried with her a decanter and glass on a silver tray which she placed upon the mirror-shine surface of a mahogany side table, poured blood-red wine into the glass, and offered it to George, who accepted it with a sorrowful expression and watched as the woman drifted back into the semi-dark. Richard, regarding this, smiled and shook his head. "It has always puzzled me, how you, a self-proclaimed man of God, have nonetheless failed to recognize His proper order of things."

"On the contrary, I understand with *much clarity and gravity* the right and proper order of things. It is *you* who fails to see it, brother. I earnestly wish to help you. I beg you to cease your ambitions for this undertaking, for no doubt it will this time lead to certain prosecution and punishment."

"Undertaking? I must confess I know nothing of what you speak."

"There goes about a rumor that the *Sarah* is being loaded with one thousand demijohns of rum, swivel guns, rice, shackles. I wonder what sort of cargo you plan on servicing with such supplies? I appeal now to your better reason, Richard—quit once and for all this detestable business while there is still time!"

Richard chuckled. "It baffles me how it could escape you, George. You and Ezekiel Truth, processing your Negro-plucked cotton—'lords of the loom partnered with lords of the lash'—are no less entangled in the same sordid business of which you decry. It is your own self-righteousness that forbids this recognition, indeed acts as a blindfold. Are *you* yourself not engaged in the exploitation of the same labor, indirect and removed though it may be? Ah! George. At least I am without the shame of denying what is a *necessity* for the well-being of myself and my family. At least I do not attempt to feign moral outrage or immunity from blame. We are *all*, for better or worse, connected to one another in this matter. All of us, even you and your hypocrite Friends, share in the collective crime simply by participating in our economy, in acquiring what you require for your pious daily lives."

"I can see that nothing will convince you, Richard, and so rather than listen to the pontifications of an insensitive, I shall pray to God that He will shine His vast light within you, and that you might one day become aware of its shining salvation."

"I am my own God, brother. Same as you, same as any directing man of action who recognizes that in this life his own survival is paramount and must be maintained at any cost. I ask you this: what was the purpose of making a new nation if not to create a new pantheon, one that worships commerce and prosperity, rather than the illusion of eternal life?"

"Well, then, lord of this dubious kingdom on the hill," George said, rising, "I shall leave you to your own divine counsel. May it bring you all the comforts of earthly Paradise in lieu of those you shall be deprived of in Heaven."

"There will come a day when you will be forced to face the consequences of your complacency, George. Posterity will come for you no less than for me."

George turned at the door. "Indeed, dear brother, in this you are right. Posterity will come for us, and I am quite certain judge us most differently."

As he proceeded down Richard's grand stair, George noticed between the balusters a series of crisscrossing threads, again, like the work of a spider, though without symmetry or pattern. The threads ran along the steps too, and the floorboards leading to and from the front door. George paused near the newel post, reached out a finger, touched a strand, and hissed breath between his teeth. The thread was sharp, drawing blood; furthermore, to his surprise, it produced a sound like a plucked string—a low, solitary note that resonated softly in the hall. This sound caused the threads surrounding it to vibrate, each producing its own sound, variations in pitch that rang together in eerie counterpoint. Startled, George rose and made haste through the foyer, the busts of the white gods, bound one to the other by more of the threads, gazing fixedly after him.

George descended the hill to the primary road, which had once been used as a common path cutting between the plots of the early settlers. They had buried their dead here as well, in the years before the Central Burying Ground was established. In that ground lay George's wife, but the graves of some of the earlier burials here still remained, the stones standing in clusters like monolithic stone circles from the Old World. Looming above them on either side of the road stood the great churches and houses of the town, houses like Richard's, elevated above the noise, the commotion, the poverty, and the stink of the river below.

The moon was enormous, a great disk the color of taper light, and it illumined the cobbled road that led down the hill toward George's humble home. The houses he passed were built on a slant, with sloping stone stoops, pitched side-gabled roofs, flame-lit multi-paned windows and flaming tin lanterns hanging from wrought iron hooks beside the doors. More thread festooned their façades like limp chain, rippling in the breeze rising and falling like respiration. George, trailing his own thread, continued to the Towne Road along the water where the great ships floated, hulking shadows blacker than the dark, their furled masts like great crosses rising from their decks. The thread was here too, leading from the wharfs to every house, every tavern, every business, up and along the connecting roads. But it was thickest along the docks, whose pilings appeared almost woven with it.

George walked to the water's edge, knelt, dipped his hand in and brought up a handful of the strands. They were fine as baby's hair, though he was reminded of their sharpness by the saltwater sting in the cut on his finger, and thought better of attempting to tear them out. Despite appearances the threads were somehow inexplicably sharp, perhaps unbreakable. Though his rational mind contemplated their origin, his businessman's mind began to ponder how he might utilize them at the mill. He considered this in earnest as he made his way home, mounted the steps, mucked off his boots on the scraper and stepped inside. The thread detached as he crossed the threshold. It bifurcated; the two strands, branched, then again, and again, then again in continuous, exponential ramifications.

George lit a lamp and a spermaceti taper, then the logs in the fireplace. He ate a simple, solitary meal then settled before the hearth with his long-stemmed pipe and his Bible and read in the sacrosanct silence. At length his eyes began to close, and so he put out the fine candle and changed his clothing and laid upon his bed. Instead of sleep, however, came Richard's accusations. His brother's words made him increasingly uneasy, though ultimately George decided that the notions were groundless. He had long ago confessed his past sins to God, and God had heard them and had, to be sure, punished him, but He had also been merciful, revealing to George how he might gain absolution for his previous crimes against humanity. And oh, the glory of His mercy! If only Richard could see it! Closing his eyes, George unburdened himself in grateful prayer, and then, with the moonlight shining upon him like a benediction, settled into peaceful sleep.

At dawn, while George slept on, the town began to stir. The people, the horses, the carriages, the carts, the boats, all trailing lines, these lying atop one another in complex networks. Crate to hoof, tailor to sailor, mother to mill, infant to farmer, farmer to shackle, chain to captain, cargo to ship, merchant to rudder. And starting out to sea: Richard's ship, sailing south down the river toward the bay and open ocean where, as the sails unfurled, there rose from the stern a massive hank of the mysterious thread, and with it the filament grid lain over the town, the revelation of the silent work done as if by some colossal arachnid, entangling its screaming, helpless prey in its sticky, adamantine snare.

– JOSHUA REX is an historian and the author of several short fiction collections including *What's Coming for You, Haunted Victorian America: Ghost Stories,* and *New Monsters*, as well as the novella *The Inamorta* and the novel *A Mighty Word*. His fiction has appeared in *McSweeney's, Nightscript, Pseudopod, Tales to Terrify*, and others. He lives in Ohio.

Under the Frozen Sky

Brennan LaFaro

Silver moonlight reflects off the surface of the Seven Mile River as it rushes ever forward. The torrent runs dark as the night, its depths hidden but patient. On a well-worn path, lined by barren trees and safe from the icy cold water, Emma kicks a pebble and watches it skip across packed dirt before it plunks into the current.

A ghost-white plume of frozen vapor swirls toward the sky. It's cold enough for breath to freeze, and although the air is rich with the crisp, woodfire smell of impending snow, the midnight blue sky shows no sign of snowflakes. Sticks crunch and dry leaves skitter and scratch in the bleak winter night.

1:53 reads Emma's phone, and no missed calls or frantic texts. She rolls her eyes, performing a show of confidence for an invisible audience. In truth, she's never done this before, and wandering a moonlit dirt trail with just over five hours before school begins twists her gut with a thrilling mix of fear and adventure. Yet she makes no move to turn toward home.

The paper-thin walls of her house amplify the arguments, the harsh whispers that often cut deeper than the shouting. Screaming and yelling are emotional reactions. A product of the moment, as any twelve-year-old knows. To have the foresight to lower one's voice before insulting a loved one is to pull back the curtain on a cultivated and tended thought.

A notion she'd gleaned from her counselor.

It hadn't always been like this, though, and perhaps it wouldn't always be.

Emma smiles even as a tear forms at the corner of her eye. She pauses, the rubble of Slattery Mill drawing her attention. Broken teeth stick out of the earth in a crooked smile. Little remains of the historic building but crumbled stone and stories.

They made children work there. Emma had learned it in school, but her father dropped the nugget into conversation with increasing regularity and arched eyebrows, a barely disguised hint at their financial troubles and his attempts to shift blame.

Another bit of sage wisdom from her counselor. Sometimes people say things they don't mean to project their own problems onto those around them. Even when those around them are barely old enough to shave their legs.

"Asshole," she whispers, watching the river's hypnotic motion, and shoves her bare hands deeper into her pockets.

"Aren't you cold?" The words come from everywhere and nowhere all at once.

Bare branches clack and rattle at the wind's insistence and below, the water mutters like a television from another room. Emma's eyes skate from tree trunk to tree trunk, pulse racing, as she searches for the source of the voice.

"Down here."

The same voice, distant with an echo-like quality. This time, there's an anchor.

Her gaze settles on the riverbank. Facing the water sits a girl. If she's older than Emma, it's not by much. She wears a sepia-toned dress splotched with mud, or something equally grimy. Long hair the color and consistency of faded straw trails out from a gray scarf, wrapped around her head to keep the cold at bay. The girl turns toward Emma, her cheeks drained of color. Either cold or worry. Something has driven this girl out at night, the same as Emma.

If not for the girl's arctic blue eyes, she could be taken from a timeworn photograph.

Emma stares, heat gathering in her cheeks, knowing she should say something, but her mind is a blank page lorded over by an author with a terrible case of writer's block.

With a gentle pat on the frozen earth, the stranger invites Emma to join her. Emma's legs carry her down toward the sweeping water, stopping short of its chilly spray.

"I'm Emma," she says, as she drops to the ground.

"Thea," says the other girl. "Do you live around here?"

The aroma of ozone seems to intensify, as though Thea comes from a place where woodsmoke mingles with sharp cold.

Emma nods. Even a simple "yes" feels as though it might open the floodgates to the obvious question. Why would either one of them be out here in the middle of the night? She can't ask without also answering.

The girls sit in silence for a moment. Somewhere behind them, the night is rent by the sharp hoot of an owl. Emma jumps, then sneaks a glance at Thea. If the noise, the cold, or the company of a stranger phase her, she hides it well.

"Do you think the sky is frozen?"

Emma wrinkles her brow. "I…I'm not sure what you mean?"

"I've always heard that the higher you go, the colder it gets." Thea shrugs. "If something as alive as the water can become hard as stone simply because the temperature drops, what happens to a place way up there, content to sit still and watch over us, if it gets cold enough?"

A chuckle escapes Emma, and she claps a hand to her mouth, embarrassment settling in her stomach. "I didn't mean to laugh. I've just never thought about it before."

The corners of Thea's lips twitch, hinting at a smile, but her eyes remain the same. "It just seemed like something to say."

"An icebreaker."

"Pardon?"

"In school, when a teacher is trying to get to know their students, they ask questions to start a conversation. It's called an icebreaker."

Thea stares into the river for a moment, seemingly entranced by the ripples. "Appropriate." She laughs, a melodious sound that twirls into the night like Emma's crystalized breath.

Emma joins her, then stops abruptly. Numbness shifts to icy prickles, jabbing at her spine. She scoots away, only a few inches, but it's enough.

Thea's laughter dies. She tilts her head to the side.

"What's wrong?"

Emma climbs to her feet, backing further away. Her breathing intensifies, filling the air like a fog machine in a low-budget horror movie.

"Your breath," she says. "Why can't I see it?"

Thea folds her hands in her lap, stares down at them for a moment, then returns her gaze to Emma and fixes her with a strange look. Disappointment might be the word. Pity might be a better fit.

"I'm sorry," whispers Thea, so softly that it's almost lost to the babble of the Seven Mile River.

Shame bubbles in Emma's stomach—over what, she can't say—before Thea's face goes even paler, nearly translucent, her straw-colored hair lightening a shade to resemble chalk.

She never lowers her eyes even as she disappears, dispersing like water droplets into the night air, and leaving Emma alone under the frozen sky.

Emma falls asleep in study hall the next morning. She dreams of ghosts flitting through the biting winter air, wonders if they freeze like the water, like the sky. Maybe they do, if it gets cold enough.

Silence bathes the house that night. As midnight passes, the walls breathe like a sleeping giant, offering safety saddled with a ticking clock.

Soft as snowfall, Emma slips on a coat and gloves and sneaks out her window and pads toward the river. The night nips at her skin, but her thrumming pulse and blood, rushing like the unfrozen current, keep her warm.

"You came back," says Thea, standing with her back to the water, eyes wide with wonder. "I didn't dare hope you would."

"I wasn't sure I would," whispers Emma. "You're dead."

A joyless smile slips onto Thea's face. "And you say exactly what you mean, don't you?"

Emma shrugs. "You weren't breathing, then you disappeared. Hard to start a conversation any other way. How long have you…" She bites her lip, lowers her eyes. "I'm sorry, is it rude to ask?"

"Probably." Thea fixes her gaze on Emma. The blue of her eyes seems to mimic the movements of the river below. "I don't know any ghosts. Any other ghosts."

"Why are you here?"

Thea's eyes drift away from Emma, up the bank and past the trees to the stone ruins lining the path.

A weight drops in Emma's stomach. "My dad says kids used to work in that mill. You didn't—"

A flicker of excitement appears in Thea's eyes. She rubs her hands together as if seeking warmth. Then a sadness overtakes her and she nods, slowly.

Emma covers her mouth, the fuzz on her gloves tickling at her lips.

"A long time ago, of course," says Thea.

"And…" Emma's brows knit in concern. "And now you can't leave?"

Eyebrows raised and lips pursed, Thea stares at Emma. The look of a teacher willing a student toward a conclusion.

"You died in there." Emma's voice emerges so softly, it's almost swallowed by the river's murmur.

Thea's legs wobble and she sinks to the ground, shaking her head and inching toward the rushing water. Emma joins her. "You don't know what it was like."

"We learned about it in school." She moves to shrug, then freezes, afraid it might appear insensitive. "Some details, anyway. Mostly the good stuff, I think. Industrial revolution. Jobs for the people of Slattery Falls. The working conditions were mentioned, accidents inside and at the river. Drownings, I guess."

Thea's eyes widen. "You learn about things like that in school?"

"Town history, Greek mythology, the branches of government. You name it. Anyway, our teacher mostly glossed over the deaths. Like someone reading the possible side effects on one of those medicine ads."

Emma squirms. Her new friend won't know what an ad is, never mind the specifics.

Friend?

Wrapping her arms tightly around her body, Thea lets her eyes wander the landscape. "I saw horrible things in there. Rarely a week went by without someone losing a limb to the machinery." She raises her head. "You wouldn't believe how much blood a body can lose and still draw breath. I saw. Horrid enough when it happened to the grown-ups, competent men and women who understood the dangers they signed up for. But the boys and girls? Sent by their parents, right along this river with nothing but a lunch pail. They tried so hard, that was the worst part. When they reached into the machines to fetch spindles—just following directions, and…" A shudder ripples across Thea's shoulders and Emma suspects it has nothing to do with the temperature.

Would lost limbs be returned to a ghost?

"And, of course, some children were taken by the river." Thea's eyes drift toward the water. "It was almost a mercy."

"Is that what happened to you?"

Thea looks up. Her eyes glisten.

Can a spirit weep?
Can their tears freeze like the river?
Like the sky?

"I don't know," says Thea, finally. "I remember so much from there. Maybe not every detail; some things are…unclear. But the last thing I recall?" Her gaze lands on the river, always the river. "Darkness."

"Darkness," mumbles Emma, and a vision of home passes through her mind.

"What are you thinking?" asks Thea. Crystal blue fills her eyes. No more hint of tears, but a flicker of…something new.

Emma gazes up through the trees. Is that the first hint of sunlight or the last glare of the moon?

"I'm thinking if I don't get home soon, I'll be in deep shit."

Thea holds Emma's eyes, doesn't so much as blink. "They care about you there. They want you home because they love you."

Laughter slices the early morning air and a beat passes before Emma realizes it came from her.

"I'm not sure they care about anything right now. Especially me." She pats the phone in her pocket; its stillness tells that she is not missed.

For a moment, Thea says nothing. Her eyes swirl.

"What if you could stay here?"

A chill breeze follows the words, seeping through Emma's skin and settles into her bones.

"I…I don't think—"

"Of course," whispers Thea, lowering her gaze. "You need to go. I just get so lonely. The water moves so quickly, Emma, it never freezes. Not all the way. When I have someone to talk to, it dulls the sound. Even just for a few minutes."

"I can come back. Tomorrow night."

"They'll find out eventually. They'll steal you away." Thea's voice grows huskier with every word, its light, fluttering tone nearly unrecognizable by the time she finishes.

Impulse takes over as Emma reaches forward, squeezes Thea's hand. Both girls jump at the contact.

Freezing, thinks Emma. *More frigid than the air.*

"I'll come back," she says.

Promise.

The word materializes in her mind, unbidden.

Emma shivers. "I promise."

"You promise," says Thea. It doesn't sound like a question.

Icy nips sting Emma's hand. Pins and needles.

It's just the cold, right?

When Emma eases her window open and slips inside, a dash of breeze and a hint of sunshine at her back, her father is sitting on her bed. Waiting.

She already knows how he'll start. *Things are hard right now, but they'll get better.*

But things are always hard.

Hands folded, eyes staring over Emma's shoulder and out the window, he says nothing, not right away. Somehow, that's worse.

That night, Emma lies in bed. Visions of Thea dance in her mind.

Is she sad? Alone? Angry? Hurt?

Eyes drifting toward the window, Emma considers the guards. Two hunks of plastic screwed into the frame. No more than a few dollars at the hardware store, and yet, they keep her window from opening more than a few inches.

She's tried.

Being made to go to school after a sleepless night was bad enough. To then come home to a makeshift set of prison bars on her window?

Emma had locked the door, refusing dinner and eventually crawling into bed to wait for the sun to set.

As she lies awake and watches the clock count away the night, there are no shouts from the other room, no cracks or slaps. Only whispers and eventually, even those dissolve into the quiet hum of a suburban residence in the small hours of the morning.

Eyelids heavy and mind churning with guilt—*I'll come back, I promise*—Emma fights sleep for as long as she can, but playing the role of both student and midnight wanderer for days on end has dampened her spirit.

She blinks and, this time, her eyes remain closed until sunlight rouses her from troubled dreams.

No one mentions the boards on the windows the next morning, how they've curbed Emma's midnight outings. Nor do they bring up the missed dinner. Like none of it ever happened. Looks are passed and avoided. The air drips with tension. Emma and her parents spend their Saturday bouncing around the house like the pins of a juggler, dodging each other's presence to keep the whole charade from crashing down.

Her parents don't notice when Emma spirits a Phillips head screwdriver into her pocket and secrets it beneath her pillow.

The sun goes down, the streetlights flicker to life, and out in the living room, the drone of the television cuts to silence. Minutes later, a muffled shouting match ensues, gradually falling to whispers as her parents wear themselves out.

When the comfortable quiet of the house replaces the bitter words, Emma's eyes flick toward the clock. She forces herself to wait twenty minutes. Each second lasts an hour, but she is patient, and when the digital numbers tell her she's waited long enough, she slinks out of bed and toward the window.

Emma knows every inch of carpet in this room. She steps on only the quietest secret keepers.

As she loosens each screw, she braces for the squeal of metal against wood, for the door to fly open, and this time, there will be anger, not just disappointment. Instead, the window locks cooperate, and the pane slides open as softly as ever.

Emma drops to the grass outside, crunchy with a layer of frost. The blades bend and snap beneath her weight as she starts toward the river.

Overhead, the first snowflake falls.

The wooded path that runs alongside the Seven Mile River is deserted. Brittle branches creak in protest at the sharp wind, and the ghost of the Slattery Mill watches.

"Thea?" She doesn't quite shout. The lonely woods echo her call back.

The stone ruins of the mill peek down through the trees. Is Thea hiding among the rubble?

Snow sticks to the ground, reflecting the moonlight and illuminating the sky like a movie set. The darkness that surrounds the stone debris remains complete. A fluttering curtain teasing movement.

"I'm so sorry," says Emma, surprised to find tears gathering in her eyes. "I tried to come. They wouldn't let me."

The wind howls in response, pelting her skin with a barrage of tiny flakes that melt and drip down her cheeks.

"I'm sorry," she whispers this time.

"I waited."

Emma spins, turning her back on the stirring black sky swimming between trees and the remnants of the Slattery Mill. On the river's bank hovers Thea.

She no longer looks like herself.

Her irises move as though they have their own current, so deep, Emma fears she might fall in. Thea's straw-blonde hair is matted to her head, dripping wet and several shades darker, as is her sepia dress, its dark spots washed away.

Her head scarf is gone, thinks Emma. *I can see all of her.*

Then, *she's been swimming.*

A stupid thought, but the only one Emma can summon as she takes a step back.

"I waited," says Thea again. The voice is not her own. It gurgles and crashes. The sound of a rushing tide slapping against rocks as it courses downstream.

"I know, and I'm sorry. I really am. I tried." Emma takes another step back. Suddenly, she doesn't want to be anywhere near the river.

"So cold out here," says Thea. "So lonely. You don't know. Alone out here for years. Years!" She shouts the last and the waters churn behind her, raging like a tempest. Snowflakes flutter down, impossibly calm amid the squall.

Emma stifles another apology.

"I watched them build it, you know." Thea tilts her head toward the ruined mill. At her feet, water collects, running back toward the river like a slug's slime trail. "Watched for years as workers came and went, grew old. Died. I remember the day it shut down. Like you said, too many accidents. Drownings."

Emma narrows her eyes. "I don't understand. How could you…"

Thea's face twists into a familiar look. Disappointment, pity. The same expression she wore the night they met. "I was here before the mill, here before the town. Before the first settlers."

"No." Emma shakes her head. "No, that doesn't make any sense. You worked in the mill. They mistreated you. Didn't care about you. Until you died. You drowned." Her voice fades at the last two words. The trail of water at Thea's feet. It's not running backward. It's climbing the bank.

"Emma." Her voice is soft, scratchy. "I belong to the river."

Sent by their parents…

They tried so hard…

They.

"You didn't drown." Emma stiffens.

I saw.

"I never said I did."

Siren.

The word floats through Emma's mind. Did Thea put it there?

"You're a siren."

"To some. A river spirit to others, and the river demands sacrifice," says Thea. "It gets so hungry."

Emma's lip quivers. "I want to go home."

Things are hard right now, but they'll get better.

"I can take you home." The words slur and burble as dark water pours from the corners of Thea's mouth.

Emma turns to run. Shimmers of snow light the path, beckoning her forward. Eyes set, she pushes off, but her back foot slips from underneath her and she crashes to the ground. The world goes dim for a second, and when it flickers back into existence, Thea stands over her, piercing blue eyes staring down. Holding her in place.

Somewhere deep in those eyes, there is still sadness.

"What if you could stay?" whispers Thea. The raging river is gone from that voice. Innocence returned. A kid.

Bitter cold seeps through Emma's clothes, icy river water cutting at her skin. Her body begins to slide down the bank. She claws at the frozen ground but finds no purchase. The pull of the current is too strong. It engulfs one leg, then the other, drawing her in. It's almost welcoming.

The chill reaches her chest, her shoulders.

What she wouldn't give to be safe in bed.

She opens her mouth to scream, and water flows in. Emma's heart races, threatening to beat out of her chest as she chokes on the ink-black river water. A hand squeezes hers. It's cold as snow, cold as death, but it's there as the river swallows her.

Water rushes over the top of Emma's head as Thea pulls her down. Arctic liquid floods her lungs. Emma sinks, but she can still see the sky.

The frozen sky, she thinks, as darkness clouds her vision. Air runs short. As her lungs ache for oxygen, bursts of light erupt before her eyes.

They look like snowflakes.

And then they're gone.

– BRENNAN LAFARO is a horror writer living in southeastern Massachusetts with his wife, two sons, and his hounds. He is the author of the *Buzzard's Edge Saga*, the story collection *Illusions of Isolation*, and the *Slattery Falls* series. You can read his short fiction in various anthologies and find him on Twitter at @brennanlafaro or at www.brennanlafaro.com.

Darkness Repeats

L.E. Daniels

December, 1944
Ardennes Forest, South of Bastogne, Belgium

Joe scrambled low across the belly of the trench and grabbed the lapels of the German's corpse. Milky pre-dawn darkness and thick fog blanketed him and Mike, the tank gunner, under stripped boughs of oak and willow. A dusting of snow fell across the capsized wreckage and flattened vehicles of yesterday's skirmish, but the Nazi ambush had barely slowed the march of Patton's Third Army to Bastogne.

Clawing at the stiff wool, Joe was past shivering now. Alternating waves of heat and chills swept beneath his cotton tank driver's uniform. Inside the thin leather gloves, his fingers were numb. His shoulder screamed from the blow it had taken when a mine tore the treads from his tank.

After one night exposed under their Sherman, he and Mike, whose gashed thigh leaked through its wrapping, were blanched with frostbite. They were the only ones in their company of five who'd survived the blast.

While Joe tugged at the German's overcoat, Mike fumbled with the plank-frozen legs. The woods were crawling with Nazis and if they were caught stealing a coat, they'd be shot on sight.

In rising metallic light, Joe crouched and swept a sharp kick to the torso of the corpse to loosen where fabric, blood, and frozen slush had melded. With a crackle of ice, the body shifted.

Mike splayed his hands, signaling to listen. Freezing cold, disoriented, and clumsy, they could easily attract a bullet.

Joe exhaled a slow mist at the ground, knowing that even a

puff could reveal their position. He paused, then as one, the men continued their attempt to wrench the coat from the corpse. Peeling back the wool, Joe looked into the broken skull, gray and deep purple in this strange light.

A *tap-tap-tap* bounced in the fog.

The men hunched, looking only at each other.

Mike clung hard to the corpse's legs.

Through the falling snow, another burst resounded.

Joe glanced upward and pointed. Mike followed his gaze. The dark shape of a large woodpecker flitted higher into an oak, the tree hanging in parts by twisted heartwood and bark. Joe couldn't help but consider it: *Good wood for building*.

Mike tugged on the soldier's legs, a signal to keep going. They had to work faster. Dawn was lighting up the fog.

While Mike worked on the corpse's boots, Joe tore the coat free and stared into what remained of the rictus grin of the German. He was young. Maybe eighteen? He had good teeth. His wool coat, riddled with sawdust and stiff with bodily fluid, felt fine and thick in Joe's hands.

"*Danker shane*, you bastard," Joe whispered in a broad New England accent to the cadaver's broken face and stuffed the coat down the front of his jacket. The son of Polish immigrants, he had never cared to learn much German.

Mike tore at the snowy laces but the boots didn't budge. He was flagging so Joe motioned to quit and follow him.

With his submachine gun poking ahead of him, Joe peered over the trench. His shoulder shrieked as he belly-crawled through six inches of snow along a wall of briars.

Back at the roadside, just near their tank and the hole they'd been living in since the ambush, Joe spotted the body of another German, his body raked into frozen slush by the vast treads of a Panzer. A pale hand with curled fingers jutted from the churn, fingernails dusted in snowflakes. On his elbows, Mike poked at the edge of the wool coat with his trench knife but shook his head.

They slipped into the darkness beneath their tank and fought to stay warm under the shared coat.

Through a crack between the scored earth and ruptured tank, and to the soft sounds of Mike's morphine dream, Joe watched the somber dawn unravel against a weighted sky. As the woodlands slowly expanded before him, a physical pang of homesickness unfolded within him. A few songbirds raised a feeble strain and Joe knew them as the wrens and bullfinches like those back on the farm in Rhode Island, where his parents, his sister, Kasia, and her husband lived with their toddler. Home reached for him, and he saw himself slip from his window at night to meet his Christina.

But, all around the burned debris, the air filled with flurries and a sudden firefight echoed in the distance. An abrupt light flashed in the fog between the trees. Joe tightened his grip on his weapon and craned his neck as far as his shoulder allowed. He looked back at Mike, but he was out, snoring softly.

Another tremor of light, and Joe thought it was the muzzle flash of gunshots, but it was soundless and steady. The woods fell silent, aside from distant exchange of artillery.

A figure parted the fog, lit up ghostly white as if by strange sunlight and not in uniform. It moved between the cleaved trunks and sprays of soot. A woman, her arms shining and bare, glided up over a broken slope of ash and snow and through the remains of the Ardennes.

Thinking it was Our Lady of Fátima herself aflame, Joe squeezed his eyes tight and blessed himself.

But when he opened his eyes, she was there, approaching him, eyes bright as firelight and fixed upon him in his secret darkness. Joe recoiled, bumping against Mike.

It was no vision of the Blessed Mother. This woman's eyes were hungry. Her mouth was opened wide as if to scream.

It was his Christina, his bride, and she was ablaze.

Licks of bright flame consumed her body, shimmering with

orange embers. The fire swooned her blackening palms into swirling ash, charring and crumbling her arms and legs into a serpentine trail of dust.

Joe threw himself back into the dirt of the trench and convulsed.

Mike roused and threw his weight onto Joe, pinning him. He breathed, "Shushh, Joe...shushhh..." but Joe bucked.

Joe slammed his knees and boots into Mike again and again; all the while, Mike whispered, pleading for Joe's silence.

August 1944, Four Months Prior
Spectacle Cloak, Spectacle Cove, Rhode Island

When the soldier is hit by a cannon ball, rags are as becoming as purple.

Christina hated that line from Henry David Thoreau's *Walden* but still, it bounced around her thoughts as she leaned into her sewing machine. It made no sense and conjured terrible images of her husband, Joey, out there somewhere in Europe, fighting for the rest of them.

Sometimes sentences ricocheted in Tina's head to the sticky racket of one-hundred-and-twenty treadle-operated Singer sewing machines in one-hundred-and-twenty-degree heat. While she drove her hands along her machine, she refused to think about the crawling, electrical sensation that plagued every inch of her skin. Here she was, allergic to wool, working in a wool mill while a heatwave broiled New England without pause and compounded her misery with a vicious heat rash. The mill that manufactured the olive drab winter overcoats for the war effort had become an oven: its gray granite walls luminous with fibers and its thick oak doors locked to prevent the seamstresses from wandering off for a cigarette break or even a breath of air.

Teen to middle-aged seamstresses surrounded her, all packed into tight rows. The women pedaled the treadles of their sewing machines, ankle-deep in the six inches of fuzz that blanketed the machine-oil-soaked floor. The whole place smelled like bodies and burning oil.

Sweat stung Tina's eyes but she didn't dare lift a hand or dry her face on her shoulder, not since she'd run the needle right through her fingernail yesterday. Once was enough.

"Oopsa-daisy," the foreman had breathed his coffee and tobacco breath over her shoulder, an unlit, hand-rolled cigarette pinched between his crooked lips.

After pulling her finger free, Tina clutched it, pounding, to her chest.

"Don't bleed on the coat." The foreman patted her shoulder. "Let the soldiers do that."

Kasia, Joey's sister, muttered in Polish, "Kapusta głowa." *Cabbage head.*

"English, Dolly." He poked a finger into her purse. "Or I'll help myself to your tickets."

Today, Tina pushed wool along the slide plate, a little more mindful of the plunging needle, attaching one sleeve at a time to an overcoat. Despite her injury, she was still the fastest seamstress in the mill, bringing nineteen dollars a week while most of the others only made five to ten. She had Joey to think of, and every single coat was for him.

Beside Tina, Kasia's machine choked, and she whipped her machine apart again. The sooner she could fix it, the sooner she could get back to work without holding up their assembly line. Still, Tina worked faster to cover for her while Kasia flicked the stop latch and spun the hand wheel for the fifth time before lunch. Kasia twirled the bobbin winder and wiped everything down with a filthy rag she kept pinned under her thigh. With the tiny oil can she kept in the fold of her skirt, she oiled each one of the pieces and joints, dripping everywhere except on the coat sleeve splayed before her, and with a swift *tap-tap-tap,* she locked each part back into place. Again, Kasia was pedaling, and tossed her completed sleeve into the cart to roll along the line to Tina.

The seamstresses worked piecemeal, assembling the coats bit by bit. An army of X-frame carts cradling white canvas bags rolled the pieces along the lines. Most seamstresses grabbed the same pieces to keep the pace high: backs or sides; lapels or sleeves. When a machine snarled up and while the seamstress oiled her machine with a little can she refilled at home—critical in keeping the metal and belts from growing too hot—the other seamstresses doubled down to keep the line moving and the foreman away.

For each completed job, the seamstresses tore a three-inch perforated ticket from the item and dropped it into their purses perched in the wool tide under their machines. Each ticket was worth a penny.

It wasn't Kasia's fault she had a bum machine. When they paused for five minutes to unwrap and eat their sandwiches from oily paper, Tina slipped her sister-in-law a handful of tickets and the ritual commenced.

Kasia refused them in Polish.

Tina pushed the tickets back, muttering in Italian until Kasia accepted and they traded half of a kielbasa on rye for half of a peppers-and-eggs sandwich.

The American seamstresses took out their peanut butter and jelly and the lines slowed to a crawl. The foreman crossed the floor with his metal lunch box, lighting his cigarette as he unlocked the doors for himself and left.

Kasia called him a cabbage head again but Tina, determined to make Kasia laugh with her mouth full, called after him, "Coglione."

"What's that?" Kasia mopped her forehead with a napkin before folding it into her purse.

"More vulgar than your cabbage head." Tina mimed grabbing his manhood with a twist then squeezed. They snorted and cackled and when they finished eating, started pedaling again.

But soon, *Walden* twisted around Tina's thoughts as she tried not to think about the crawling itch that plagued her body.

When the soldier is hit by a cannon ball, rags are as becoming as purple.

It was Joey's idea to exchange pocket-size copies of Thoreau's *Walden* on their wedding night. From their hotel room near the courthouse, they had watched the sun rise on their only night together, twin books mixed in with the rumpled bed clothes. Christina's head was resting on Joey's chest when she asked, "How can a boy with so little chest hair go off to war?"

"I have enough." From his voice, she could tell he had his eyes closed.

"Mother said we should exchange Bibles."

"I couldn't write all my love notes in a Bible. Besides, this is about the life we'll build together when I get back."

Christina flicked through the pages of his underscores and drawings of tiny pumpkins with curly vines, then stopped. "But look at this. I don't want to read this when you're gone…" The reality of his imminent departure struck in waves. She pointed to the sentence, turning her face into his body.

Why should they begin digging their graves as soon as they are born?

Joey took the book. He squeezed her to him as he flipped to a sentence he had underlined twice. "Here. When you miss me, think of the pumpkins we'll grow, big enough for your majesty."

Now, as she rounded the shoulder seam along her needle, she turned her thoughts to Joey's line.

I would rather sit on a pumpkin and have it all to myself than be crowded on a velvet cushion.

And with a deep exhalation through an itchy nose, she let that big, bright orange pumpkin roll round and round in her mind.

December 1944, Day Two
Ardennes Forest

During Europe's coldest winter in thirty years, Joe, tank driver and technician 4th grade, and Mike, a corporal and gunner, were the only two of their five-man crew who were still breathing under the carcass of their Sherman M4A3 while Patton's forces marched to aid the Twenty-Eighth Infantry and 101st Airborne Divisions in Bastogne. In just a few days, they'd arrive and beat the Nazis back toward Berlin—without Joe and Mike.

Before they had found themselves in this wreck, their crew had made it from England, through the hedgerows of Normandy to Carentan. They'd dodged what would have been a fatal tangle with a Tiger tank by reversing straight into a French farmhouse, crashing right through the floorboards, and crawling backward from the root cellar undetected. They'd laughed about it all the way to Mainz, Germany, before they got the call to head back to help the Americans encircled at Bastogne.

As the crew joined Patton and rolled northeast, the temperature dropped, and the men mumbled about a lack of rations and winter gear. George, the radio operator, delivered the bad news, "Supplies are SNAFU-ed at the quartermaster in Antwerp. Winter coats. K-rations. Munitions. We gotta make do with what we got."

That was last week. Now, with much of their supplies gone with the mine—except for one first aid box and some morphine Joe had scavenged from the wreck—they faced another frigid night sucking snow in the Ardennes, wrestling with hypothermia and dehydration. Somewhere, shells were falling. Nothing else moved in the woods.

Mike licked bouillon powder from a foil pouch from under the coat they shared. When he removed his gloves, his fingertips were black.

Joe shifted his weight around his injured shoulder and inspected his own fingers. They were bleach white. He couldn't feel his toes either and in that cramped space, he couldn't take off his boots to look.

He pulled his gloves back over his hands and looked at Mike. His face looked gaunt, the skin pocked and peeling. Stubble and dark circles gave his face a sunken look.

Joe regretted the panic that overtook him earlier, the nonsense of it. He was sure he'd kicked Mike right in his wound, but the gunner hadn't said a word. Mike hadn't even asked Joe what it was about, not that Joe would tell him.

"I'm sorr—" Joe began.

"No." Muffled against the shared coat, Mike snapped a bar of chocolate and handed half to Joe.

Joe gave him their last packet of sulfanilamide tablets for infection. They were just holding out for the Red Cross to show up and it would be tomorrow, they had decided. The medics would come in the morning.

When Mike's breathing rolled into the shallows again, Joe took the morphine syrette from his lap and pulled the coat over him.

In the growing darkness, Joe suddenly wondered where his copy of *Walden* had landed. He dared not look in the tank where his brothers were in pieces, but he remembered that one line.

Why should they begin digging their graves as soon as they are born?

Joe cradled his gun and kept watch through the crack in the deepening fog. When they had been hit, they were told to stay put and wait for the medics trailing the march. Now, it was hard to tell if the shells were falling before or behind them.

August 1944
Spectacle Cloak

Descending the stairs of the mill after their shift, Christina and Kasia trailed the troop of damp, sweaty seamstresses. Tina rubbed her nose viciously and stopped to scratch her shins on a landing.

Once she started, she couldn't stop. The tangle of pleasure was hypnotic, searing pain a relief against the itch.

Kasia gently touched her shoulder. "Stop, Tina. You're bleeding."

Christina straightened, blood under her nails. Her skin burned. "I'm sorr—" Tina began.

"No," Kasia said. "I see you, my sister."

When they reached the ground floor, Tina and Kasia waited for the crates to stream from the elevator to the loading dock. Trucks took the coats to a ship in Spectacle Cove Shipyard and from there, they were bound for New York then London.

Tina wiped a hand across her brow, and through the manager's open door, she read the headline on his desk—"Death Valley Days"—but she didn't need a newsie to tell her how hot it was. Her shins bled into her socks, and her entire body tingled and burned. She'd just have to wait and see how bad it looked when she got home.

Then she had a dark thought. At least Joe wouldn't see her like this—scored flesh and blisters welling. He'd run screaming, she thought, and raked her fingernails hard across her arms.

"Jim is trying to get us a job," Kasia said. "We just need to hold on a little longer." Kasia's husband was one of the managers at the nearby Frontier Parachute mill. His name was Zigmund but in America, everyone called him Jim.

Tina tried not to limp, her feet aflame now, as she exited the great oak doors, the sparkling granite blinding in the late-afternoon glare.

The two of them walked toward Tina's home, where she would live with her mother until Joe returned. Her mother took in sewing and ran a daycare for the children of the millworkers, including Jim and Kasia's two-year-old boy, Andrei. They'd made it as far as the front path before Andrei burst from the door and wrapped himself in his mother's skirts.

Kasia scooped him up. "Oh, you smell like strawberries!"

"Look!" Andrei held a plump berry to his mother's lips.

"Mm, thank you, my sweet boy." She turned to Tina. "I'll see you in the morning."

Tina took to the backstep of her house, but nightfall brought little relief. Cicadas buzzed in the dark, a relentless, mechanical sound. Tina stripped while her mother brought her a pan of water with baking soda and a cloth.

She sat in her brassiere and slip, scratching the soles of her feet ragged on the lip of the concrete step. Beside her, *Walden* was face down, cracked at the spine.

Her mother handed her a towel. "Oh, figlia mi', you're only making it worse!"

Tina grunted. "Pain is better than this godforsaken itching."

Blisters oozed and blood peppered her arms and legs but worst of all were the gaping sores under her breasts. Carefully, with her injured finger extended, Tina unhooked the clasps at the back of her bra and peeled the satin trim from the crust of her wounds. She lifted one breast at a time and patted the lesions with the baking soda rinse. Again, the deep prongs of the stinging were far better than the itch.

Finally, while she soaked her feet, she slipped into a cotton camisole. She examined her arms in the light from the kitchen window and pulled tiny wool threads from where they had lodged in her pores. She then patted herself all over with corn starch knowing she would do it all over again tomorrow.

She glanced at her clothes in a heap, then placed the book in her lap and scanned a line.

All costume off a man is pitiful or grotesque.

She laughed.

Behind her, her mother let the screen door slap.

"Is there no relief from this heat?" her mother asked, shaking the hem of her night dress on the step. She pointed to the little book. "Most couples exchange Bibles."

"It's Joe, reminding me of the house he's going to build me in the woods."

"With what? He didn't even buy you a decent ring." Her mother lifted Tina's hand into the light. "This costume jewelry has already turned your finger black."

Tina pulled her hand away and curled her injured finger into her palm.

"I wish you hadn't married him like that before he left." Her mother sighed. "You should have waited."

They'd eloped to the town courthouse with Kasia and Jim as witnesses, the day before he shipped out for basic training in Georgia—something that was never done in this family. Her mother would never forgive her, and Christina accepted it as a fact.

"He loves me, Mama. He's smart. He'll keep the tank on the road and come home to me. He promised."

"They all promise, figlia mi'." Her mother withdrew back into the empty house. "Your father promised too. You married nothing but grief."

December 1944, Day Three
Ardennes Forest

It was dawn when Joe felt the rumble of machinery. When he tried to sit up, his hair and clothes clung to the ground. He didn't know if it was the Germans or the Allies or if he was having a seizure in the darkness beneath the tank.

Joe nudged Mike but he didn't move. He peered through the crack and saw first light and black tires grinding up slush on fat trucks through the fog. Sloppy, green canvas hung off the trucks and they looked American, but he wasn't sure.

His eyes were blurry and felt frozen open. Then the voices started: a garble. Joe went to rub his ears, but his fingers weren't his own.

When he tried to grip his gun, his shoulder pinched with spasm and he fumbled along the stock and trigger guard. He pulled off his gloves and held his hands close to his face. They were as black as Mike's.

Joe tried to free himself from the ground, but the frost held cloth and flesh. He kicked out his legs and remembered kicking the German for the coat.

Mike's head fell to the side and a stench leaked from under the coat.

Joe thought *Christina Christina Christina* and wondered if he burned when she burned. He thought maybe they had both been dead for days because he couldn't feel anything except the scream of his shoulder and the fog that still rolled all around them.

He saw that German's head blown apart, a boy with good teeth, probably farm-raised on milk and fresh eggs and bacon his father had hung in the smokehouse every autumn.

Boots passed his view, and he heard men rounding the wreck. He turned his head, his heart drumming.

A face appeared, and Joe waited for the muzzle and the shot.

Instead, hands reached for him and pulled. Hard.

Joe opened his mouth. His throat was so dry, he couldn't make a sound. Someone poured water, freezing, into his mouth and down his chin and he coughed.

When he found himself in milky sunlight on a stretcher, he saw the big red cross on the truck. A medic packed and strapped his bleeding shoulder, put a drip into his arm, and placed the bag on his chest.

Joe turned his head to see Mike on another stretcher on the ground, sound asleep. Past him, two medics pulled the remains of his brothers from their tank and finally now, he wept.

Beyond the trucks and milling men, wending through the slopes of snow and skeletal oak streaked with ash, again she approached without touching the ground.

Christina was ablaze, her eyes and mouth pale and wide, the shimmering contortions of flames consuming her all over again.

August 1944, Lunch Break
Spectacle Cloak

Time twists in on itself for the dying. Darkness repeats until somehow, it breaks open the very seams of life; torn and rent, a multitude of threads burst from this great chaotic loom of which Christina was but one.

In the roar of flames and whoosh of ash, the screams emptied into an inexhaustible tide. There followed a moment, a stirring silence, when the incredible pain stopped and there was, before everything collapsed like spent cinders, one last explosive expression that reached across time and space.

Earlier that day and for no visible reason, every single one of the seamstresses stopped their treadles simultaneously; their needles paused, and the women looked at one another. Usually, a few plunged ahead for a handful more of tickets, but not then.

In the dry heat of the mill, Tina's sweat evaporated like beads on a skillet. She noticed the eerie silence, as if the mill itself held its breath. A tingle of amazement shuddered through the dust motes, and the seamstresses began to smile. They held the moment a second longer, then turned to fish their lunches from their purses.

Five minutes to eat.

As they had done before, Tina traded half her peppers-and-eggs with Kasia's kielbasa as the real Americans bit into peanut butter and jelly.

"What's it taste like?" Tina introduced herself to the teenage girl beside her, a thin blonde who the foreman also called Dolly and whose name Tina had never bothered to ask.

"Here." She offered her sandwich. "Skippy and strawberry jam. Our own strawberries. I'm Joan."

"What's Skippy?" Tina took a bite before handing it to Kasia. "Oh my God."

"Oh," Kasia said, "the jam…"

Bread was torn asunder. Fried green peppers dangled in curls. Olive oil melted with the sweat on Joan's chin and the mill rushed with noisy chatter.

As she savored the last bite, Tina saw the foreman swing the big oak doors closed and lock them, cigarette pinched between his lips, his brow furrowed. She felt her own smile fade as smoke expelled from his nostrils, as if from a bull guarding its winter field.

The foreman's lunch box was gutted and its contents half-wrapped, as if the noise of the women had prompted a swift return to the floor. Tina saw him suck hard on the rushed cigarette, the hand-rolled paper canoeing. The bright, shining cherry fell, and tumbled into the sea of wool that spanned the floor.

In a flash, a carpet of fire swept across the floor.

Autumn 1955
Army-Navy Surplus, Spectacle Cove, Rhode Island

"Need any help, mister?" A young salesclerk emerged from behind gray curtains at the back of the store with a shining Brylcreem hairstyle. He approached at a clip.

"Ah, no." Joe turned toward the clothes racks, hiding his scarred face.

The clerk rested his hands on the hangers. "Well, if you need anything, just give me a holler."

"Thank you." Joe shot him a look out of politeness and saw the recognition on his face.

"Thank you, sir, for your service." He put out his hand.

Joe sighed. He pulled his hand from his pocket and extended it, the tips of his fingers missing.

The young man gently shook it before retreating. "Twenty percent off for vets," he called.

A sign on the wall above the rack read, *Our Very Own Spectacle Cloak!* and Joe felt the crackle of those words under his ribs. He thumbed through the rack until he touched wool.

Outside, an automobile rumbled over the cobblestone street, slowly passing the large storefront window. Its windshield caught the sting of the afternoon sunlight, the glare falling sharply across Joe's eyes.

He saw her, his Christina, burning, embers crumbling to ash, and his breath caught. He ran his hand down the sleeve, squeezing it hard.

As he broke down, the clerk disappeared behind the curtains.

– L. E. DANIELS is a Bram Stoker Award® nominee for short fiction and an American author, poet, and editor living in Australia. Her novel, *Serpent's Wake: A Tale for the Bitten* (Interactive Publications) is a Notable Work with the HWA's Mental Health Initiative. Lauren co-edited Aiki Flinthart's *Relics, Wrecks and Ruins* (Cat Press) with Geneve Flynn, winning the 2021 Aurealis Award and with Christa Carmen co-edited *We Are Providence: Tales of Horror from the Ocean State* (Weird House Press), a 2022 Aurealis finalist. Recent publications include "Silk" in *Hush, Don't Wake the Monster* (Twisted Wing Productions) and "Hangman's Coming" in *Where the Silent Ones Watch* (Hippocampus Press). Lauren's personal essays appear in *Holistic Horror, Quick Bites,* and *34 Orchard*. Her recent poetry is published in *The Cozy Cosmic* (Underland Press), *Under Her Eye,* and *Mother Knows Best* (Black Spot Books), with "Night Terrors" (HWA) a finalist for the 2022 Australian Shadows Award. Lauren runs Brisbane Writers Workshop.

Mill Dues

Jason Parent

Running.

Aron had been doing it his entire life—first from his violent drunk dad and schoolyard bullies, then from former friends and now-estranged family members after he riffled through their wallets or pawned their things for a fix, then finally from the cops as he turned to scamming and stealing to feed his addiction. He had pretty good cardio for a junkie and all the taut muscle his five-foot-nine, one hundred twenty-pound frame could hold.

This time, though, he was running for his life. Shaky and in imminent need of a fix, Aron would have traded the billfold of cash—a few thousand, he'd guessed, though he hadn't paused long enough to count it—for one more blessed gallop through the snow. His heart raged against its cage, the adrenaline almost distracting him from his need.

Almost.

Who am I going to buy from now? He cackled, then threw a hand over his mouth to silence his hysterics. Still, the irony that he'd stolen from his dealer forced nervous laughter up his throat, even as tears clouded his eyes and snot smeared his upper lip. Vic had just left it sitting there on the kitchen table, too preoccupied with his cuddle puddle in a back room to notice his return customer. Door unlocked, Aron had just walked right in, the money positioned in front of him like a worm on a hook. All he had to do was grab it and back out of the apartment as quietly and as unobserved as he'd entered, and he would have been set for a few weeks, if he didn't get too stupid.

A toilet had flushed as his fingers folded around the bill stack. He'd already pocketed the wad in his likewise-stolen North Face jacket by the time Gage, Vic's steroidal enforcer, entered from the hallway opposite the entranceway. Gage froze, his belt ends unclasped in his hands. His gaze shifted to Aron, then to the table, then back up.

Cue running. Aron had been running since. He ran past the gym, the CBD shop, and the other businesses that had taken over half the space in one of Fall River's former mill districts. The other half remained un-redeveloped, ruins of the past with little hope for a future. A lot like Aron in that way, equally untouched, corrupted, unclean, and always in regress.

A perfect place to hide.

Aron ducked behind the struggling businesses, moving farther away from the street. The shadow of the Braga Bridge beckoned him beneath its dark canopy, toward a watery dead end, but he resisted its call, instead heading deeper among the dilapidated structures, all ninety-degree angles except where supports had crumbled. He turned and headed toward an opening in the chain link fence at the opposite side of the lot, where the industrial revolution had come and gone, its existence all but forgotten.

"Over there!" someone called, closer behind him than Aron had hoped.

He swung his arms and strode faster. Ignoring the NO TRESPASSING signs and barbed wire ringing the top of the fence, he barreled through the cut-away opening, spun, and crashed down hard on the other side. His jacket tore free from one arm. Pain seared through his shoulder. As he prodded it with his fingers, they came away wet with blood.

His breath hitched as heavy boots thudded on the pavement. Aron scrambled to his feet, but as he tried to resume his flight, his jacket tugged back, caught in the pronged and twisted remnants of the fence. He slid his arm out of it and sprinted away in his yellowed T-shirt, leaving his jacket behind.

Aron hurried across cracked pavement, weeds sprouting high as if trying to undo the destruction civilization had brought to them. He ducked behind a corner of a massive building with window upon window marching in parallel with each floor. With their glass broken or missing entirely, nothing but pitch black behind them, they looked like rows of chipped and rotted teeth. Listening for signs of pursuit, he stopped to catch his breath.

"The dumbass left the money!" Gage said back at the fence. "It's all here."

Aron patted his non-existent jacket pockets. His shoulders sagged and he rocked his head back against the wall, desperation having dealt him a crushing blow. He felt as used up as his supply, ready to curl up like a pill bug and take his licks.

"Should we head back?" Gage asked.

"No," Vic said. "Gotta teach the prick that he can't steal from me and get away with it."

The chain link fence rattled in the otherwise dead silent night, Aron's hunters stalking their prey. He slid his back down the wall and sat on the cold cement, resting his head in his hands.

"Over here," a small voice called, soft and melodic like a distant song carried on the wind.

Aron looked around and saw no one, sure he'd imagined the voice in the first place. It hadn't been the first time he'd heard things that were not there, though he was usually high when that happened. Just how much he'd scrambled his brain over the years was something of which he couldn't be sure, and it had often been one of his many reasons to stop using that wouldn't stick.

To his right, about ten feet away, a small rectangular window sat just above the granite block foundation. A light like a single star against a sky of black twinkled from somewhere inside the lowest depths of the mill then vanished. Aron thought he might have imagined that as well. What he was sure he hadn't imagined was the all-consuming darkness inside that mill. He could lose himself in that lightless night, become lost and unable to be found.

Footsteps pounded louder. Aron saw no other chance at escape. On palms and soles, he scrabbled over to the window. He winced, expecting a loud crash as he kicked in the glass, but it instead broke more like a sheet of thin ice without much more than a crackle. He swiped away as many shards as he could, earning him several superficial cuts to his hands, before sliding into the darkness.

He did not expect the drop. His feet hit the floor after just enough time for him to think they might never. His right foot rolled, sending stabbing pain into his ankle. It gave, and he collapsed onto his hip then shoulder, his face smacking against cold, unforgiving stone. Grime smeared his cheek. A powdery dust, undisturbed for decades, wafted over him, coating his lips and burning his eyes. The taste of brackish mud filled his dry mouth. His nose instantly clogged, a foot-fungal, sweaty gym sock odor trapped inside behind a plug of mucus and filth. He hacked out whatever had gotten into his mouth, every breath stinging his throat and lungs as if the air were made of thumbtacks.

Aron blinked rapidly as tears squeezed from the corners of his eyes. Unable to see, he used his T-shirt to wipe them clean, not knowing if he was doing more harm than good.

"Where the fuck did he go?" Gage's voice came from above. "In there?"

"Probably," Vic said.

"You want to go in?"

"Not yet. Circle the building. If you find him, text me. Otherwise, meet me back here. Cockroach ain't getting away that easy."

Aron crab-walked until his back hit a wall. He couldn't see a thing, not knowing if his blindness was due to the absence of light or whatever had gotten into his eyes. A beam of light answered that question.

"You down there, asshole?" Vic's hand came through the window. In it was his cellphone, its flashlight illuminating little as it panned over an open floor space. Beyond its range, Aron followed its trajectory, taking in as much of his surroundings as he could before the light went out again. He saw no weapons, no fixtures, no furniture, no nothing—just a seemingly endless space covered in spider webs, dust motes or spores as big as snowflakes, blackish muck, and—

A flash of something white fled the light. Vic seemed to have noticed it too as his flashlight panned in the direction of the movement. "That you, motherfucker?" Vic's head blocked the light through the window. "Aw, man. It stinks like a mass grave down there. You'd better not make me come in after you, or it'll be your corpse stinking up the place. If you come out now, I'll at least let you live."

After a moment, through which Aron held his breath, a large rat scurried into the light, rising up on its hindquarters as its nose twitched at the air.

Something gripped Aron's finger. He imagined pointed teeth burying themselves to the bone and bit his own knuckle to stifle a shriek. Nevertheless, the light beam swiveled his way.

The sensation lessened, but the touch remained. He felt no pain, but its absence did little to calm his nerves as his mind raced through nightmarish scenarios of what could be clinging to him in the dark. His instincts screamed at him to pull away, but he fought against them, his fear of Vic barely trumping that of the eerie unknown so close to him in the dark.

He closed his eyes and tried to will both troubles away. Despite all the poison he'd willingly ingested over the course of a wasted life, Aron didn't want to die. And what kind of cruel god would make him face his death sober?

When he opened his eyes, Vic was still at the window. The pressure around his finger remained. No matter how hard he tried to ignore it, Aron had to look at his hand. In the faint light of the window, a small, glowing blob, its shape blurred by the poor light, encircled his index finger.

Some kind of white slug or leech, he thought, leaning closer to it, his curiosity making him momentarily forget his trepidation. Thin black striations ran nearly equidistant from one another as they curled around his finger. Turning his palm, he examined their polished white, porcelain-like ends.

"Shhh," a voice whispered, seemingly inches from his face.

Aron shrieked. His stare rose to meet two marble-black orbs in a circular moon face. A finger lifted over a small pouty mouth, the digit matching those of the tiny hand that held his.

"What's the matter, crackhead?" Vic called. "Making some new rat friends?" Metal glinted in the moonlight as Vic aimed something though the window. A loud blast was immediately followed by the *ching* of a bullet ricocheting off the floor. It didn't sound all that close, but Aron scrambled away without thinking, crying out as he tweaked his injured ankle and causing a second shot to come much closer.

A tug came at his finger. "This way," the tiny voice whispered.

Aron knew too well how badly he needed a hit, so he didn't think being high could explain the apparition in front of him. He couldn't rule anything out though. Maybe he'd finally had a psychotic break or something had somehow triggered a residual or delayed trip. And this was one trip he didn't care for. Whether what he saw was a little person or a talking doll, he couldn't be certain, but either way, he had to be hallucinating at a time when he needed what little wits he had about him.

Or I'm finally losing it. He pushed a dirt-caked hand through greasy hair. *God, if you get me out of this, I swear I'll get clean.*

"Hurry," a high and squeaky voice, like that of a little girl, called from the darkness in front of him.

A shot whizzed by him. He wished muzzle fire would offer some light to show him his way like it did in the movies. Instead, he only heard the gunshot, the report echoing through the empty sarcophagus of the mill.

The voice beckoned him into deeper darkness, away from the window. He saw no choice but to follow.

His hands and knees squished and slid over what felt like mud-covered stone. Occasionally something would skitter out from beneath his fingers or crunch under his palm. He tried not to think of it, his mind instead focusing on his wheezing as his breath crackled like burning leaves, turning to ash in the fire that ignited inside his lungs. Dry coughs seemed at odds with his stuffed and running nose and watery eyes. He wanted to wipe them but resisted, knowing whatever was on his fingers could make them worse. Pushing forward, hand over hand and knee over knee, Aron crawled to where he hoped no one would follow and the bullets couldn't reach.

Until his forehead hit a wall. Something tugged his shirt. "Down here," the soft, child-like voice called.

His eyes caught a glimpse of a blurred thing standing roughly a foot and a half tall. The object slowly came into focus, a faint bluish glow emanating from somewhere near the floorboards, illuminating a figure in its ghostly light. He could see it now—a doll, yes, with porcelain skin and a pristine white dress, a corona around her bonneted head like a halo. An angel, no doubt. His savior.

Is an angel better than a delayed trip? He tried to blink the hallucination away. But the doll remained, pointing into a doghouse entrance-sized cut-away in the wall from which the bluish light resonated. It darted inside the hole.

"Wai…" The word fizzled on Aron's tongue. He shook his head, feeling stupid for trying to talk to his new imaginary friend. He laid on his stomach and peered into the hole. Sure enough, no doll, talking or otherwise, was lying inside. But what he did see was a much better lit room connected to his by twelve feet or so of tunnel. He slid into the opening, using elbows and toes to shimmy himself forward, his ankle protesting with every push.

After what seemed like hours, he pulled himself into the room. By then, every inhale felt like a porcupine burrowing through his esophagus, every cough-peppered exhale as if he were trying to vomit up a coral reef. A bluish haze seemed to cloak everything in the room, perhaps resulting from the watery sheen over his eyes. He pulled off his shirt, already of little consequence against the cold night air, and used its relatively cleaner underside to dab his eyes.

He gasped as the room came into view. Moonlight poured in from the ceiling, through a gaping circular hole that penetrated five more ceilings on its way up through the roof as if a meteorite had plummeted straight down to the basement and vaporized upon impact with the stone floor.

At the room's center sat a standard folding table, candle stubs aligning it as if it were some kind of altar. Black sludge marked most of the table, but as Aron looked closer, he saw the clumpy substance formed what looked like hieroglyphics or runes, maybe geometrical shapes or some language Aron had never seen. The circle itself seemed to be one giant sigil, but aside from many eyes around its circumference, he could not make out what was depicted beneath the goop.

Piles of bones and rusted manacles were arranged around the four walls, all which lacked doors or windows. Chains hung neglected from railroad spikes hammered into each façade, in some cases still attached to a forearm. Although the bones no longer connected to form true skeletons, Aron could easily identify them as human, the torsos and rib cages dead giveaways. Scraps of fabric interwove the piles, though if they'd once been garments, time and teeth had long since eaten away at them to the point of unrecognizability. He counted a dozen or so piles, though their skulls were noticeably missing.

He found them behind the table, arranged in a circle, each with a doll standing sentinel beside it. Although their mostly Victorian-style dresses, hair, and bonnets varied in color and material, all were like in size and composition such that they were likely constructed in the same era, if not by the same maker.

Like the rest of the bones, the skulls were fleshless. Strange runic markings were etched in the floor inside the circle. At its center, a large rat was slit open, its innards oozing from what looked like a fresh gash in its belly.

Aron recoiled at the sight, together with the ongoing stench of the room, but he sensed no immediate danger. Though he had no idea how long it took skin and muscle to rot, he figured the bones must have been there a very long time. And the person or persons who had caused the bones to be there would also likely be long gone.

As creepy as he found the place to be, it was also his salvation. He doubted Vic would follow him in there, so he would just have to bear the room's awfulness until morning or whenever Vic and his crony decided to pack it up and leave. The bones were just bones, and the dolls were just dolls. Old-fashioned, sure, from an age well before Cabbage Patch Kids and Barbie, but silly, inanimate, unspeaking toys, nonetheless. Each wore a dress down to its feet, somehow as unmarred by time as their bisque doll arms and faces and hair that looked as real as his own. Nothing supernatural, nothing angelic, nothing alive.

And yet, they all seemed to be staring at him. He groaned, his sandpaper tongue scraping against the roof of his cotton-dry mouth. He coughed again and tasted copper. His head began to spin, and he keeled over.

When he righted and his vision cleared, a dozen pairs of glossy eyes all fell on him. As if whispered in his ear, the voice came again. "You are safe here…with us." Not one of the dolls had moved its lips.

Of course they didn't. They're just dolls. The thought came with little comfort. Someone unseen had still spoken to him. No, he was tripping, maybe from something in the air, on his clothes. *In my mouth?* Had to be. He spat. *Pull yourself together, man.*

"Safe here… with us," a multitude of whispers said, as if echoing each other.

Aron sucked in a breath. Goosebumps tingled over his arms. "Who are you?" He shifted his gaze about the room. "*Where* are you?"

His eyes fell upon one of the dolls, the same one he thought he'd seen or had imagined previously. Though it stood motionless, lips equally unmoving, Aron could sense on some subliminal level that the stronger voice belonged to it, perhaps having been projected like a ventriloquist's. He knew how crazy that sounded, but he couldn't shake its truth.

"What are you?"

The dolls did seem to move then, ever so slightly, their gazes not so much shifting rather seeming to alter due to the way the light glinted off their lifeless eyes. Each had a hand resting on a skull, which Aron could have sworn had not been the case a moment earlier.

"We found an escape," the voice whispered. "We can help you escape, too."

"Can help you…escape, too," several other whispering voices echoed without unison.

The dolls shimmered like black-and-white televisions going in and out of focus. When they came in clear again, they each were a step closer.

"Escape? How?" Aron studied the skulls once more, one for each doll. *Do they want to make me a doll, too?* "I'm good." Hands out in front of him, Aron took a step backward, his body fleeing from what his mind couldn't fathom. His breath hitched and his coughing intensified, amplifying further when the dolls phased out and phased back in closer still. He gasped and clutched at his chest, his coughing fit straining his rib cage to the point of bursting. A semi-solid, semi-liquid black substance, like mucus-coated gelatin, jettisoned from his mouth onto his hand. As he studied it, it slid across his knuckles as if alive.

He flung it off his hand with a jerk. While he'd been distracted, the dolls had moved in around him, staring up in a semi-circle of ghastly light. He took another step back and bumped into the folding table, leaning away from the figures so much that he nearly fell upon it. His head spun, and the room spun, and he vomited more of the thick, brackish gunk. He turned, tried to run, but his sudden sickness rendered him dizzy and weak. He braced himself on the table before his hand slipped in its filth and collided against its edge as he fell to the ground.

His breaths came short. His lungs felt like water balloons under a faucet that wouldn't turn off. Gurgling wheezes emitted from his throat as gelatinous slime oozed from the corners of his mouth.

As his eyes blinked in and out of focus and his voice failed him, he glimpsed the dolls around him, their tiny porcelain hands reaching.

A camera focuses on what appears to be an altar in a dilapidated room, sun shining in through the ceiling and through an absent wall to the left, where dust and debris are thicker.

News Anchor: "A grisly scene was discovered in Fall River today as demolition crews uncovered what police have described as a serial killer's trophy room in a long-abandoned mill on Globe Street. Apparently operating sometime in the 1920s or '30s, the killer or killers appear to have targeted young women, with multiple remains suggesting over a dozen victims.

"Also among the dead, a homeless man, yet unidentified, who is believed to have made the macabre setting his home. Though the investigation is ongoing, the man's death seems unlikely to be related to the century-old homicides, with asbestos and/or mold poisoning being the likely culprit. Although an autopsy has yet to be conducted, the medical examiner set off more protests outside city hall with his comments about the extent of the asbestos and mold that had plagued the deceased, presuming years of prolonged exposure that may have been avoided had the city taken action to remediate the longstanding dangerous conditions the condemned mill sites continue to pose. Mayor Ferreira has pledged to level all remaining abandoned properties, calling them junkie dens and deathtraps for our curious children and homeless communities."

As the camera zooms in on the altar, a large rat stares back from its perch thereon. Its eyes gleam with an intelligence unbefitting the base creature. As it scurries out of sight, it seems unaffected by the gash running down its belly and its exposed entrails dragging in the grime.

– JASON PARENT is an author of horror, thrillers, mysteries, science fiction and dark humor, though his many novels, novellas, and short stories tend to blur the boundaries between genres. From his EPIC and eFestival Independent Book Award finalist first novel, *What Hides Within*, to his widely applauded police procedural/supernatural thriller, *Seeing Evil*, to his fast and furious sci-fi horror, *The Apocalypse Strain*, Jason's work has won him praise from both critics and fans of diverse genres alike.

The Cleaner

Victoria Dalpe

The tall man unlocked the gate and waved Lee in her van down a narrow alley lined with trash cans to the door at the back of the mill building. The boxy three-story structure was long ago painted a pinkish hue, the kind of color that had been labeled 'flesh' in the crayon box when she was a kid. It was the color of *no one's* flesh, of that she was certain. Lee maneuvered the rickety old van so that she was backed up close to the stairs. The man watched anxiously, occasionally spitting on the ground.

Up close, he was rail thin, his shirt and pants rumpled as if they'd passed the night on the floor before being tossed back on. It was clear he'd spent a lot of time outdoors, and it was hard to guess his age. Could have been thirty or sixty. He didn't say anything to her, just squinted, and she fought the urge to fill the silence with chatter. She hated long awkward silences. He fished out a ring of keys and flicked through them as he made his way up the cracked cement stairs to the rusted metal door. Only when he found the right key did he turn and look at her, as if really seeing her for the first time.

"It's bad in there. Are you all alone?" he asked.

When she nodded, he looked surprised. Then again, they usually were. She was a petite woman, barely five feet and a hundred pounds, the kind often described as "cute." She wore an oversize gray coverall and a big backpack that was nearly the same size as her.

"They tell you what to expect?" he said, sizing her up, his face humorless.

She lifted the bucket filled with additional cleaning supplies. "Yes. It's the job."

"I don't get paid enough for this shit," he muttered.

"Same," she said with a forced smile.

With his duty done, he nodded curtly. He did not open the door though; instead he stepped as far back as he could in the narrow stairway and stared off into the distance. She waited.

"Don't think this will be the last one. Seems they are getting braver by the day."

"Or hungrier," she supplied and he grimaced.

"Yeah, I told the owner not to let people move in. But he didn't listen. Just lock up when you're done and put the key in the mailbox there." He pointed to the rusty mailbox on the wall: R, Jenkins. Then he pried the key from the ring with shaky hands, his grimy nails chewed down to the quick. He opened the door and a belch of hot foul air rushed out. It was too dark to see anything inside. She'd stepped toward the doorway when his arm shot out and grabbed her. His hand was warm and strong through the sleeve of her jacket.

"Hey, uh, *it's all still in there*. All of it, you get me?"

She swallowed. "Yes. It's the job."

He squinted at her, meeting her eyes for the first time, his hand still on her arm. This close, she caught his sour smell which was a mix of alcohol and not washing himself enough.

"Don't stay after dark. I warned all those artsy idiots as they moved in. But they thought it was a big joke."

She met his bloodshot eyes. "I'll be out by dark and this place will be good as new soon enough. Now, if you'll excuse me." She glanced at his hand on her bicep. He dropped it and stepped back.

"Okay, okay. Be discreet...we got business neighbors there and there." He pointed to the squat auto repair shop with bay doors open and rock music playing and across the parking lot was a generic brick mill building, some sort of precision machining from the sign. "I don't need any more trouble from this situation, you got me? I'm just trying to make an honest living here as the property manager. I don't need the cops and fire inspectors coming around."

She doubted he was making an honest living—anyone living there was illegal—but also knew it was none of her business. Hers wasn't to ask questions, it was to erase the problems.

She forced a smile. "Discretion is part of the job description. Now, let me get to work so you can go back to your regular life, okay?"

He nodded as he headed down the rest of the steps. Finally, Lee went inside, shutting the door behind her.

The smell was a complex bouquet of floral rot, cigarette smoke, trash, and stale sweat. There had been a heat wave the last few days and it felt like stepping into a recently used oven. Or a garbage incinerator. The telltale bloom of human decay was a scent that she'd come to know very well. It was sweeter than other mammals. Her dad said it was the fat.

Lee felt around the wall until she found the switch. Banks of dingy overhead lights clicked on, barely chasing away the thick shadows. The windows, what few were there, were covered.

There was a lot of blood. Everywhere.

There were also a lot of bluebottle flies, attracted to death and gore. They buzzed around her face and she shook her head to shake them off. She hated flies and found them absolutely maddening. She thought of horses she'd seen as a kid, vainly trying to swat the flies with their tails, but they were never long enough. The flies walked all over their faces and congregated on their actual eyeballs. She waved away a few more flies and pushed her disgust away.

The mill space had been converted into an illegal living space, with a hodgepodge kitchenette consisting of a grimy fridge and mismatched cabinets with a hot plate and ancient coffee pot. There was a rickety bistro set, more likely to be seen in a garden. The kitchen had a mound of dishes in the sink swarming with yet more flies and skittering roaches. There was a slab of melted butter in a dish on the counter. There were even a few inches of coffee left in the coffee pot. An open newspaper was on the small table.

The newspaper had blood spatter and she noted the corner of the kitchen counter had a ribbon of skin and a tuft of hair. Like someone had fallen against it and shorn off a chunk of scalp. The flooring was heavily scored wood that was soft under her feet and spoke of the many years this place operated as a factory. From the give when she pressed with her foot, it was most likely rotted.

In the corner near the fridge was a hole big enough for a person to crawl through. She could see the gnaw and claw marks from below. They must have been working to get in for some time. She toed the edges around the hole; the floor felt secure enough around it. Now she knew how they got in.

She played out how it happened: Night Shift must have busted through the hole while he was reading the paper. He jumped up and then fell back and cracked his skull on the counter. He got up and tried to flee…

…into the "living room space" with rough plywood walls plastered with posters and graffiti. The other side of the wall was a bedroom. On the back wall was an open doorway to a bathroom. The living room had an ancient revolting brown carpet that had gone black in the areas where blood had soaked in. The walls were streaked with blood, as was the partial drop ceiling above. She sighed at that, because the porous material of the asbestos tile made it so hard to clean well. *Trash. The ceiling tiles would all be trash.*

She followed the blood toward the bedroom, finding a finger lying on the carpet like a little worm. She knelt and poked at it, noting the rough edge at the knuckle.

Must have been bitten off, she mused. *Odd, they didn't eat it.* She slid it into a rubber glove and put it in her pocket.

She noted the tatty orange plaid sofa and a wooden spool that must have held phone lines or something similar once but now functioned as a coffee table. A television sat on a rickety rolling cart, a floor lamp leaned, and a bookcase made of wood and cinder blocks was filled with books and records. The trash was overflowing and the recycling box on the floor was filled with liquor and beer bottles. Piles of shoes lined a wall: sneakers, combat boots, loafers, flip flops. Looked to be the same size and all male.

She followed the trail to a bloody handprint on the bedroom door. Missing the ring finger, she noted.

The bedroom was a small sad space with stained off-white walls, a mattress on the floor and unmade bedding. A large mirror perched on a dresser overflowing with clothes. The dead man was half on, half off the mattress. He wore a T-shirt, torn open at the neck and a pair of boxer shorts. They gaped open giving her a glimpse at his withered manhood. She was surprised they hadn't eaten that too. They usually did. He was in his mid-thirties, soft in the middle, with messy brown hair. He had a lot of tattoos.

There wasn't much of his face left; his lower jaw was gone as was his tongue. His neck was chewed open, and his stomach had a bowling ball-sized hole in it. A tendril of intestine hung out, but she doubted there was much of his organs left in the cavity. They must have been scared off, because there was plenty left of him to eat. This man looked to live alone so had they timed things better, they could have eaten him down to the bones without much trouble. Then again, that would involve planning and efficiency, and that was not their forte. The Night Shifters were brutes with big stomachs and small brains. It was just a fact. She wouldn't say it to their faces, but then again, there wasn't much she would say if confronted with them.

"Let's get to it shall we?" She addressed the body.

Overall, it was not the hardest job she'd had. That had been at a small mom and pop restaurant. Over *twenty* bodies practically painted every inch of the place with gore. Not to mention the challenge of discreet disposal. Now that had been a big multi-day project. She'd needed backup for the bodies alone.

The trick she'd found over the years with this type of work was taking it bit by bit. Otherwise, the jobs were overwhelming. She put an audiobook on, then brought the bucket and cleaners in from the steps. From her giant backpack she pulled out her plastic coverall and booties. She stripped the dead man naked then wrapped the body and the finger in a plastic sheet and dragged him to a clear corner. She would deal with him last. She knew other Cleaners who dealt with bodies first, but she found the quality of work was much shoddier overall when she did that. Better for the body to be last. That was her rule.

She quickly worked up a sweat in the hot space wearing cotton coveralls and plastic ones on top. Her mouth tasted of salt. Damned heat wave. Had the weather stayed cooler, she wouldn't be so uncomfortable, nor would the swarms of flies be so bothersome.

With a grunt, she moved the couch and then rolled up the gross old rug. It stuck to the floor tenaciously in a few spots. Then she went about with a trash bag to gather any obvious bloodstained items. She stuffed the newspaper, the posters on the walls, the books spattered on the shelf. Lee hated to throw out the books, but there wasn't much to do about it. The record covers she could wipe down, but paper pages? There was no way.

Although it was time consuming, she washed all the old dishes and put them away. Then she was able to wipe down all the surfaces properly with a blood-dissolving cleaner. She tossed the hunk of scalp in the bin.

Then, she'd had to retrieve her ladder from the van to get the drop ceiling down. So much trash. She stripped the sofa and soaked the cushion covers in the bathtub. The bedding was tossed into the tub as well. Then she sprayed the mattress down, pleased with the speed the blood lifted and disappeared. The new cleaning compounds were pretty impressive for blood.

Outside, the sun was blinding after her time in the dark space and it took a few moments of blinking before she could see well enough to scan the area for witnesses. It was easier to work at night, but with the building infestation of Night Shifters, she didn't want to end up in a tug of war over a dead corpse. No, better to clean up while they slept, even if it upped the risk.

The garage was open, but she couldn't see anyone coming or going, so she started hauling the rug and trash bags to the van. After enough trips up and down that her legs and back burned, the space was nearly clean. She'd been working for hours and the sun was already midway across the sky.

Need to be done by dusk.

They had an uneasy truce, the Cleaners and the Night Shift. They helped each other in their own way, but they weren't friends.

She'd had a lot more calls to these old mill buildings as the transients and artists moved in. She couldn't blame the people who needed cheap places to live, rents were crazy high everywhere. But the landlords knew better and were courting danger, as the Night Shifters had long lived in and used the tunnels beneath the neighborhood to nest. As long as these old mills had been operational, there had been a strict 'in by dawn, out by dusk' rule. The Night Shifters slept through the days deep underground and left the people above alone, but at night they woke hungry and climbed out. It wasn't safe to be in their territories after dark.

But people had short memories and the factories and mills were long vacant. Opportunists saw whole swaths of the city abandoned like a ghost town. And more government types were looking at the blighted land they sat upon as prime real estate for luxury condos, for affordable housing, for a new bigger school. She had a feeling she would be getting a lot more work if they broke ground on any of that.

Lee sniffed. *Good luck. Night Shifters could do a lot of damage fast.*

And like the sucker fish riding along the bodies of sharks, wherever there were Night Shifters, there were Cleaners. They left the mess and the Cleaners tidied it up. Scavengers to some, opportunists to others, but forever linked to the Night Shift. She didn't hate it though. Lee liked that she had a purpose and a place.

Her job meant something.

She hung the couch cushions over the shower rod to drip dry. The couch was hideous but could be reused now. The rest of the bedding she decided to bag up and toss. She cleaned the bathroom; it hadn't gotten bloody but was disgusting and she liked to be thorough.

After a walk-through, she was pleased. Her watch said it was four-thirty, keeping her on schedule. She worked hard and was tired and hungry. Now she could deal with the body. But first she rolled the heavy spool table over and covered the hole through which the Night Shifters came up. It wouldn't stop them, but it would deter them.

Then, from the van, she retrieved her cooler and knife set. She unrolled the plastic, what blood remained had congealed and a mess of flies swarmed in excitement as his naked pale body tumbled out of his tight wrappings. She examined the man, deciding to start with the soft meat of his backside. She laid out her knives and got to work.

Lee was precise, her work always quality. She cut the hands and feet off, bagging them. She knew someone who liked to use them to make soup stock. Then out came the eyes, the soft parts of the cheeks and the brain. She slid the skin back and expertly butchered the remains. Each piece she wrapped in wax paper and stacked in the ice cooler like little gifts. Only when he was little more than bones and gristle did she allow herself to eat a bit. She'd saved herself a piece off the glutes, which was her favorite. She ate it slowly, savoring it, occasionally waving her hand to scatter the flies.

It was a shock, to say the least, when Lee learned of her family's business and heritage. Her father owned a commercial cleaning company that he'd inherited from his father and her mother worked at a funeral home. She'd never thought much about it until she'd turned thirteen and gone through a growth spurt. She couldn't seem to get enough to eat and no matter how much or how often she ate, the hunger burned deep inside, never sated.

Her father took note and made her a special dinner, a pasta Bolognese, which was still one of the most delicious meals she'd ever eaten. Even all these years later, Lee could close her eyes and taste the soft noodles, the sweetness of the tomato, and the ground meat, perfectly seasoned.

Only after the meal and the first good night of rest in a long time did her father explain that the meat had been that of a dead man.

"We eat the human dead," he said as simply as if he was telling her the time. "I hate the word ghoul, but it is what it is."

Ghoul. It was an ugly word. She learned that her family preferred the term Cleaner and that they often worked closely with those in the know who didn't want to cause a fuss. People who wanted bodies disappeared. Oftentimes these were bodies created by Night Shifters, or criminals.

"We aren't doing anything wrong," her father told her the first day he'd taken her to work. She'd stared down at the body, a young woman, partially eaten, her wounds wriggling with larvae. She should have found the sight revolting but it made her stomach rumble instead. She fought the urge to drop to the ground and bite into the dead flesh with her blunt human teeth.

"I know how you feel, but in this day and age, we must treat every corpse as if it may be our last. We need to gather up all the meat to freeze and share with those of us who can't hunt on their own. The butcher, Mr. Mitchell? He sells our cuts to specific clientele. So today I'll show you how best to carve up a person."

And from then on, this was her job and life. She cleaned the bodies that the monsters, authorities, gangs, or whomever did not want found or investigated. She erased their deaths and helped her people to survive in a world becoming harder and harder to live in.

"In the old days, the bodies were buried in pine boxes or even better, simple shrouds. No chemicals, no nothing. You get a job as a gravedigger, like my great-great grandfather, and you could feed your whole community. Easy. No harm done, no crime done, nothing. Could just dig up your dinner with no one the wiser. Now, we have to rely on the scraps of the fucking monsters and mobsters."

Monsters and mobsters.

Once she finished, she noted the time and started to clean up from her meal. The sun was dipping low, the sky a riot of oranges and plums. The bones were gathered. The skin she put in another container. The meat was secured tightly in the cooler. She wrapped the scraps in plastic for disposal and hauled it all to the van. The machine shop appeared to be closed, but the garage was still bustling with music and cars. She moved as fast and efficiently as she could. She had just slid the cooler in and closed the van when someone called out, "Excuse me?"

Lee clapped a gloved hand to her mouth to hold in a scream.

The girl was in her mid-twenties, same as Lee, with a shaved head dyed yellow and a few star tattoos on her cheek. She had a septum piercing and wore all black denim. In one ear was a dangling knife earring.

"Yes?" Lee said, thankful that she'd stripped off the plastic coverall and booties on her last trip. Though she noticed a smear of blood on her rubber glove and quickly put her hand behind her.

"Um, who are you? What are you doing here?"

"I'm helping clean the space after the last tenant left," Lee responded coolly.

"Bullshit. Rich didn't just leave. I saw him Friday, and we had plans tonight."

Lee shrugged. "I don't know what to tell you. I was hired to clean up this space. No one has been in there all day but me."

The girl pushed past Lee calling out Rich's name as she went. Lee decided to follow in part to see how well her clean-up job appeared to someone who knew him and his home. She watched the girl stomp through the space, sticking her head in the bathroom and bedroom, but it was basically a big box without many places to hide.

"See?" Lee said. "Just me here, cleaning up."

"Cleaning up what? Where is Rich?"

"I wish I could tell you. I was hired to come and clean up, that's all."

She narrowed her eyes on Lee's hand. The hand that had blood on it.

"Look, I have to go. Was supposed to be done by now, and I need to lock up. I don't know where your friend is."

"I want to wait for him," she said, chin jutting up defiantly.

Lee's eyes cut to the wooden spool in the corner. "I can't let you. Should I call the landlord and tell him you're here? Or the police?"

The woman shook her head. "No. No. I have a friend who lives down the street. I'll go over there. I'll just come back later." Lee was tempted to warn her away from the neighborhood entirely, knowing that the Night Shifters had a way into the building, but held back. Wasn't her job.

She walked the woman out, turning off the lights and locking the door. "I'm sorry your friend wasn't here," Lee told the girl, who looked like she was going to cry.

"Me too," she said, jamming her hands in her pockets as she walked away.

"It's not safe around here at night, so you should hurry." Lee dropped the key in the old mailbox. The last tendrils of sun dipped behind the garage, which had closed in the time she was dealing with the girl.

Only once she was driving away did she breathe a sigh of relief. It may have been a trick of the light, but she swore she saw something moving along the alley. A hunched thing with a shock of white skin.

She took a sharp turn and the cooler slid along the floor of the van, reminding her of its contents.

Her stomach growled.

– VICTORIA DALPE is a Providence-based horror writer and painter. Her short fiction has appeared in over forty-five anthologies. Her previous books include a short story collection, *Les Femmes Grotesques*, and the gothic horror novel *Parasite Life*. She is a member of the HWA and the New England Horror Writers.

The Circle

Christa Carmen

Foster, Rhode Island, 1893

There was something about drying and mixing the herbs, no matter how many times she'd done it, that calmed whatever turmoil might twist through the forest of her mind. Dolly Cole poured the caraway into a satchel, the oblong seeds as crisp and carapaced as tiny insects, and promised herself it would all be okay.

Mabel toddled into the kitchen, cheeks ruddy, blue eyes bright. "Mama," she said, and Dolly marveled—for at least the thousandth time—at the melodious lilt of her daughter's voice, at its ability to bring joy to her heart no matter the circumstances.

"Yes, my love?"

"Books? We weed books by da fire?"

Dolly looked to the window to find night was almost upon them. "Yes, my love," she assured her. "Mama's almost done with this work."

Tomorrow, she would bring the caraway seeds, along with lemon balm, catnip, motherwort, and ginger, to Edith Fisher for the purposes of easing her monthly malaise. Dolly provided many of their neighbors with elixirs and remedies, to their boundless gratitude and great relief. Only recently had the whispers started; the occasional curious look tinged with suspicion and malice. Now Dolly held her daughter's hand a little tighter on their walks through the woods or the town square, pulling her close no matter whom they passed.

It's the mill, she decided. *Something in the mill is turning them against us.* For, wasn't it those who worked at Ramtail Factory who were the most contentious, who shot her the cruelest and most disagreeable looks? Those who labored in the home—or the schoolhouse, the library, even the police station—they were still engaging with Dolly, still appealing to her for her modest and well-wrought remedies. The men and women of the mill held animosity in their eyes, tiny blazes fanned by the heat to which they were subjected in the large, airless rooms, feeding the machinery with as many broken dreams and mangled fingers as they did spools of wool and cloth.

Dolly shook her head to clear her thoughts, finished tying off the satchel, and placed it in the pocket of her shawl for the next morning. She wiped her hands on her apron, scooped Mabel up, and carried her to the bookshelf.

"Which story would you like, my little raindrop?" She pressed her cheek to her daughter's and knelt, knees popping, so they could peer at the spines together.

"Dis!" Mabel cried, and Dolly took hold of the one she was pointing to.

"*The Light Princess?*" Dolly asked, and Mabel nodded her head fervently.

Dolly had abridged the Scottish fairy tale herself, bringing the illustrations to life—with berry-juice-blacks, dandelion-dust-yellows, and rusty, metallic-smelling reds—by candlelight over the course of several evenings while Mabel slept, choosing which scenes to depict with the same care she used to prune the stalks of echinacea and lavender spikes in the large back garden, then binding the parchment with twine.

Dolly carried both book and child to the worn rocking chair in the corner. "If it's the Light Princess you want, then the Light Princess you shall have," she said, breathing in Mabel's lilac-and-honeyed scent.

As they settled in, Dolly tried to revel in the tickle of her daughter's curls against her neck and the warmth of Mabel's hand pressed into her forearm. If she focused hard enough on those sensations, maybe she wouldn't have to see what was in her head. Wouldn't have to see the figure that had been plaguing her for months.

"The only time the princess could remain tethered to the ground was when she was submerged in water," Dolly read. "To break the curse, it was thought that the princess needed to cry. But this was the one thing she could not do. And so, the light princess despaired, without love and without even one ounce of weight to her body to hold her down."

Twilight pressed in on the windows. The image on the page shimmered, and Dolly was no longer seeing the outline of a young maiden but the figure that haunted her. It was an impossibility, all silvery-white and wet, trailing spray like an angry swan rising from the water. She shouldn't be surprised it came to her now; the figure accosted her every waking thought and filled her sleep with visceral, dread-inducing nightmares. Earlier that very evening, it had escaped the confines of her skull and rushed, pell-mell, right at her, as she stooped at the brook's edge for a pailful of water.

The ghostly figure had reached for her—too-large hands outstretched and stream-damp hair trailing like vines. Dolly had yelped and fallen backward onto the rocky bank, certain whatever fate awaited her at the hands of the specter was a dire one. But when she'd opened her eyes, the brook was empty. No fast-moving water-woman, bare toes dragging along the otherwise placid surface, no shriek that seemed to sound both all around her and only in her head. Dolly had looked around, blinking and wondering if the vision had been sent by a vengeful God or from some deep, damaged fold of her brain.

"Mama," Mabel warbled, and Dolly realized she'd paused in her reading.

"Sorry, my love." Dolly cleared her throat and pushed the silvery ghost from her mind yet again. "The sorceress discovered that the princess adored the lake," she continued, "so she set out to dry it up, along with the springs and the rain. The princess's one love was taken from her, her one weakness used against her."

Dolly finished the story and then two more. The night wore on, and Mabel's earnest questions were replaced by the child's slow and rhythmic breathing as she slumbered in their shared bed in the corner. Dolly's thoughts turned to the men and women who poured from the mill like ants each afternoon, their faces lined, their voices bitter.

The visions—and dreams—of the specter on the water had begun around the same time that the townsfolk had turned against her. She'd made it a point, ever since, to avoid the water when the mill let out for the afternoon. To never be close enough to hear the things they called her.

But their words followed her all the same, stuck into her skin like the fine, fierce stingers of wasps:

"Wretch."

"Wench."

"*Witch*."

Foster, Rhode Island, 2023

"Bitch."

"Excuse me?" Calista Stone had been called worse by a client, but this was her very first session with Marjorie Taylor. When they'd spoken by phone, the woman had been practically bursting with excitement at having found a licensed psychotherapist in the area. Now, Marjorie seemed wary, as if she feared someone might have seen her coming into Calista's office and would judge her accordingly.

"Sorry." Marjorie had the decency to look sheepish. "I'm just telling you what I heard."

Calista nodded slowly. "So, let me get this straight. People in Foster are calling me a bitch because I opened a marriage and family therapy practice, but I'm not from the area?"

Marjorie shrugged. "What can I say? We're incredibly suspicious of outsiders. Oh, and anyone from the city."

Calista closed her eyes. She prayed Theo was having a better time of it at the high school, but for some reason, she doubted it. If only Theo would open up to her again, like she used to, before adolescence had rendered her as closed off as—

Calista's thoughts were interrupted by a familiar crackling. When she opened her eyes, Marjorie Taylor was on fire in front of her. Flames engulfed the woman's face, climbing her cheeks, her hair, charring her flesh, melting her features. The smell of burnt flesh and fabric stung her nostrils, and the shriek that emanated from Marjorie's—no, not Marjorie's, the charred woman's, for it was her, the woman from her dreams—black mouth seemed to sound both all around her and only in her head.

Goosebumps rose on her arms. Tears of terror and helplessness welled in her eyes. She tried to breathe, but the air caught in her throat, and Calista thought she might be on fire too.

"Dr. Stone, are you okay?"

Calista blinked. Marjorie's hair and skin were back where they were supposed to be. There were no flames, no shrieks of agony, though she swore the smell of burnt flesh still hung in the back of her throat. She coughed. "I'm fine." She willed herself to actually *be fine*. "Now, what was it you were saying?"

"Oh, um, just that this office space is right where the old mill used to be. Did you know that? It was demolished years ago, but so many of us in Foster have connections to the place. Generations of family members who worked there." Marjorie smiled, but it looked a little pained.

Calista nodded, desperate to get the session back on track. "Did you have family who worked there? Or your husband? I know you came in today because you wanted to talk about troubles you were having with him."

Marjorie's jaw tightened. "We're beyond trouble at this point. We're separated. He's got a new girlfriend. Some nutjob named Lana. Fancies herself a regular Lorraine Warren."

At Calista's blank expression, Marjorie squawked, "You mean to tell me you don't know Ed and Lorraine Warren? You've never seen the *Conjuring* movies?"

Calista stiffened. The fiery figure flashed in her brain. "I'm not really a fan of horror movies," she replied.

Marjorie looked as if she wanted to say more but changed her mind. "Regardless," Marjorie said, "this nutjob Lana, she likes to hold séances, spend the night in the cemetery, debunk supposedly haunted houses, stuff like that. She's pulled my Joe into everything. They do it together, now, like a regular business. It's ridiculous."

Marjorie spent the rest of the session talking about how she should earn a portion of Joe and Lana's 'ghosthunter earnings,' since she was technically still married to him. Calista listened as best she could, half-haunted by the image of the woman on fire and half-distracted by the knowledge that she'd been officially elected to the role of town pariah. How was she going to earn a living for herself and her daughter if the people of Foster equated working with a psychologist to some sort of witchcraft, unfit for the reputable citizens of the town?

Five minutes past the hour—and fifteen minutes past the time when Marjorie's appointment should have ended...for someone who was suspicious of outsiders, Marjorie sure could talk a lot—Calista was finally able to bid the woman farewell. She watched Marjorie exit the building, closed the door and picked up her cell phone.

Theo answered on the first ring. "Hi, Mom. I was just about to call you."

Calista relaxed at the sound of her daughter's voice. "That's nice to hear. So are you all set then? I just finished my last—" she did not tell Theo her *only* "—appointment of the day, and wanted to see if you were ready for me to pick you up."

"I'm actually helping out with an after-school project."

Calista paced before the mirror, careful not to accidentally look inside it, where the figure of the burning woman might wait. "Oh, that's great, honey. Have fun with the other kids. What time do you need me to pick you up?"

"I can get a ride. Is that okay?"

She wanted to say no. She wanted to pick up Theo herself, right now even, and bring her safely home, away from the thinly veiled malevolence of the town. But she also didn't want to ruin Theo's chances for a life here, if she was on track to have one. Not to mention that Calista had sunk all their savings into moving to Foster, believing its fewer providers per capita would work in their favor.

Calista swallowed her fear and forced a smile into her voice. "Of course. I'll see you for dinner?"

"Sure," Theo said. "See you then."

Calista hung up and looked across the county highway, a potholed, mostly deserted stretch of road where, beyond its curves and crests, the Westconnaug Reservoir lay like a quiet cauldron. *Makes sense there used to be a mill here*, she thought. *Though, not so much that the people who've lived in Foster since those mill days haven't evolved beyond their tribalist thinking.*

Calista closed her appointment calendar, walked several textbooks and case studies to the bookshelves in the room's far corner, then collected her jacket, purse, and keys.

She may be an interloper, but she'd remain on the outside looking in for an eternity as long as Theo found her place. Calista walked out of the building alone and, if she were being honest, lonely, thinking of the men and women who, once upon a time, would have streamed out of the mill doors together, that sense of community, comradery.

Please let Theo find more in common with the folks in Foster than I have, she thought as she drove away, the sun in her rearview mirror like a ball of fire.

Foster, Rhode Island, 1893

Edith Fisher lived north of the brook, her small abode flanked on either side by farmland—the Rhodes' place to the west, the Vaughans' place to the east—and Dolly enjoyed the damp spring morning, rife with birdsong and the scent of dogwood blossoms, as she walked. One hand was in the pocket of her shawl to ensure the various satchels of herbs remained in place, the other clutched Mabel's small fingers.

Her daughter was imitating the loud, two-parted whistles of a cardinal, her little-girl voice turning the trills into something comical and vague. They'd left early, and so she allowed Mabel's near-constant stooping to collect myriad treasures: a pebble here, a feather there, various acorn caps and sticky pinecones. The trinkets would keep the girl entertained while Dolly explained to Edith how to best prepare each remedy. The woman was busy with several young ones of her own and often forgot Dolly's instructions from one month to the next.

But when they got to Edith's door, Dolly was surprised to see Edith already waiting, her round face pressed to the front window like a flower moon. Dolly helped Mabel onto the stoop and waited, straightening her shawl and smoothing Mabel's hair. The door opened an inch, then another. Edith had seen them. Why wasn't she welcoming them inside? Then Dolly saw the hard, hawkish look on the woman's face, and the way she peered over Dolly's shoulder, as if keen to determine if anyone had followed Dolly, or watched them now.

"Edith?" Dolly started when the woman still didn't greet her. She unearthed one of the satchels and held it up. "I brought your remedies, as promised."

Edith's eyes darted to the woods again, then back to Dolly. "I won't be needing them." Her tone was curt, if not a little apologetic.

Dolly laughed lightly. "Whatever do you mean? I added lemon balm this time, like we talked about. That, with the motherwort, will have you feeling better right quick."

"No. Like I said, I don't need your spell work." Edith's tone was as cold as the brook in January. Dolly tried to catch the woman's eye, but Edith was looking everywhere but at her face. "Don't come back here, Dolly Cole," Edith continued. "Martha Wescott saw you by the water at midnight. She told me. You was under a full moon, mixing things in your pail, and you was naked!"

Dolly scoffed and resisted the urge to cover Mabel's ears. Luckily, the girl was distracted by two squirrels chasing one another along the branches of an elm. "That's the most ridiculous thing I ever heard," Dolly said. "Not to mention, what was Martha Wescott doing by the water at midnight? Surely the overseers at Ramtail don't abide late workers. I can't imagine Martha made it to her shift on time after galivanting along the brook in the middle of the night." She half-expected Edith to laugh and was disappointed when she didn't.

"So you confirm it, then? You were at the brook at midnight, cavorting with whatever Dark One gives you the recipes for those spells?"

Dolly scoffed again. "Good heavens, Edith, of course not."

Before she could say anything further, try to appeal to Edith's good sense, or convince Edith to let her in so they could discuss this off the front stoop and over a nice cup of tea, like the friends they were, or, at least, like the friends Dolly had thought them to be, Edith opened the door wide. Rather than gesture Dolly and Mabel inside, Edith took hold of a broom by the doorframe and shooed them off the stoop as if they were dogs.

"Leave here, Dolly Cole," Edith growled. "I won't be havin' the good Christian people of Foster seein' you on my doorstep. I won't be havin' those men and women who toil in the mill to make a decent living thinkin' I'm takin' shortcuts. The mills represent forward thinking and industrial progress. You trade in magic and superstition. Go on, now. Git!"

With this final word, Edith aimed the broom at Mabel, catching her in the chest and sending her toppling back into the dirt. Mabel's face twisted, first with outrage, then with fear, then finally with pain as her hands went to her backside, and she started to howl.

Dolly turned a look of shock and abhorrence at Edith. She reached into her pocket, grasped the bags there, and threw them at Edith Fisher's face. A curse was on her lips, and she was ready to heave it at Edith, to bury her in her disappointment and rage, but before she could open her mouth, Edith's form flickered.

The drab browns and greys of Edith's dress and apron shifted to something silvery and slippery, like the underside of minnow that'd jumped from the water to catch the sun in its scales. Edith—but, no, she was not Edith any more—flew down the stoop and right at Dolly, who shrieked and shrank back. Rather than the coarseness of the woman's skirts, she felt water, cold, shockingly cold, enveloping her as she sank. Dolly turned away, flailing for the ground, desperate to feel dirt beneath her fingers and not more water, gasping for breath. But the bite of the rising water did not come. Rather, she felt Mabel groping for her, heard her baby calling.

"Mama, Mama. Leave, lady. Les leave lady."

Dolly blinked. She was on the ground in front of Edith's cabin. Edith was not the figure from the brook, and she was not on top of Dolly. Edith stood on the stoop, staring at Dolly as if she truly were the evildoer she'd been told she was by the likes of Martha Wescott. Dolly swallowed, climbed to her feet, and scooped Mabel up, pressing her to her hip.

"Yes," she whispered to Mabel. "We leave. We leave this lady." She turned and glared at Edith. "We leave this lady and all her lies."

Edith backed into her house and closed the door.

Dolly did not put Mabel down until they'd crossed the brook, which bubbled as if in response to the indecencies Dolly and Mabel had suffered. When she did set her daughter down, brushing off her bottom and checking her arms for scratches, she found she was afraid to turn and look at the water. What if the figure was there, rising from the rocks, full of all the malice Dolly was finding the people of Foster felt for her, despite her having always been kind and helpful to them?

"Are you all right, my little raindrop?" Dolly asked. She knelt beside Mabel and cooed in her ear. The little girl took a piece of Dolly's hair between her fingers and worried it, a method of self-soothing she'd engaged in since she'd gained the coordination to do so. Dolly brushed her face against Mabel's and took her hand. "Come on, my love. Let's go home."

She led Mabel up the small hill toward their house, and at the top, she gathered her courage enough to look behind her. The brook coursed eastward, toward the Westconnaug Reservoir, formed when the owners of Ramtail Factory realized they'd turn a far larger profit should they control more than just their employees. Sometimes, oftentimes, Dolly wished the dam would burst.

Anger coursed through the brook of her own veins, swiftly, loudly. She saw the broom hit her daughter's chest and Edith turn into the silvery specter, and her vision went silvery-white with rage.

Let the people of Foster work their mill. Let them hold her back, as if by a dam. She would break free of them. And she would carry her daughter away from here. Toward safety. Away from whatever was haunting her. Pushing her back. Warning her.

Though, warning her of what, she did not know.

Foster, Rhode Island, 2023

Calista paced the kitchen. It was after eight o'clock and still no word from Theo. With a sickening feeling, she realized she didn't have the phone number for a single parent of Theo's classmates, didn't know the names of any of Theo's friends. Finally, she jumped in her car and drove to the school. She circled the building once and was halfway around a second time when she saw a small group of students milling by the senior parking lot.

"Hey," she called, rolling down her window. The students— two boys and a girl—fixed her with similar looks of boredom but sauntered over.

"Yeah?" the shorter boy asked. He looked to be sixteen or so, about Theo's age.

"My daughter, Theo, Theodora Stone. Do you know her? She said she was staying after school for a project, but that was hours ago, and I haven't heard from her."

The boy exchanged a look with the girl while the second boy glanced toward the woods beyond the squat brick building.

"Do you know where she is?" Calista pressed.

The girl seemed to decide something, sighed, and rolled her eyes. "She's with Joe Taylor and Lana Morgan. Lana is shooting some YouTube livestream tonight. Something about the Witch of Ramtail Factory." She paused, looking thoughtful. "Or maybe it was a vampire? I can't remember."

"I thought it was about the ghost of some cross-dressing prostitute that used to haunt the stream by the old mill." The tall boy said this flippantly, as if trying to get a rise out of Calista. She, of course, couldn't care less what sort of nonsense Marjorie's cheating husband and his mistress were filming. She just wanted to know where Theo was.

"Why would Theo be with them?" she asked.

The girl rolled her eyes again. "Lana came looking for someone to help with the livestream. You know, set up the tripods, manage the different cameras, that kind of thing." She shrugged.

"But why Theo? Did they offer to pay her?"

The girl looked at Calista with some mixture of pity and incredulity. "Why wouldn't Theo go? It's not like she has any other friends to hang out with. Sometimes kids, the losers, anyway, and the fuck-ups, go too, to watch whatever craziness goes down. But everyone else knows not to get mixed up with Joe and Lana. They're like Ed and Lorraine Warren, but an Ed and Lorraine who microdose on LSD."

The dread that'd been pooling in Calista's stomach rose like a flood. "Where are they shooting?"

The girl flipped her hair. "On the Westconnaug Reservoir somewhere."

"The western bank," the short boy added. When the girl shot him a look, he reddened. "What? Lana's hot. I might have watched a couple of her livestreams before."

Calista didn't thank them before peeling out of the lot. All this time, Theo had been struggling, and Calista hadn't known, too wrapped up in her own isolation and her failing practice. Had the students she'd just conversed with contributed to Theo's ostracization? Calista couldn't know, but she was sure of one thing: Nothing good could come of Theo out there in the dark with a pair of druggie hucksters and a bunch of kids circling the production like sharks hungry for blood.

With anxiety shooting through her bloodstream like a high voltage current, Calista pulled onto the 102 and pressed on the gas.

Foster, Rhode Island, 1893

The days passed with an aggressive mundanity after her run-in with Edith Fisher. Dolly tended to Mabel, and to the garden, but she made no deliveries, afraid of running into someone from the mill as she was. She needn't have worried, however, because after more than a week of this hermitude, spent venturing no farther than her garden—except, ironically, for quick jaunts to the brook for fresh water under the cover of darkness, always with an eye out for both callous neighbors and vengeful water spirits—Dolly was interrupted at the kitchen basin by a knock on her front door.

Shooting a quick glance toward Mabel, who was sitting at the center of her favorite braided rug, chattering to a floppy-necked ragdoll she waved around in one hand, Dolly dried her hands on her apron and crept to the window.

Outside stood three men, nary a friendly face among them: William Vaughan, Zachariah Rhodes, and Robert Wescott. Dolly considered her options. She could hide somewhere in the house and hope they went away, creep out the back door and into the woods, or answer the door and see what they wanted. She desired this last choice least of all, but this seemed the only option she could get away with. Dolly hurried over to Mabel, scooped her up, and placed her in the bassinet the girl hadn't slept in for over a year.

"Stay here, raindrop," Dolly whispered. "Play with your dollgirl. Mama will read you *The Light Princess* when I get back. Here." She reached for the book on the shelf, opened it, and placed it in Mabel's lap. "Look at the pictures for Mama, all right? I love you."

She ruffled the girl's hair and returned to the front of the house. Squaring her shoulders, Dolly lifted her chin, pushed open the door, and shut it behind her. She regarded each stern-faced man in turn. "Mr. Wescott, Mr. Vaughan, Mr. Rhodes, what can I do for you?"

"Dorothy Cole," Mr. Rhodes said, wasting no time. "We're all for progress in the township of Foster. My mill demands it." He smiled, but there was no joy in it. "You know this. And you know the people onto whom you've pushed your witchcraft, they're displeased with being forced into your brand of healing."

"I never forced anyone into anything," Dolly said.

Mr. Rhodes held up a hand. Mr. Wescott cleared his throat. "Now then," Mr. Rhodes continued. "We need some sort of pledge from you that you'll put this dark magic aside. That you won't go corrupting the good people of Foster with the Devil's tinctures and tonics."

Dolly felt something drop within her: dread plummeting down the river of her body to settle, like stones, in her stomach. "How do you suppose I'm to make a living, Mr. Rhodes?"

He chuckled. "Well, now, that's just it, Ms. Cole. That's why I came here. To offer you a good, wholesome position at Ramtail Factory pushing wool and cotton. You'll make a nice wage. And we'll be able to keep an eye on you. Make sure you're abiding by the same rules as every other unmarried woman in Foster." He looked past Dolly, into the window of her house, as if searching for the child he knew she had.

Silvery sheaths of water fluttered at the corners of Dolly's vision. *Not now*, she thought. For the moment, at least, the terror-inducing figure of the water woman stayed away. "Thank you, Mr. Rhodes, but I cannot accept," Dolly said. There was a tremor in her voice that was hard to control.

Mr. Rhodes' expression hardened. Mr. Vaughan cleared his throat. "We're not going to take no for an answer," Mr. Rhodes said.

"Well, you'll have to," Dolly replied. "Because that is my answer. No today. And no tomorrow, should you ask me then too. My business is healing and midwifery. I'd be no good to you in the mills. Now, good day to you, gentlemen. I must be getting back to my daughter. Thank you for calling." And with that, Dolly turned, slipped inside, and closed the door behind her.

She spent the rest of the day and all of that evening looking over her shoulder, glancing out the windows and into the golden sky of early twilight, certain she'd see someone else from Ramtail Factory coming to make the case for her to start work there. But no one came. By the time she put Mabel to bed, she was beginning to wonder if they'd leave her alone after this afternoon. They'd tried to scare her. They'd tried to strongarm her. When they found they could do neither, maybe they'd grown resigned to the idea that she would quietly return to helping those who needed her. Dolly doubted it, but as long as their brand of intimidation stayed firmly in the camp of dirty looks and rude outbursts on porch stoops, she could live with it.

Mabel was snoring lightly. What Dolly wanted more than anything was to soak in a warm bath. Wash away the uncomfortableness of the day. She glanced in the direction of the brook. She didn't like the idea of being in the water woman's domain after such a tumultuous afternoon. But, in the same way she wouldn't let Zachariah Rhodes push her around, she wasn't going to shrink in the face of fear—or Martha Wescott's ridiculous accusations. Dolly reached for the bucket by the hearth and slipped her shoes on. Before leaving the house, she walked over to the bed and leaned over Mabel.

"I'll be right back, my Light Princess. Dream your dreams of weightlessness, free to embrace that which you love."

Mabel did not stir when Dolly left the house.

The night was like something out of a fairy tale, pencil sketching-sky, trees like snake scales and abstract shapes like crouching cats. Dolly walked quickly, but she wasn't scared. So when the pail was full and reflecting the moon like a face in its surface, Dolly found she was tempted to stand a spell over the brook, letting fireflies wink in her periphery and spring peepers pierce her thoughts like sewing needles. She dug her bare toes into the muck and felt that something had shifted, some energy in the air. No longer would she be fearful of what the mill folk said. They could do nothing to her. The water woman was merely a projection of her fears, and she had conquered them.

No sooner had she thought this, then the water downstream began to swirl and collect. Simultaneously, she heard noises behind her, in the distance, also collecting, like voices growing in courage, ideas growing in unity. She smelled smoke. *People*, Dolly thought. *They're coming. They're coming for us.*

A maelstrom rose from the brook bottom.

Mabel, Dolly thought.

The water swirled into the shape of a woman.

She rushed Dolly so fast and deliberately, Dolly had only one possible direction she could go in. But it didn't matter. By the time she crested the hill between the brook and her house, the house was already beset with flames. Dolly rushed for the door with the same singlemindedness as the water woman had shown for her, but Zachariah caught her on one side. Dolly wasn't sure if she felt shocked or vindicated to find that it was Edith Fisher who held her on the other.

They restrained her while the house burned, Dolly fighting like a salmon in a bear's grasp, and when they felt it had burned beyond the point where she would go for it, they let her go.

Dolly went for it anyway. Through the mouth of fire that was the door, directly into the flames.

Light of spirit, by my charms,
Light of body, every part,
Never weary human arms—
Only crush thy parents' heart!

The curse brandished against the Light Princess played like a hymn in Dolly's mind as she held what was left of her daughter. Her arms were heavy with flame, and the pain was like water, rushing over her in waves, curling, liquifying, carrying her forward. Finally, the fire drove her, like the water woman, back—or was it forward?—and out of the house. Dolly heard whispers. She heard a nascent hum, like that of a spinning wheel. She wheeled around but could see nothing. She believed she carried Mabel in her arms still, but she couldn't be sure. Either of whether she held anything, or whether there was anything there with which to hold.

Somehow, she lurched, on feet of flame, her heart ice in her chest, to the edge of the bubbling water. She collapsed at the brook's bank, the ash of her body mixing with the clay and silt and sand and sediment. The world turned from red to silver. She blinked, feeling the end. The river woman was upon her, hoary-white and wet, but yet still and peaceful. Any rage she had once carried had been spent, taken up by the men and women who'd come for Dolly. Who'd come for her from the mills.

She was warning me, Dolly realized. *All along, warning me.*

Dolly took the water in the ruin of her fingers, the water that fed the mill, and she poured all her rage and hatred, her sorrow and regret, into it, as if a dam had burst. With every last ounce of her strength, she whispered:

"Heavy of spirit, by my charms,
Heavy of body, every part,
Always weary human arms—
Forever crush thy traitors' heart!"

And Dolly died, while the curse, once a prayer that had been whispered into the sleeping ears of a little girl to direct her dreams, was carried downstream by the water. It would enter the mill. And exit it.

Enter it.
And exit it.
Enter the people of the mill.
And exit them.
In a circle.
Forever unbroken.

Foster, Rhode Island, 2023

Calista saw the lights before she noticed the turnoff, and when she jerked the wheel to the right, a spray of gravel flew up from the wheels. Calista leapt from the car, leaving the door open, groping for her phone, trying—and failing—to enable its flashlight. The path was dark, even with the lights up ahead, and she stumbled as she tried to find its opening.

She'd just managed to eke out the general direction of the path when the area before her went up in flames. Calista sank to her knees, her skin prickling under the intense heat, water welling in her eyes. From the flames, a woman's arms reached forward, gripping her, and though the pain, the heat, was astronomical in its intensity, Calista felt it was pulling her forward to help her, to warn her, rather than to harm her.

A scream sounded in her mind, melding with the crackling of the fire, and through it, she heard voices, words. "Action!" "Move the camera back!" "Aim it that way! That's where Dolly Cole, the Witch of Ramtail Road, will appear from! See her? See her ghostly form?"

Somehow, Calista knew these words were spoken by Joe and Lana. But just as quickly, their words were drowned out by a slew of other, crueler voices. "That's no witch. At least, not a ghostly one. It's that fucking Theo chick! Stoner-Ed-and-Lorraine put her up to this! She's a fake!"

The flames licked through Calista's mind, writing understanding in ash upon the walls of her skull. Her Theo. Her everything. She'd been clothed in a gossamer dress, face painted to appear corpselike and drawn. Not hired as the camerawoman but the ghost. To be recorded on the banks of the water for Joe and Lana's latest hoax. Calista saw it all within the fiery vision as if she'd been there.

The flames exploded outward, then condensed, until Calista was staring, eyes burning, at the woman engulfed by flame. The figure circled her to push her forward from behind. Just when Calista could stand the heat no longer, the flames winked out, as if sucked into a vacuum, and all she was left with was the smell of smoke.

Calista blinked, felt her body for burns, but there was nothing. Up ahead, the voices, kids' voices, came again.

"Get her! She's an outsider! Drown the witch! Send her back where she came from!"

She ran, toward where the light had been, though, now the light was gone. In another moment, she saw why. A man who looked to be in his forties, and a woman, significantly younger, were shoving recording equipment into bags, panic smeared across their faces.

"Where is she?" Calista screamed at them. "Where's Theo?"

Neither Joe nor Lana answered. Lana abandoned the equipment altogether and ran, up the path Calista had just descended. Calista started screaming at Joe again but stopped when she heard the splash. Eyes darting to the water, she saw the black shapes there, about a hundred feet out.

Calista sprinted into the water, trying to high-step through it to keep up her speed, a desperate salmon thrashing against the stream. The deeper she got, the more panic threatened to consume her. She gasped for breath, while all around her, the spray of water from her wild charge morphed into flames that were subsequently smothered by the air.

There were four of them ahead. Indiscriminate, though human, shapes. As she neared them, they dispersed, two to each side, like beads of oil shooting out around a stream of water. Their attention was directed down, toward a concentric series of ripples. The ripples turned into a ring of flame, and Calista dove into its center.

Through the orange-white brilliance, she saw Theo, hair fanned out like the rays of the sun. Her body was deep, almost at the bottom of the reservoir, but floating upward. Calista reached for her, found her, pulled her up, through the flames and to the surface. When they broke the surface, the fire was water once more. The four bodies that had surrounded the scene of the drowning were gone. Calista turned toward land. Joe was gone. Lana was long gone. She was alone. Alone with the body of her daughter.

Calista carried Theo to the bank, where she stroked her cheeks. Her forehead. Her hands. She smoothed her hair. Felt the heat of her body as it was replaced with a dull coldness, as if Theo's flesh had become the river. She felt weightless. Though, hadn't Theo's gravity returned to her in the water? There, she'd been so heavy. There, the curse of their Otherness had been lifted.

Calista rummaged through the recording equipment Joe and Lana had left behind. She found the right sized rocks, encircled them with extension cords. Carrying them along with her daughter was easier than she anticipated. They, too, were apparently weightless.

She brought them out as far as she could swim. Far enough so that, once she gave them back their gravity, tethered them to it, there'd be no escaping it. When she released the rocks, they drew down like raindrops, cutting through night air. Calista felt the water in her fingers, the water that had once fed the mill, and she released all her rage and hatred, her sorrow and regret, into it, as if a dam had burst.

And Calista succumbed, the world turning from silver to red, like the fire-red skin of the charred woman who had haunted her. She sank alongside her daughter, to the place from where what had once made up their bodies would be carried upstream. It would enter the reservoir. And exit it.

Enter it.

And exit it.

Enter the people of the small town.

And exit them.

In a circle.

Forever unbroken.

– CHRISTA CARMEN lives in Rhode Island and is the two-time Bram Stoker Award-nominated author of *The Daughters of Block Island*, *Something Borrowed, Something Blood-Soaked,* and the forthcoming *Beneath the Poet's House*. She has a BA from the University of Pennsylvania, an MA from Boston College, and an MFA from the University of Southern Maine. When she's not writing, she keeps chickens; uses a Ouija board to ghost-hug her dear, departed beagle; and sets out on adventures with her husband, daughter, and bloodhound–golden retriever mix. Most of her work comes from gazing upon the ghosts of the past or else into the dark corners of nature, those places where whorls of bark become owl eyes, and deer step through tunnels of hanging leaves and creeping briars only to disappear. Visit her at www.christacarmen.com.

In the Belly of the Mills

Elizabeth Devecchi

A penny for a candy
in the belly of the mills.
I leave my mother's side to walk the rows:
sugar buttons
lemon drops
rootbeer barrels
bottle caps
I search my empty pockets and resist.

A shadow brushes past me
cool air turns thick and stale.
The outlets fade to darker times
in the belly of the mills.

Grandmother's stories echo
through the whirring of machines.
In the tinny air around me
floats the stench of broken dreams.

A child for a doffer
in the belly of the mills.
She leaves her mother's side to walk the rows:
empty bobbins
wisps of cotton
spinning jennies
broken threads
Despite her empty pockets she persists.

– ELIZABETH DEVECCHI spent her formative years in Rhode Island, setting out after high school to travel and gather degrees. She writes in a variety of genres and styles. Her debut poem, "Oh, Brother," appears in Black Spot Books's *Under Her Eye*, and Wicked House Publishing will be releasing both her debut horror novel, A Whisper in the Dark (October 2025), and her debut thriller, A Twist of the Lens (mid-2025). Elizabeth is a member of the HWA and currently resides in Colorado with her family. For more info: elizabethdevecchi.com
Facebook: https://www.facebook.com/esdevecchi
Instagram: https://www.instagram.com/themoonthesunandlittleman/

The Gourmand

Mr. Michael Squid

When you are a young punk musician, money isn't falling into your lap. In 2004, I measured success on diet, lifestyle and vinyl repertoire. I wore my band buttons and patches with pride. Any man daring to catcall me would receive a rage-filled berating, and an occasional lesson on boundaries which I used pepper spray to demonstrate. I'd carved out a little angsty niche where I felt cool enough, savvy enough, and sarcastic enough to really enjoy pretending not to enjoy life and all the chaos it delivered daily. Then I realized I'd only been skimming the surface of a much deeper ocean of counterculture after moving into an old factory converted into a show space.

Carla was the friend who'd indoctrinated me into the rebel coven of eccentric starving artists and musicians. She was the first person who guided me into the vinyl section of our local music shop. She'd brought me to my first show, and cared for me when a skinhead elbowed me in the face, jostling loose a tooth that later fell out. She wiped crusted blood from my swollen lips and gave me a tampon to plug up my bloody nose as we blasted "Nazi Punks Fuck Off" and moshed around on my childhood bed.

She was my first everything. First show, first crush, first time drinking, first time puking from drinking, first time leaving Ohio. I'd never have told anyone, of course, but I wanted to be her, or a mirror of her, in every way. I'd followed her to Providence, and she invited me into the cliques and crews that thrived just below the surface of its college-town streets. She invited me to The Refinery, a punk paradise known for the floor-to-ceiling Marshall Stacks and legendary shows that no licensed venue could ever get away with. It had its share of fistfights, fires, nudity, and noise complaints, even though the closest house wasn't even visible from the old brick and steel building used as a refinery during the industrial revolution. Some claimed when it was running, workers often went missing, supposedly dissolved into vats of lye. It was condemned in the 1970s and thirty years later, converted into the punk paradise.

The warehouse had been divided into rooms by the starving artists who had lived there before me. Every surface was decorated with colorful stickers, silkscreens, childhood toys and outsider art of the tenants. I had my own thin-walled room, and the rent was only $150 a month. I never said it, but I would've paid more for that dingy room that smelled of sweat and glue than any upscale living situation. I felt like I was actually home for the first time.

I was used to being ostracized. I was called Freak, glowered at by the normies. The cuts on my arms drew giggles and whispers back in high school. I was always the square peg in a town filled with perfectly smooth cylinders who seemed complacent. Not me. I hated the mall, I hated the church, and I hated the prom, the sports, the nightclubs and the stink of cologne and bland generica those cylinders all seemed to accept. The Refinery was a place for square pegs, and the more splintered, the better.

Cigarette filter earplugs let me sleep the nights bands stopped by. Spilled beer always found its way under my poorly-constructed door, drunk up by my mattress and the little bedding I had to survive the winters. One thing I didn't foresee was how cold the space got without proper heating. A space heater from the Salvation Army kept me from freezing, at least until I woke up to the smell of smoke and realized I'd nearly incinerated myself one night.

I became friends with all of the residents of the repurposed mill. There was Izzy, a loud and snarky chick with a goth aesthetic and arms striped with scars. Pete's quiet voice and tall, lean figure seemed like some clean-cut, Rockwellian variation of punk. Scarred and Ferret were charming goofballs who were always forming new bands; they were young and loud, always practicing music so distorted and squealing that I kept ear plugs in my pockets at all times for the frequent sonic assaults. Sarah and Faye were both working all the time or in their rooms, so I rarely saw them. They were kind and soft-spoken, both talented painters.

Two of the most tenured residents, Jeff and Henry, were big in the underground music scene. They put on shows, did a lot of promotion, and had links with some of the most legendary punk labels, so they would always have a plethora of reviewer pre-releases before they hit the shelves for us to dig into. It really was a punk-rock utopia, and I'd never felt more comfortable in my life than the short few months I lived there. That third month in December, as students abandoned the city to head home for winter vacation—the place I'd come to feel so comfortable in—shifted into something entirely foreign.

I walked up the four flights of concrete stairs, lugging my second used bike after learning the hard way not to lock it outside for the thieves with bolt cutters. My arms and legs were tired after a long day of hauling bags of soil that had arrived at the hardware store where I worked. I was emotionally drained after an impatient customer demanded to see my manager, insisting I was being rude (I was not), and I was worried I'd be let go. I told myself I'd practice not reacting when some silver-spoon-fed preppie laughed at my half-shaved hair. I told the manager too, but got a warning nonetheless. Aspirations for a better job or higher pay, and the obstacles in their way, danced in my head, but when I got to our floor, my focus was redirected to the voice calling out in a panicked tone.

"Carla?! Carla? Oh my God! Oh my God!"

My pulse quickened and anxiety spiked. Was she hurt? I dropped my bike on its side and walked in the entryway of our dimly lit living space. Izzy was pacing, her bony hands clutching her thin arms. Her mascara bled down her face, which happened every time she cried.

"Izzy, what's going on?" I asked.

"C-Carla's gone, but I don't understand how!"

Izzy was walking back and forth in an odd dance of dread, feeding into my own building paranoia.

"Like, it makes no sense," Izzy added.

"What do you mean, she's gone?" I thought of Carla just splitting without telling me, and the lost puppy she'd always called me manifested. Was she upset with me? Was I acting too needy, or too clingy? Before I could enter my usual spiral of self-loathing, Izzy grabbed my jacket with desperate fingers.

"No…no…NO!" Izzy's voice raised in frustration. "She was *here*, she never left, but she isn't here anymore. I feel like I need new meds. Jesus."

Izzy was intense and quick to panic, occasionally magnifying inconveniences as a crisis worth screaming over, so I hoped she was just confused, having missed Carla slipping out for a trip to the store or something equally benign, but I walked over to Carla's door all the same, weaving past pillars of stacked art supplies and amplifiers. Cold moonlight beamed through the old art-covered windows, bathing the trinkets and souvenirs of a thousand curbside trash pickings in an eerie glow that, for the first time since moving in, felt unwelcoming. I knocked on the thin plywood door covered in bumper stickers and show posters, hearing no reply.

"Carla, are you in there?" I called.

Izzy's raised voice immediately followed. "*She's not here!* I've checked and listened and called and checked again." Izzy picked at her scar, something she did when her anxiety was turned up all the way. "*I checked and checked and checked!*"

"Okay, well don't fuckin' shout at me! I just got home from a shitty day at work."

Izzy, who was perpetually between jobs, looked down in guilt, apologizing under her breath before storming off.

"Carla?" I asked, twisting the doorknob to find it unlocked. She always locked it before leaving. I pushed the door open and felt a shiver ripple through me.

Carla's room looked like the same aftermath-of-an-explosion it always did, but it was far too cold. I glanced at the windows, which had been covered with blankets and band posters to insulate the space from the New England winter air. They were all closed tight. I walked past a frog-shaped ceramic ashtray spilling over with butts to Carla's bed, which was empty. She didn't appear to be home, but her worn leather boots were on the floor, kicked into their usual space. Her coat sagged on the chair at her desk, and most chillingly, her wallet and keys sat on her desk. She never went anywhere without them.

As I stood in the cold room, staring at the details in the shadows, the dread within me grew into a full-body shiver as I noticed the hole in the floor past the edge of her bed. A five-foot wide hole in the floor inspired the fear that she'd fallen through and was grievously injured on some lower level, or worse. Reluctantly, I approached to get a better view.

The hole was deep, but oddly enough, it wasn't a puncture through the levels of the building. It seemed to contradict the way buildings are structured, and my mind raced to try and understand it. The hole in the wooden floor was warped inward; the angle was gradual like the start of a funnel, and it seemed to continue past where the other rooms of the warehouse might have been. The hole was Daliesque; a bizarre warping of the wood that should've been impossible unless it'd been made of plastic, melted and pulled out of shape.

"Carla?" I yelled down, praying my voice would summon a response. I dropped to my knees and opened my fraying messenger bag, feeling my way past keys, pepper spray, and buttons from shows I'd attended. I located the small flashlight I kept for roadside bike repair and shone the beam into the orifice in the floor.

The angle was sloping at least, something that brought some relief. If Carla had fallen in, she might not be critically injured. I leaned in to get a better look at the floor beams that all seemed to retain their width and spacing despite their odd curves. Fear for my friend caused me to act rather than plan. I attempted to inch forward, but my boot heel landed at an angle it wasn't used to from the warped floor beneath it, and I flailed my arms for balance. Too late. I fell onto the ground and slid into the dark hole.

Imagine a waterslide but take away your vision. Add icy cold air and jagged splinters, a foul stench and the dread of impending demise, and you might get close. My flesh was battered and bruised as I slid down into the unseen depths of the hole. Panic screamed in my skull as my fingers scrambled for purchase, the wood soft and slimy like the waterlogged beam of an abandoned train track. I felt death's presence, like any moment I'd freefall down into some lower level where my skull would shatter against concrete. Maybe it was the surging adrenaline slowing time, or maybe it was really just that long, but it seemed to go on forever; a slide into a dark cavity that seemed to defy architectural reasoning.

When my aching body finally slowed to a stop, my eyes fought to adjust. The sickening stench of decay permeated my nostrils and lungs, and I vomited, adding to the miasma. My fingertips throbbed, stinging wet and warm, and it took a second to realize I'd lost a few fingernails in my attempt to stop my descent into the depths of this dark oblivion.

"Carla?" I wheezed out. My chest was heavy and sore. *Maybe a broken rib,* I thought, as tears stung my eyes. There was no light to see, and I felt around in the darkness.

The warping floor, or walls, or whatever this structural anomaly was, gave little information. Direction failed me, and had it not been for the coarse wood beneath me, I'd have no sense of gravity at all. I struggled onto my hands and knees, feeling at the wood and the lack of it in order to find a passage in order to progress. I could hear my racing heartbeat pulsing in my ears due to the grim lack of sound, something I'd never thought I'd experience in that old building full of loud and brazen punks. I inched forward in the one clear direction possible. I felt my bag at my side, and hope ignited within me as I fumbled through it blindly. I found a pack of matches, and removed them, striking the phosphorus with a spark.

It was surreal to see the wood warp and bend into a winding tunnel in the ochre glow of matchlight. The form of the hollow was almost organic in the wavy passage; a stark contrast to the right angles and minimal construction of a strictly utilitarian space. Any sense of wonder was quickly stamped out by shivering horror when I realized the brittle black sticks that had collected on the bottom of the space were bones. Some small ribs and femurs or rats long decayed. Most were clearly human.

"Carla!" I shouted, my voice boxed in and small in the contained space. The pain of my burning fingers caused me to drop the match, and the sulfuric smoke as it went out was welcome in the foul air of the enclosed space I was trapped in. I sucked on my still-stinging fingertips, tasting the copper and feeling the bumpy wound where the nail of my index finger used to be. I reached into my purse, lit another match, and screamed at the wide-eyed, frozen face staring at me from further down the tunnel.

It was hideous: lidless eyes and a hole where the nose should have been if the cartilage wasn't missing. A terrible, lipless grin was fixed on the unmoving, hairless skull. The skin was pink and translucent, revealing winding veins and the crimson muscle beneath. If it wasn't for the cut-off shirt she'd bought after the first show I'd attended on my sixteenth birthday, I wouldn't have recognized her: Carla.

I let out a wail at the sight of her decomposing body. My skin began to sting in little nibbles of pain I attributed to friction burns from my descent. I forced myself to crawl closer to the horrific remains of my best friend. I nearly vomited again as I saw her internal organs visible through the semi-transparent skin and muscle of her abdomen below the bottom of her shirt. My vision began to blur from what I first thought were tears. But then it began to click, and I realized how she'd been so mutilated in such a short time. Carla wasn't rotting; she was dissolving. The stinging of my skin grew more painful, and I whimpered.

So was I.

In a dizzying panic, I scrambled forward. The match went out, a relief from the image now seared in my mind of what became of Carla in the dark, awful depths of the building's innards. My flesh burned, nerves alight as I scrambled over ancient bones and climbed on in search of a way out.

"It's eating me," I whispered, dumbfounded, as I pushed past my friend's partially digested body, feeling her sticky, flimsy skin no thicker than a water balloon about to burst.

It might have been hours, or maybe just minutes as I squeezed through the narrowing wooden tunnel that veered left, then up, then down in the bitter, burning blackness. The pain was everywhere; my armpits, my privates, the backs of my knees, the insides of my ears. Every single centimeter of my body burned and screamed in pain, and moving made the pain louder, but still I squeezed my chubby tummy through the narrow passage. I wondered how long until my lungs dissolved, or my throat clogged with blood, but I wriggled on like a fat worm as the passage finally turned again.

My temples throbbed as the tunnel pitched down, blood rushing to my head. It became harder to breathe, and harder to move. Gravity was then the sole reason I was able to continue down the hole. The horror of realizing I was being digested alive compounded upon reaching a dead end. There was no exit; no wooden orifice from which the tunnel led. There was no escape. I screamed.

I refused to accept it. There was no way I'd make it back up, and I turned to the floor beneath me. I clawed on the damp, slippery boards beneath me and more fingernails peeled back. I punched and bit at the old wood planks, feeling splinters pierce my gums and the tender meat where my nails used to be. Breathing hurt and my fingers were thumping, throbbing digits that didn't feel like my own.

A cracking sound was followed by another, and I struggled to move my defiant, sluggish limbs to claw at the floor toward freedom. Finally, it gave under my weight. Another cracking sound as I fell downward through the strange floor of the warped wooden passage. My stomach lurched into my throat as I plummeted. Pain erupted and pulsated in my skull when my head connected with a cold, concrete floor. It hurt when I shivered, and my breath billowed out in a vapor cloud from my aching lungs. I wondered if I was on the third floor, or maybe the second for a bit, my mind unable to process the horrors that had just ravaged it, and then I lost consciousness.

I awoke in the hospital. Tubes in my arms and nose, bandages covering me like a weeping scab quilt. My vision was blurry, but I could make out the look of surprise on the nurse seeing me awake. I eagerly took a plastic cup of water with gauze-wrapped fingers, finding relief despite the burn as the cold liquid went down. I was told of my first and second degree burns, which affected the majority of my skin. Some might heal in time, some would not.

I was there for a week, staring at the faint brown water stain on the drop ceiling as my wounds slowly healed. They let me use the phone, and I called my parents who later came to visit. The old mill was evacuated of tenants and condemned. I spoke to the police, but they seemed eager to label me a drug-addled youth more concerned with substance intake than looking into my preposterous claim. I eventually was discharged from the hospital and had to couch surf with friends who didn't believe me. The only thing worse than experiencing a nightmare is having nobody believe you. In all fairness, I wouldn't have believed me either.

I grieved for a while. Many nights I screamed into a tear-soaked pillow. I struggled to process her loss, magnified by unexplainable events that had transpired. I tried to find a logical reason. I tried to rationalize the floor that had eventually eroded inward, having sponged up years of hydrofluoric acid from the mill's industrial usage. That it was just some terrible accident of years of caustic chemicals being absorbed into the warping wood, but no amount of therapy or rational thinking will grant me closure for long. Every so often, the illusion shatters, and the possibility that all is right in the world gives way under my feet.

I'll pass by some black-and-white photo of a smiling stranger on a telephone pole with the word that brings it all back: "Missing." My stomach twists and I remember that mouth in the floor that would have been impossible for Carla to miss. It hid in wait, only revealing itself when it found what it was hungry for and only ideal conditions were met. The hairs on my neck raised with an icy chill as I understood why only some went missing and only occasionally from The Refinery throughout the decades. I'll shiver uncontrollably when I think about how it would lie in wait for those it hungered for.

I wasn't the only one with good taste.

– MICHAEL SQUID is a horror author and filmmaker living in Providence. His short story collections, such as *Darkest Dimensions*, contain tales he's adapted into short films. He's working on his first feature now.

The Spinning Mule

Paul Magnan

The old wooden door jammed in its frame when Stu tried to pull it shut. Likely, he'd done damage when he broke the lock. He tightened his grip on the brass knob and yanked. The door slammed into place and the knob came away in his hand. The knob on the other side clattered to the concrete ground.

Shit. Stu tested the door with his shoulder. It was wedged shut. At least it couldn't be opened from the other side. Then again, this massive building probably had many doors.

Fuck it. That was something to worry about later. Stu wished he hadn't tossed his gun in the store dumpster, but he didn't want it on him if the cops caught him. For now, he had to get his bearings and figure out what to do next.

He turned to take in the wide room that reeked of dust and old oil. Much of the glass in the large, multi-paned windows was stained brown, with several pieces cracked or broken. Rocks and chunks of macadam littered the wooden floor, no doubt thrown by bored kids who targeted empty buildings such as this. Outside, the sun had set; the residual light of the gloaming cast shadows over the brick walls and reflected off a small mirror propped up in a corner. Stu's reflection was hazy from red brick dust on the leaded glass. Ancient mortar pushed flakes of green paint from the walls.

Chunks of the floor were torn away. Stu figured it happened when they removed the machines that used to manufacture finished thread and yarn for clothing. Rhode Island was home to many old mills like this. He had heard stories of the horrible working conditions from his grandmother, who had emigrated here from Scotland as a child. At the age of twelve, she lost the tip of her left index finger in the gears of a braiding machine. Many others, she told him, were maimed worse.

The shadows lengthened. It would soon be full dark. Stu had a small flashlight in his pocket, but he didn't dare use it. He had to stay out of sight. He looked for a place to sit but found nothing. The wall on the far side opened to another room. Within, the dim light from the windows reflected off something metallic.

The machine was huge. It appeared to be made of two long sections, thirty or so feet in length, connected on either side by metal rails, and upon which rested heavy steel rollers blackened from oil and years of use. The carriage closest to Stu had several empty spindles. Metal hooks curved like claws over the frame. The piece against the wall was larger, with thick horizontal rollers running the length of the machine.

Its stillness reminded Stu of a hibernating predator. So long as it was asleep, all was well, but if awakened, it would be starving. The thought sent ice through Stu's heart.

"Hi!"

Stu jumped and reached for a gun he no longer had. On the far side of the room was a child, a boy no more than five or six. He wore faded overalls over a plain linen shirt. On his head was a dirty newsboy cap. The child smiled and walked closer. His feet were bare. Lanky dark hair spilled from beneath the cap, framing a thin face covered with freckles. The boy's eyes sparkled with curiosity. "What's your name, mister?"

What the fuck is this? Stu struggled to speak. "What are you doing here, kid? You lost or something?"

The boy shocked Stu by laughing. "I'm not lost. This is my home."

The sun was gone and a full moon, bloated and white, shone through the filthy windows. The whole scene was like something from a hallucinogenic nightmare. "What do you mean, this is your home? Where are your folks?"

"They're dead. They've been dead a long time."

The moon's dull luminescence hid the room's hungry shadows. "Kid, I don't know what's going on right now, but I can't help you."

The boy laughed again, the sound bouncing off pitted brick walls and echoing into darkness. "You're funny, mister."

The hairs on Stu's arms rose. "I'm outta here." He stepped back, keeping his eyes on the spooky kid.

The boy's smile disappeared, and his gaze fell to the floor. "Please, mister, don't go. I haven't talked to anyone for so long."

Faint police chatter crept in through the gaps of old masonry. A flashlight beam stabbed through the dirty glass.

Stu flattened himself against the wall underneath the window and beckoned the kid to do the same. He held his finger to his lips.

Wood creaked from the other room. Someone was trying to push in the door that no longer had a knob. Stu forced himself to breathe slowly. Would the kid give him up? He looked over. The boy was still and silent.

The cop gave up on the door. Stu hoped there wasn't another doorway nearby. Despite the chill in the building, Stu's body was slick with sweat.

After several long seconds, Stu heard tires crunching on loose concrete. The sound dimmed and vanished. He chanced a peek out the window but saw nothing but building silhouettes and distant streetlights.

"Wow, mister!" the kid whispered, a wide grin on his face. "Are you on the lam from the coppers?"

On the lam? Coppers? "What are you, a fan of old movies?"

The boy frowned. "What are you talking about? I ain't never seen a movie."

Stu wanted nothing more than to get out of this building, but the cops were too close. He was stuck here, probably for most of the night, with a rugrat that gave him a serious case of the heebie-jeebies. What was this kid doing here all by himself, anyway?

"Look, kid, I don't know why you're here, and it's none of my business. I appreciate you not giving me away to the cops. But who takes care of you? Are they around?"

"Nobody takes care of me."

He didn't look tough or weathered enough to be a street kid. Stu reached into his pocket and pulled out a crumpled package of Outdoorsman Beef Jerky. He always had some on him for an occasional snack. There were only a few pieces left, but he offered it to the kid. "It's not much, but if you want it, here you go."

"I don't need food, mister." This was said with such serious earnestness it took Stu a moment to process it.

"What do you mean, you don't need food? Everybody needs food."

"Only folks who are alive need food. I haven't needed any for over a hundred years."

What. The. Fuck. Stu slowly put the jerky back into his pocket. "Kid, I take a joke like anyone, but I'm getting sick of this."

"My name isn't 'kid'. It's Claude."

Stu shook his head. "Okay. Claude. Since we're now on a first name basis, my name isn't 'mister'. It's Stu. Either way, I'm getting sick of your games. I'm gonna find another room to sack out in for a while. Do us both a favor and leave me alone."

A low, deep growl shook the floorboards. A terrible grinding noise erupted from the machine. Flakes of rust fell away as rollers, long dormant, squealed on dry rails and sent the front carriage sliding into the stationary back portion with a *clack!* The moving part glided back and reset in its original position.

"I don't want you to leave," Claude said. "And neither does the spinning mule."

Stu's heart thundered in his chest. There was no way the kid could have turned on the machine. He was standing at least ten feet away from it.

Claude walked to the spinning mule. He raised his arm and

his hand passed through the metal. A ghost. Stu was looking at a fucking ghost.

"You see, mister...Stu...I used to work as a scavenger for this mule. I crawled under the fibers that were spun, collected loose bits of cotton, and cleaned up oil and dirt. Adults couldn't fit. They needed someone small, like me. I had to time it just right. I had to know when the carriage was going to move, like you saw. I would lie flat with my face pressed to the floor, and hope it was enough for the carriage to miss me. My friend, Eddie, didn't lie down flat enough and the mule tore out his hair. Some kids got hurt even worse."

The machine growled again.

Claude's gaze dropped. "Mr. Drezer always said I was too slow, that I ducked too soon before the carriage moved. Sometimes he smacked me good for it. I was more scared of him than the machine. I tried to stay up longer so Mr. Drezer wouldn't belt me, but..." The boy paused. "I didn't duck in time. The carriage nabbed me and dragged me. It hurt so much, then I was floating above my body. I saw my head squished between the carriage and the roller beam. There was a lot of blood."

Claude turned away. A perpetual trickle of blood dripped from his ear.

"I'm sorry, Claude. You were dealt a bad hand. You never got to grow up. But, still, I can't help you."

Claude looked up, and his eyes sparkled. "Maybe you can."

Stu shook his head.

"Maybe we can help each other."

Stu opened his mouth to say how foolish this was, but all that came out was "How?"

"You're hiding from the coppers. Didja rob a bank, or something?"

Stu looked out the moon-tinted windows. "I didn't rob a bank. I aimed lower. I held up a convenience store."

Claude mouth twisted. "What's a convenience store?"

"A small place that sells food and lottery tickets. You know, ah, uh, a general store."

"Why did you rob the…convenience store?"

"Why does anybody rob anything? I needed the money."

"How did they catch onto you so quick?"

"Things have changed in the world. While I pointed my gun at the clerk and stuffed bills into my pocket, he pushed a panic button under the counter. I ran. Within minutes, I heard the sirens. I ditched my mask and the gun. I've been pinched for robbing convenience stores before, so I'm at the top of the local cops' suspect list. Now I need a place to lay low, and then leave the area for a while until things blow over."

Claude's eyes were wide with awe. "Wow, you're a regular Jesse James!"

"I'm just a guy trying to survive in a world that's screwed him over. But you said you had a way to help me."

"A way to help us both. But we need the mule."

The machine thrummed with restrained energy.

Stu held up his hands. "No way. I'm not going near that thing."

Claude shrugged. "Have it your way. The coppers are gonna catch you, you know. Then you're off to the slammer. For years, I bet, all because you're scared of something that's bolted to the floor."

Fuck! "I'm not touching that thing."

"You don't have to. Just stand next to me."

Stu didn't like it, but he walked over. The spinning mule hummed, as if eager for his presence. "Christ, it's as if that thing is aware of me."

"It is," Claude said. "I don't know how, but after it killed me, the mule came to life. At first, it wasn't nice. It was evil. It enjoyed hurting other kids. But then the mill closed down, and the other machines were taken away. All the kids left. Only the mule remained. It was forgotten, like me. All these years, we've only had each other."

Claude tried to touch the machine, and again his hand passed through it. He sighed. "When I lost my body, I lost everything. I couldn't grow up. I couldn't see all these changes you say happened in the world outside. This building, like me, doesn't change at all, except to fall apart as it grows older. Someday, this building is gonna be gone. And me and the mule will be gone with it."

The machine shook with a clatter. Stu jumped back a step.

"The mule knows it will be torn to pieces or rust away. Now it doesn't hate so much. It feels bad about the kids it hurt. Especially me. It wants to give me back my life. But it needs you to help."

Stu had difficulty catching his breath. He wanted to run as far away from this building as he could. But this time, a conviction would land him in the state pen for at least twenty years.

"Why does this thing need me? It can run on its own. Anyway, how does staying here with you help me out?"

"You'll walk out of here without being recognized. No one will know who you are. The coppers won't look twice at you."

"Is this contraption a plastic surgeon? Will it give me a new nose, new cheeks, new eyes?"

Claude's face reflected a weary maturity gained from decades of spiritual stasis. "Does it matter? You'll be free. No more time spent in prison. Make up your mind, mister."

Stu looked out the window. Cops were patrolling the next street over, shining spotlights between buildings. They would be back to search the old mill, probably sooner rather than later.

"Okay, Claude, what do I gotta do?"

"Stand next to me. The mule will take care of the rest."

Stu didn't like this but felt he didn't have a choice. He went to the ghost child, standing between him and the machine.

"Now what?"

"Now the mule does the job it was made for, spinning raw material into threads ready to be sewn into a new shape."

Stu looked at the spinning mule. "What raw material?"

"You."

The machine roared. Two of the large metal hooks spun on their frame and snagged Stu under each arm. He was yanked off his feet and thrown several feet to the frame against the wall. His left side jammed between two heavy metal rollers. Stu screamed and thrashed as the hungry rollers bit deep. The carriage hissed and rolled forward. The rollers spun against each other, tearing at Stu's skin.

"No! Make it stop!"

The hooks dropped and pulled away thin strips of flesh from between the steel cylinders. The carriage clacked back on its rails, stringing along the bloody threads, and wound them on empty spindles. The cones spun, twisting the meat around them.

Stu's left arm and leg were torn from his body. His torso was pulled between solid metal tubes that pulped ribs and organs.

"The mule took away my adulthood," Claude said, "and now it's giving it back."

Blood bubbled from Stu's lips. The carriage clattered forward again, and the fallers pulled away more of Stu's body. Bones crunched and brain matter splattered as his skull splintered between the rollers. Within minutes all that remained were glistening red strings, dotted with patches of clothing, threaded between the spindles and the rollers.

Claude glided to the floor between the carriage and the rollers. He rotated in place. The bloody strings adhered to him, and he spun faster. The spindles turned in the opposite direction, providing more material. Bones formed, then tendons. Organs spun into being within an emerging torso, quickly covered by a thin layer of muscle that knitted thicker into arms and legs. Veins and arteries threaded through the flesh and filled with blood. Skin and hair wove over the whole. Clothing was spun and settled over the new body. Free from all traces of Stu, the rollers and spindles ground to a stop.

Claude stopped spinning. Now physical, he looked at his adult-sized hands, flexed them, and gasped. The decades-long ordeal of nothingness was over. He stepped forward, tentatively at first, then with more surety. He rejoiced in the sensation of climbing out of the silent spinning mule. The clothes he wore were the same ones that had belonged to Stu, but Stu was gone. He was Claude, and he was grown.

His new stomach growled. Claude had forgotten what it was like to be hungry. He pulled out the package of Outdoorsman Beef Jerky and stuck a piece in his mouth. It was tough and had a bit of a rancid taste, but his teeth and saliva soon softened it. He swallowed and ate more.

The spinning mule growled. Claude had to clear his throat a few times before he could speak.

"The debt is paid. You can be at peace."

The machine hissed and its parts settled under the weight of a hundred years. The metal parts oxidized and fell to the floor in rust-brown shards. The large rollers collapsed and disintegrated. Empty spindles rolled to dark corners. Within minutes, nothing was left but formless scraps.

Claude marveled at the strength of his new legs as he strode to the next room. He found the mirror and wiped away the accumulated grime. The face that looked back at him was not Stu's; it was his own, aged about thirty.

Something pounded on the wooden door behind him. It burst open, and two police officers entered, holding flashlights and guns in close, two-handed grips. One of the flashlights swung at Claude.

"Freeze! Don't move!"

Claude held out his hands to show he wasn't a threat. Several other cops entered and fanned out through the room. Claude was surprised to see that some of them were women.

Calls of "Clear!" echoed throughout the mill. The cop who had spotted Claude approached him. Claude wished the man would get the light out of his eyes, but the beam didn't waver.

"You got some identification?"

Claude wasn't sure what he was being asked, so he said no.

"What's your name?"

"Claude."

"What's your last name?"

Claude had to think about that. What was his last name? Oh, yeah…

"Morneau."

"Uh huh," the cop said, not hiding the skepticism from his voice. "What are you doing here, Claude Morneau?"

"I live here."

Another cop came up to them. "What do you got?"

"I think it's just some homeless guy. He might be giving me a false name, but I don't know for sure."

"You want to take him in, fingerprint him, see if he's got a record? He's trespassing, regardless of whether he's homeless."

The cop pulled out a photo. "You see this guy around anywhere, Claude?"

It was Stu.

"No, sir," he said as politely as he could. He couldn't stop looking at his hands.

The cop watched him with wary eyes. "Anybody else in here with you, Claude?"

"No, sir."

The other cops returned, all reporting the place as empty.

"Well, Claude, if you do see him, don't approach him. He's armed and dangerous. Just give us a call. You got a phone?"

A telephone? "No, sir, I don't. Only rich people have those."

The cop shook his head. "Whatever. Just don't be here when we come back."

"Yes, sir."

The cops funneled out through the shattered doorway. Claude heard several cars drive off. They were much quieter than the cars from years ago. He exhaled, shaking a bit from excitement.

Claude walked to the doorway. The moon looked the same. So did the stars, but not as many were visible as when he was a child. There were more lights on the horizon and in the nearby streets.

Claude took a deep breath. The air tasted more acrid than he remembered.

Claude walked out of the emptiness of his past. The world had changed, but it didn't matter. Claude was going to live his life. Now that he was an adult, he would take anything he wanted. Nothing was going to stop him.

– PAUL MAGNAN has been writing stories that veer from the straight and narrow for many years. He is the author of the four-volume dark fantasy series, *Kyu, The Unknown*, as well as the short story collection, *Veering from the Straight and Narrow*. He has had many stories published in various venues, including in the anthologies *Violent Vixens: An Homage to Grindhouse Horror* and *We Are Providence: Tales of Horror from the Ocean State*.

Gourd Guy

Rick Claypool

We were hiking in the woods when my brother Jake first warned me about Gourd Guy. I must have been like six and he was in high school. Dad was always making him watch me, which I'm pretty sure he hated. But me, I loved when Dad was like, "Jake, why don't you take your brother and go somewhere else."

I loved our hikes because I loved my brother Jake, and because I understood that when Dad said this, what he meant was, You boys are bothering me so much I'll start yelling and punching walls, so it would be better for us all if you weren't here.

When Dad was in a mood like that, I also preferred to be someplace else, especially since Mom was gone.

It was November. The woods were sloppy from excess rain but the sky was pure blue. I couldn't stop looking up. I couldn't help it. Which, I'm sure, is how I accidentally stepped in the largest pile of dog shit I'd ever seen before or since.

And then I started running.

I think I thought running as fast as I could would get the shit off my boot. I thought the faster I went, the cleaner my boot would get. Instead, I tripped and found myself caught in a green-brier tangle that cut my face and stabbed through my jeans and hand-me-down sweater.

"Slow down, Captain Poopy Boots," Jake said, removing his gloves. He pinched the brier stems one at a time, pulling them back so I could wriggle free. Almost as soon as I was out, I tripped over a big warty gourd. It must have been rotting along the trail for weeks.

"Gross! What is that?" I asked.

And Jake, very casually, replied, "You don't know about the Gourd Guy, do you?"

Now when I was a kid, for some reason I hated admitting anyone else knew anything I didn't. So I played it cool and said, "Yeah, I know about the Gourd Guy."

Jake smiled. Under the rim of his ballcap, his eyes looked like hollow slits in the creases of his cheeks. He ignored my lie and continued as if I'd asked him to tell me all about the Gourd Guy. I appreciated it, though I didn't show it.

He told me the Gourd Guy haunts the old mill ruin in the woods behind the soccer field. He's a cursed thing made of pumpkins and gourds and he lurks the streets searching for children every Halloween. Those he catches, he drags back to his hideout where he turns them into pumpkins and squashes and all kinds of gnarly looking gourds and adds them to his body. The longer he goes without children, the more rotten he gets.

"I know! I know! I know!" I told Jake because I wanted him to stop. He was kind of freaking me out.

Jake picked up the rotting gourd. Pill bugs scattered. A fat slug clinging to its underside withdrew its eye stalks. He winced at the smell of the thing, and I could tell he was holding it carefully so his fingers didn't puncture its slimy flesh. "Of course, the grownups all work together to try not to let him get any kids. And usually, they succeed—by dismembering the Gourd Guy." He dropped the gourd with a thud.

We started walking again. "The gourds and pumpkins you see scattered along trails in the woods," he said, "are all parts of Gourd Guy's dismembered body. But every year he somehow reassembles himself to turn new children into gourds. And, every year, at midnight on October thirtieth, the grownups take him apart so he doesn't get any."

By then, he'd drawn me into the spell of the story. I couldn't pretend I knew everything anymore. I had a question, and I had to ask it: "But why don't they just destroy the gourds or whatever so Gourd Guy never comes back? Like, burn them or something?"

Jake's smile stretched into a sinister grin. "They don't destroy the gourds because they say the children's souls are still attached to them—so SATAN gets the souls if the gourds are destroyed."

This, I remember, is the precise moment I became sure my brother was full of shit.

Years later, the old mill ruin Jake said Gourd Guy haunted became what they called a mixed-use complex with apartments, a brew pub, and a FedEx Office.

Meanwhile, I'd grown up and gone to college and moved out of state. I only came back on holidays, but family gatherings felt so awkward that I'd leave as soon as possible.

There was always something inexplicably uncomfortable about sitting at the table with Dad and Jake, some distance between myself and them I could never quite bridge.

We'd drink some beer. Then eat some food. Then drink some coffee.

And that was it. And then I left.

My thoughts always turned to Mom during those long nighttime drives. One thing or another at Dad's always wound up reminding me of her, rooting those hazy, intrusive memories in my mind. The hypnotic pattern on the old Formica table where we ate. The spoons she used when serving me soup when I was small and sick. The strangely menacing macrame thing hanging on the cellar door.

I clearly remembered her spending so much time on the other side of that door. But the memory of her face, or anything at all about her appearance, inevitably melted into something my mind could never quite grasp.

My forgetfulness made me furious. I came to despise the reminders.

Eventually Dad got sick and sold the house. Work kept me from making it back to help with the move. Dad wasn't big on talking on the phone, but I spoke with Jake most days.

"Don't just think about yourself," he said, insisting I return as soon as possible. "Think about your family."

I came back as soon as I could. Months later, unfortunately.

Jake had moved Dad into a little rent-stabilized apartment in the mixed-use complex that used to be the old mill ruin.

Over the phone I'd asked Jake how he got Dad in there. Those rooms were scarce. He answered by saying, "Well, you know, I know a guy..." After that, I'll be honest: I stopped listening.

I thought I understood and still hated admitting that anyone else knew anything I didn't.

It was raining when I arrived. Something about the building's size and aggressively rectangular structure reminded me of a mental institution, the kind where people used to lock away their demented relatives. There were hardly any windows aside from the FedEx Office, which was made up almost entirely windows. The brew pub was closed.

I didn't want to be there, but I was worried about Dad, and I wanted to show Jake that I really could be there for my family when it mattered.

Inside, I followed a dark hallway and a few flights of concrete stairs to a lower level, where Jake had told me Dad lived now. The place was new, but it already felt outdated, like an abandoned mall. Dad's door was at the end of the hallway. It was made of some kind of metal, and when I pounded on it with my fist, the booming noise echoed horribly.

No one answered. It wasn't locked so I let myself in.

The inside of Dad's apartment was unbearably dim. An earthy stench stung my nostrils. The damp air was hard to breathe. Cardboard boxes were stacked along the walls. I stepped over what looked like random piles of dirt.

I followed the sound of TV commercials until I found Dad in a makeshift living room. He was lying on a gurney, covered in blankets, his head so swollen it looked like some kind of awful, sweaty squash. His color looked all wrong in the glow of the TV screen. His shallow breathing came out in ragged gasps. I stood next to him.

"My son," I thought he said, but his lips didn't move.

Someone else was in the room with us.

My eyes adjusted. A humanoid shape glistened against the wall among the boxes. It stood, then shuffled into the light.

It looked like a person-sized pile of pumpkin guts. Each step forward squished against the floor. It reached out a goopy, glistening arm. Its hollow face made a horrible expression.

"My son," it wheezed.

I turned to run but tripped and fell to the ground. When I tried to stand, I found my foot was tangled in a snarl of roots. As I freed myself, I saw that the roots were growing out from under the pile of blankets at the foot of Dad's gurney. I pulled away the blankets, thinking I should save Dad from the invasive roots before saving myself from the being still shuffling toward me.

My hands shook. Dad's shallow breathing continued. The wet footsteps came closer.

Under Dad's blankets, I was shocked to see that, instead of his feet being tangled in roots, his legs somehow *were* the roots—the roots and my father were somehow one and the same.

"My son," the shuffling abomination whispered beside me.

This time, when I ran, I did not trip, following the roots growing from Dad out of the apartment and down a dark corridor and deeper into some kind of sub-basement with a dirt floor.

I flopped to the floor and crawled, tracing the root into darkness, searching for the place where it sunk underground.

The root twisted along the floor to the far wall. In the dark, I could feel the wall but not see it—its texture was rough and irregular, as if made of strange rocks. I took out my phone to use the light of its screen to see.

I gasped.

From the floor to the ceiling, skulls covered the wall, like in a catacomb. From their small size I could see they were children's skulls. I stood and turned to get out. The oozing pumpkin horror blocked my way.

"Myyy sonnn…" it gurgled.

Something crashed to the floor behind me. I wheeled around and saw skulls falling from the wall, clicking and banging against each other and making a ridiculous racket as they piled onto the floor. And as I watched, the skull pile formed into a humanoid shape with arms made of skulls and legs made of skulls and a torso made of skulls and a skull for a head.

The thing took a step closer to me. "It's okay, man," it said. "It's your brother. Jake."

"What?"

"And behind you," it said. "That's Mom."

The shuffling thing dripping with pumpkin guts took another wet step forward.

"What?"

"Myyy sonnn…"

"Yeah, sorry!" said Jake. "Mom is the Gourd Guy. She hasn't been feeling well lately, like Dad…"

He awkwardly lurched toward me.

"Jake?" I asked.

"Yeah," he said. "It's really me."

I turned and slipped on the trail of pumpkin slime on the floor. I almost fell but used all the willpower I had to stay upright.

Something touched my shoulder. I turned my head just enough to see a skull grinning back at me—a skull hand at the end of Jake's skull-arm!

I wheeled around to face Jake.

"Don't just think about yourself," he said. "Think about your family."

He reached out and grabbed my nose between the teeth of the skull hand, then pulled down, unzipping my skin.

And pumpkins tumbled out.

When I woke on the dirt floor of that damp sub-basement, Jake was adding pumpkins to Mom.

I tried to climb to my feet, but I couldn't.

I tried to scream, but I couldn't.

I couldn't move at all until Jake picked me up. I felt him holding me carefully so his skull hand didn't puncture my slimy flesh.

And when he pushed me into the pile of Mom, I told myself I understood—not because I actually did.

But because I hated admitting I didn't.

– RICK CLAYPOOL (he/him) writes absurdist horror. He is the author of *Skull Slime Tentacle Witch War* (Anxiety Press, 2024), *The Mold Farmer* (Six Gallery Press, 2020), *Leech Girl Lives* (Spaceboy Books, 2017), and short stories that appear here and there, including *HAD, Maudlin House,* and *Back Patio Press*. He grew up in the industrial outskirts of Pittsburgh, Pennsylvania, where generations of his family worked in steel mills, and lives in Rhode Island. For more, visit rickclaypool.org.

Strike

Jessica P. Wick

1.

Do you remember the playground rhyme? Local historians believe it was inspired by a real fire at this particular mill.

Open your matchbox inside the mill
Before you strike, breathe deep
Your sweetheart is in the river still
Now rock you to sleep sleep sleep

At the old textile mill the first thing you notice is the river, reflective, cold, and restless in its bed. The water's low now but it floods easily, turpentine-colored water that would seep into all the buildings along the bank and pull them in, if it could.

Sleep all day, sleep all night
Your eyes swing open and you lost your sight

Next it's the squat hulk of the old building, horizon-haunting; a ruin under renovation. See how it waits above the river, how it is in the scene like a stain gets into linen. There was a bell tower once, and the real estate company that wants to turn the mill into luxury apartments makes much of the original brick.

Devil's in your throat
Devil's in your hair
Devil climbs your body
Climbs up heaven's stair
Way to knock him down
Way to rock him bye
Strike your match and watch sparks fly.

They point out that the belltower has never burned.

2.

Inside the mill, women hard at work. Ring spinning frames pouring out spools of yarn and carding machines where fiber becomes a river of pale smoke and gets into your lungs particularly, but your hair, too, and your clothes—they're *noisy*, those machines. The building amplifies every clack, clink, *clatter*, throwing a shroud over conversation.

But today, there's an undercurrent of excitement. Lillie is grinny and bright eyed whenever her eyes meet anybody else's or after John the foreman trudges past. Lillie's sister, Mary, has been talking to the other workers about a strike. Rumor is the mill's owner, who already cut their wages, is planning to extend their hours and cut their wages again.

"We aren't wheat; we shouldn't be threshed of *every* speck of grain. We work hard. Do we deserve hardness?" Lillie overheard Mary, flint and fire, say more than once.

If you didn't observe Mary speaking for the strike, you'd never believe it. She appears to be a catalog model of what a mill worker should be, according to the bosses. She's as prim and precise as the uncracked spine of a book...a clothbound book, foil-stamped, containing a precious subject like practical etiquette or how to beautify a home. Even after a twelve-hour work day, Mary's hair stays as neat as a needle.

If Mary's flint and fire when organizing, she's oil—or maybe water—when she's talking to her sister. And Lillie's whatever Mary isn't. They love each other but don't understand why.

If Lillie were a book, she would be a sketch book, hand-sewn, pages scrounged from paper used by fishmongers and endpapers from other books, half-filled with wild drawings and notes that made sense at the time. She cheerfully says excuse me to robins and makes comments to the mill's machines. "In a mood, hm?" Or "Too eager today, are we?" when the thread breaks too often and they have to wet the cotton down. She swears the spinning frame likes the conversation and is more likely to be sweet. After a twelve-hour workday, Lillie's eyes are red, her throat is scratchy, and it's best not to regard her hair. Mary usually does, a mere look inspiring Lillie to say, defensively, "I pinned it."

Nobody discusses the strike inside the mill, but it's as if the mill knows. Anything that can go wrong, does go wrong, causing work to take much longer to complete. "It's having a conniption," Lillie said to Mary as she took a small break to stretch her back and fingers. When Lillie looked at her sister, she caught Mary sharing a meaningful look with John the foreman. If John were a book, he'd be a pulp adventure with a dramatic cover, a creased paperback handled carefully but still torn up at the edges. And he'd fall open to a scene of romance, in spite of himself.

Meaningful looks have been the mill's second product, what with the speaker from the UTW coming tomorrow, the strike set (just about) for Monday, and the boss's son swanning about with his starched collar and clear belief that he is the handsomest man anybody has ever laid eyes on. But those are for the mill workers, not for a potential rat with the bosses.

Lillie sticks close to Mary when their shift is over. They're not even over the river when Mary excuses herself. "I must have left my scarf behind," she says, and Lillie cynically notes that Mary is even perfect when she is lying, for the scarf is nowhere to be seen.

Of course, Lillie pretends to believe Mary and, also of course, after Mary is out of sight, Lillie follows her.

3.

The road back is cold and furrowed, wheel tracks from carts and the boss's son's car, all treacherous rills of grey ice. The shadows are deep enough to trip over, send yourself pitching onto ice or off the bridge and into the river. The river by the mill is black, roiling like a cauldron, spinning anybody who looks at it too long dizzy.

Lillie sees no sign of her sister outside the mill, and the mill itself is silent. Lillie thinks the silence feels layered. Dig into it and it would come down on your head and make sure nobody would hear you calling for help. The silence would shove itself into your mouth and nibble on your last words. She frowns at herself, because she is not usually afraid of the mill. Buildings cannot think to hurt you, and accidents are only accidents, and when it is quiet like this it is because nothing is around to make noise—not because something is hiding in the quiet, thinking about you, waiting for you, wanting you to join it in its stillness.

But Mary went in 'for her scarf,' so Lillie goes in too. "I'll only be quick," she tells the mill, patting its wall as she enters. The brick's so cold against her bare hand; that must be why she feels as if it moves against her—strains closer. Lillie wouldn't tell you why she followed Mary, but she could. Lillie wants to catch Mary with the foreman. Not even to tell anybody, just to have the secret, to be able to choose whether or not she teases her perfect sister until finally, just once, it is Mary who is rumpled and put on the defensive by a mere look and having to comment on the state of her hair pins.

Inside is a preview of what it will be like when they strike. Cold instead of sweltering, and everything so still. In the spinning room a board creaks underfoot and Lillie feels attention swerve to her so solidly that she turns to meet it, expecting Mary. Instead, she's met with a darkness that seems to cling thickly to *that* particular corner, to clot underneath *that* spinning frame, to press fast against the clerestory windows.

"Hello," Lillie squeaks. "You really don't enjoy being alone with your thoughts, do you? Do you know where Mary is? Come on, be a good one."

Lillie doesn't expect an answer but hopes her questions will banish uneasiness. Instead the mill sets her ears ringing, pressing so hard against her voice, it's like a blow, and even the spinning frame she thinks of as hers doesn't seem to know her. The awareness of something *watching* pricks its way up her back, and the darkness moves closer. *That's it!* Lillie thinks. She's going; she's gone. Except, before she's out, she hears raised voices near the entrance to the belltower.

"—didn't know you could be so foolish."

John. He has that second-generation Irish sound, muddy silver, as if the Irish were being flat-hammered out of him but putting up a rollick of a fight.

"Didn't you tell me so I would be 'foolish'?" Mary says this icily. John should beware, thinks Lillie; Mary never backs down when she has that voice. And what is she hearing?

"No, woman, I told you because I—told you. I agree it isn't right, but neither is this strike. Monday, Mary? It's too soon. Have you thought about what'll happen to our record?"

"You were for it earlier. Your cousin's part of the UTW, the one who helped me arrange for our guest. You introduced us. He said—"

"Shhh. That was before." John sounds terrified. Lillie almost feels bad for him; Mary isn't going to go easy because he's scared. In Lillie's experience, Mary is one for forcing you through the fear, though she'll be kind as anything for a while after you've done the thing you were so scared of.

"Before what?" Mary demands.

"Certain—things."

"Oh, well, if it's *things* now, why didn't you just say? *Things.*"

"Can you stop it, Mary?" John is urgent.

Lillie has snuck close enough to see them now. John looks—big. He's a big man, sure, but he doesn't look *right* big, Lillie thinks. His bones are all—loose. He's standing like he usually does, but it looks as if he's been caught mid-fall; man-as-puppet, hanging from strings, yes, bigger, but oddly defiant of gravity, a man-shaped skin stuffed with needles and menace and the vague memory of what it was like to stand. Lillie notices beads of sweat trickling down his temple even though the mill is still cold.

Mary's chin is high, her voice salted with disapproval. "Of course I can't. But why would I even try?"

"For the mill," John says.

And though Lillie knows she made no sound, John turns his head to look right at her. Sometimes when a shift runs very late, the mill's windows glow amber, reflective as evening gathers; that glow is on his eyes, like oil on water, and Lillie wants to run, but she can't. She can't move.

"The mill takes care of itself." Mary's reply is sharp, though not as sharp as John's fingers in Mary's elbow, digging deep enough that Lillie sees them disappear into her coat sleeve, or the pressure of John's eyes on Lillie's. "Who will take care of us?"

John turns back to Mary, and Lillie rocks back behind a spinning frame.

"You shouldn't say that." Now John's voice is a crackle of whisky, smooth and entirely rotten for you without moderation. "Now, you shouldn't say that, darling; the mill will take care of us, too, for it's work, isn't it? Let's walk by the water and clear our heads, right? The air will brace you. You'll think more clearly then."

Lillie runs back through the room of spinning frames. The darkness has moved; now it is gathered under a connector, and roughly the size of a ten-year-old, but it doesn't reach out for Lillie when she passes, and she's halfway down the road before regret catches up with her. Did she really leave Mary with John? She turns back and hides under the trees by the river, watching for them. She tells herself she'll go get help if she doesn't seem them walking.

It's a while before one of them appears, and it's John. Only John. He doesn't look so big any longer, just his usual closed umbrella self, slouching stiffly toward the center of the bridge where he stands for an age. He looks and looks at the water, but Mary doesn't come. Lillie watches John jerk his hands toward the bridge's rail; fling them back, then grab for it again. He grunts loud enough that she hears it from the tree line over the water; his hand stiffens into a claw, skitters back to his side.

Lillie's heart beats hard. *Mary*, she thinks, *John Murphy's mad for you.* He begins to walk back over the bridge and down to the riverbank, and Lillie is certain that when she ran away something terrible happened to Mary. She needs to tell somebody; somebody needs to help. She races home. But when she opens the door, calling out to her brother and sister-in-law, "Serge! Janet! Mary never left the mill!" Mary is home after all.

Mary looks at Lillie. Her eyes reflect darkness; the glassy pull of water, ceaseless, falling.

"You must have missed her on the road," Janet says.

"I must have," Lillie says, but knows she did not. "Where is your scarf?"

Mary touches her throat and declines to speak, except to say, "Dust."

Lillie looks at Mary all night long, trying to unpuzzle her presence. She begins to *feel* Mary's silence like she *felt* the silence in the mill, especially when Mary does not look at Lillie. Mary coughs so often and so loudly that Serge sends her to bed. *Is this my fault?* Lillie wonders. *What should I have done? Did something terrible truly happen or did I make it up?*

4.

In the dark bedroom Mary's eyes are open but blank as a mirror in a box. Moonlight washes the room in shadow, but the shadow is nothing like the knot of darkness at the mill. Even so, Lillie stares through her lashes at Mary from her own bed.

Finally, she whispers, "Mary?"

Nothing.

"Mary, did John hurt you?"

Still no response.

"Mary, are you awake? Do you need help?"

The third time is not a charm. Lillie pushes her covers aside and kneels beside her sister's bed. She holds her fingers over Mary's arm: It's warm. The moonlight is on Mary's cheek and her nose and lets Lillie's sharp eyes see a film woven across Mary's eyes, a net of roving, and at her nostrils more of the same—wisps at the corner of her mouth, a little wet. Lillie gives Mary's arm a savage shake and the wisps pull back into her nostrils like a snail to a shell. They pull Mary's eyelids down by the lashes. Then Mary takes a deep gulp of air, startles up and looks down at Lillie, who is on the floor, staring in disbelief and terror.

Mary's eyes are wild. She begins to speak but dissolves into a hacking cough that dots her fist with blood. Lillie runs to wake Serge and Janet. Serge was already awake and is quick to follow, but they find Mary composed, sleeping with her cheek on the pillow. She opens her eyes slowly, blinks languorously. There is blood on her mouth, which she licks away as she says, "What is the matter? Is there a fire?"

"Lillie said you were coughing blood. I came to see you before calling the doctor."

Mary laughs. There is no evidence of a cough. "She must have been dreaming. I think Lillie's nerves are rattled by this silly strike."

"They are *not*," Lillie hisses. She feels anger flush through her chest, throat, cheeks, and knows it for a too strong reaction, one that nearly oversets her, but she is sure she was not dreaming even though the things her eyes told her would sit more easily in a dream. How dare Mary suggest she's not supportive of the strike?

"Then why are you waking the household? Go to bed, Lillie. We'll discuss it, and the strike, in the morning."

Serge frowns, taking Lillie's side for once. "I heard you coughing. Perhaps I better get the doctor." At the same time, Lillie says, "What do you mean, 'discuss the strike'? It's set."

"The doctor will do exactly what? And for exactly what payment?" Mary ignores Lillie, who persists.

"*What* about the strike?"

Serge pats Lillie's shoulder, but lets the question stand. He's so used to being the balance between his sisters, not the oldest, not the youngest, but the man of the house after their eldest brother died.

Mary says, "I only mean the strike isn't such a good idea after all and I wonder whether we should go through with it."

Serge frowns more deeply. "*You* wonder? After everything you said?" At the same time, Lillie cries, "Liar! Serge, she was for it just last night—she and John, they were arguing—I saw them not half an hour ago—and he...he must have intimidated her—"

"Go to *sleep*, Lillie," Mary says.

"What did he do to you? I waited for you!"

"John Murphy didn't do anything to me."

"Both of you—*enough*. Sleep," Serge says, wearily. "We'll talk about it tomorrow. John Murphy, too, Mary."

If Serge were a book, he would be a book of psalms, used weekly, and very patient, pages so thin you could see the light through them, but somehow one of those pages will carry the weight of the whole heavy book. He would contain words people returned to again and again, be passed around in the common way for comfort.

Lillie subsides until they're alone again.

"Traitor," she hisses.

Mary's gaze is fixed on the ceiling. Does Lillie see something—a film, filaments, like loose roving—crawling across her eyes? Or is that her imagination? Mary's hands are folded neatly across her ribs. Finally, she says, "*We* are treacherous, but it is not too late. John Murphy learned the truth of our obligation to the mill. I have learned it too."

Something in her tone is so dreamy, so strange, Lillie flops over to signify the end of the conversation, although she immediately turns back to keep an eye on Mary, scooting to the furthest corner of her bed. She watches until her sister falls asleep. Then, finally, Lillie closes her eyes as well.

5.

Who do you think they pulled from the river the next morning?
If you thought it was Mary, that the Mary who was found at home
was not Mary at all but a doppelgänger, a copy, that real Mary—
true Mary—was already lying at the bottom of the river while a
puppet took her place, then you are wrong. If you guessed John
Murphy, you are correct. They pull him out, tangled in the great
plumed weeds along the bank. He's fully dressed, water sluicing
from the creases of his coat and boots and pants, his skin a ghastly
blue and his hands cut up, raw red meat.

Mary held Lillie's hand with crushing strength as they watched.
Lillie looked at Mary's face, but it held none of the anguish contained
within her grip, the bones of Lillie's fingers grinding together like
kindling. "The poor man," Mary says, as if he were only a casual
acquaintance, not someone she'd argued with the night before and
was *apparently* quite close to.

"Yes," Lillie agrees. She finds herself remembering how he
kept jerking toward the bridge as if he'd haul himself up. Did he
drown himself? She finds herself remembering the figure he made,
trudging off into the gloom along the river. She wonders how soon
after she saw him he died and shudders. "Aren't you sad, Mary?"

Mary's fingers tighten even harder, and Lillie gasps. "I think
we should postpone the strike," Mary replies. "I am going to speak
with Harriet and Colin first."

"*No.*" Lillie pulls her hand away. To her surprise, Mary releases
her without a fight. "Aren't you sad?" Lillie asks again.

Mary begins to cough; she coughs so long and so loudly that
several others turn to see whether John Murphy's corpse is about
to be joined by another. She coughs blood onto her fist and,
somewhere in the coughing, Lillie hears a quiet, "Yes."

She thinks of Mary saying John Murphy understands his
obligation to the mill. "Do you know what happened to him?"

There's another long pause before she answers. Lillie is watching Mary closely so she notices her tongue and teeth: tufts of fiber slick and webbed over both. "It is a terrible tragedy. Do you want to help your sister, Liliana?"

Strange. Stranger. "Yes," Lillie says.

Mary's cheeks are flushed; she looks sweaty, a trickle of sweat near her ear. But her voice is cool: "I need my scarf. Will you fetch it for me?"

6.

Lillie goes to the mill. You and I know she shouldn't go. She reasons that it will be an easy errand, and it is daytime, so none of last night's atmosphere will trouble her. She reasons that she does not want Mary, whatever is inside Mary, to know she suspects something impossible. If the thing inside her sister knows she doesn't believe all is well, it will do something to her or Serge or Janet or somebody else. Lillie thinks if she goes to the mill she can find an answer, some proof, and bring it to the doctor or the priest, that she will know what to do.

As soon as she crosses the bridge, she realizes the daylight won't shield her. The quiet around the mill is suffocation; a stone in the gut; a threat, whispered at your ear; a blunt object used for a weapon; a warning. Neither bird nor insect song dispels the dull anger Lillie fears is crouched in that silence. She almost leaves, but then thinks about Mary staring at her in the darkness of their room while fibers coat her tongue and move her jaw, thinks about those fibers spinning out into thread, a thread which will reach from Mary's bed to her own. She thinks about John the foreman. She thought he was a rat, but now he's dead and she was the last to see him alive, and she isn't so sure. She thought Mary never left the mill, but Mary was already home. And yet, Lillie isn't so sure of that either. She *is* sure she should have stopped whatever happened last night. And that the explanation for Mary's behavior is here at the mill. She reasons a lot, but it isn't reason which finally gets her into the mill.

It's guilt.

The mill is icy, and although daylight spills in through the clerestory windows, there are still patches of darkness thickening in certain corners and under certain spinning frames.

"I am here for a scarf," she tells the mill, but she goes to the bell tower, because perhaps she can retrace Mary and John's footsteps there. "Hello?" The mill is angry, but it does not yet have a voice to answer her; it watches as she touches the wall where there is a small brown stain. Lillie thinks it could be blood. The mill knows what it is. "I am not trouble," Lillie says. "I am just here for my sister. Are you afraid to be alone? We'll come back. We're just wearing out." She trips on the stairs and feels as if the stairs tripped her. *Don't run away this time,* she tells herself, and forces herself into the carding room with its heavy iron machines. Weak sunlight lies limp across the floor and there are motes of dust and fiber drifting white through it.

"You are looking for an answer," he says behind her. Lillie whips around: The boss's son is standing there, neat and glossy in a wool flannel suit.

"I'm not here to break anything or cause problems. I'm here to help my sister, she—"

"I know. You were invited." He has none of his usual smuggery, his certainty that everybody thinks he is the sun; instead, he looks at Lillie with the same affect that Mary looked at her, and he seems big, bones loose, though not quite as loose as John. "You came for answers, and I will show you how to hear what the mill has to say."

"It doesn't want the strike," Lillie says, backing away. "Did *you* do this?"

He shakes his head and then stops, abruptly, to grab at the door and yank it closed on them. In a weary (the mill has found its) voice, "Not I."

There is a tug at her ankle, and she drops her gaze. There is a clot of devil's dust: fiber debris, small stones and thorns and dirty seed-fluff, crouching by her like a creature rather than a chance assortment of fluff. The sunlight from the window gives it a blazing head; gives the boss's son deep shadows on his face. It works its way up her leg, and she kicks it to pieces, but a speck of fiber lands, soft as a kiss, on her nose. She brushes it away and another piece lands on her eyelashes, and it is too late.

The mill in her head says, *Do not leave before you wear out.*

It was too late as soon as she stepped back into the mill.

7.

Lillie watches herself sit.

Lift her hands to the machine.

She feels her cheeks move when she smiles. There is no strike. There is a new foreman. Lillie hears herself speak, say words she'd never say, not in a hundred years. She is well-behaved and rigorous and her body aches, but she doesn't take her hands away from the machine unless her muscle spasms out of the mill's control. Wearing out. Sometimes, she tries to say something about it to Serge; to Mary, who is the same as she is. Instead, she coughs until blood's scraped out of her throat and speckles her fist. Then she feels the slimy fibers tighten around her tongue. At night, they spin away from her body, seeking, pulling at her, spreading out. She cannot stop them; no matter what she tries, she can only watch. They close her eyes, then open them, and it does hurt. Oh, yes, it does.

Serge asked Mary and Lillie whether they wanted to visit their cousins in Massachusetts. He looked concerned, his eyes soulful. She heard herself say, "I do not want to leave the mill right now," and saw his face. Serge was unlikely to argue, but she felt the mill's attention sharpen. She saw the mill in Mary's eyes. She tried to say anything else but coughed herself bloody again. The thing inside her wants to get inside Serge, too. *To keep him safe,* it thinks, and that is close enough to Lillie's thoughts that she feels no tightening of her strings.

Lillie watches herself sit.

Lift her hand to the machine.

Open your matchbox inside the mill

Because all she can do is watch, she sees the spark by the machine near a basket of cotton for the carding. She tries not to think about it and cranks the wheel so it goes more quickly, too quickly, hoping for another spark. If it burns—

Sleep all day, sleep all night
Your eyes swing open and you lost your sight

There. Another spark. But the mill is in her head: Her hand seizes, bones crack; she coughs until her vision swims.

Devil's in your throat
Devil's in your hair

Is that smoke?

Way to knock him down
Way to rock him bye

Is that fire, spreading?

Strike your match and watch sparks fly.

– JESSICA P. WICK is a writer, poet, and editor. She co-founded *Goblin Fruit* with Amal El-Mohtar, a quarterly e-zine of fantastical poetry, and is a passionate advocate for the reading aloud of poetry and fiction. Her poetry has been nominated for the Rhysling Award and received honorable mentions in Year's Best Fantasy and Horror anthologies. Her short fiction can be found scattered across the internet; recently, her novella, *An Unkindness,* appeared in Mythic Delirium's *A Sinister Quartet.* She currently lives in Westerly, Rhode Island. When she isn't rambling through cemeteries, gazing wistfully at the breakers, or working on "the swashbuckle-y novel," she can be found at the newly reopened independent bookshop where she works, across the street from a Victorian strolling park.

Blackstone

Steven Belanger

1.

The mill days are not over. Not for those like me. We walk slowly, hunched over with pinched nerves and herniated disks, coughing up plaster-dust-colored phlegm for the rest of our lives. You know that guy driving that red-rusted pickup truck with the giant tool chest stretched across the bed, trailing pot and vape-smoke, an arm crooked out the open window even in the winter, sucking on a cigarette like he's making love to his future cancer? That's me. That's a lot of us, if you just open your eyes and see.

And it doesn't matter to us what you think. If you've got healthcare, if you can sit without a piercing pain in your lower back and a cement basement in your lungs, you have that luxury. If you've got a safety net instead of bottles of little white pills, you've got the time and the energy to judge. We've lost a mother or father or uncle to this job, to this attack on our lungs, on our bodies, on our minds. And we keep doing it because that's our cage. Ten years after high school, Mary and I formed our own little demo company, because we didn't know anything else. I demoed. She retired and did the books. But it was already too late for her. She lost a father and an uncle to asbestos and plaster-cancer, and five years into our own little venture, seven years after we tied the knot, I lost her to the same damn thing.

I went into debt burying the one I loved, then joined Davis and his demo crew at a big job, December 2020, during COVID's first U.S. howl. Blackstone. A giant, sprawling old mill that needed to become Blackstone Condos, fast. Like, illegal working conditions and super-overtime fast. Twelve, fourteen hours a day, six days a week. Seven when I could. Sounds like I was working myself to an early grave, doesn't it? You're goddamn right I was. I was walking toward Mary and the bright-white lantern light she shone in my nightly darkness. Same as the women and children who'd worked in the old mills, like Blackstone. Because people like us always see the bars of our cage. Mine are covered in a fine layer of asbestos and plaster-dust. Their cage was a system of enslavement to white mill owners. I read a lot about it while on the job, even more afterwards.

The little girl and her red ball showed up on the third day of the job, exactly a year to the day after Mary died. For Mary's "anniversary," I took a Percocet with a shot of Dewars, said a short toast, then went to work. The world does not owe us a thing. I will do the damn day.

It was just me and Chris, working ourselves to the bone, smoking bones and popping pain pills and sleeping when we couldn't stand or swing a crowbar anymore. Blackstone, Inc. put us into on-site units so we could demo, not commute. Mine was right above the manager's office. But I was rarely there. I slept on my feet, covered in plaster-dust and breathing it in. In work, as in life, I didn't build, I just tore down. The race was on. By mid-2021, Blackstone Mills had to become Blackstone Condominiums. Conveniently (and very expensively) located between Routes 146 and 295 in suburban Smithfield, Rhode Island. All units pre-sold. I got to work so often I didn't have to feel. Or think. Or remember. I was tunnel-visioned. I saw Mary's lantern light at the end of my tunnel and I ran toward it.

The first time the girl appeared, that was a busy day with lots of people. Davis, the crew-chief, was in and out all day. So were Blackstone reps, contractors, electricians. Tons of people trample through a demo site. I ignored them all and figured some idiot didn't have a babysitter and brought their kid.

I'd been hearing children, in the distance somewhere, singing and playing. A man and a woman talking. Murmuring, really, in soft voices that got louder, then lower. Closer, then further away. I was clawing plaster I'd loosened the day before, in the hall outside the little museum-to-be, next to the first-floor manager's office. I pried the last dusty block of stubborn old asbestos-filled wall with my crowbar. The block chipped and split and floated to the floor in a blizzard of thin, white flakes. I remember thinking, *That floor's from about 1850, eleven years before the Civil War. That's a great floor. Don't damage it, asshole.*

Another chunk of plaster and asbestos thudded at my feet amidst the fluttering flakes. I knelt to the floor to check the boards for damage and I saw two small feet in two small tan shoes. Pieces of leather held together, really. White socks sagged below bony ankles. Thin stilts of legs and there she was, a little girl with a bowl-shaped haircut and a burlap sack top and pants. A malnourished gray to her cheeks. She cupped that red ball in her small hands, looking at me with those sad eyes, as the voices and murmurs got louder. Closer.

I thought I was about to pass out, and I was annoyed at whoever brought their kid to such a potentially dangerous place, so I shooed her away with a wave of my white-dusted hands. I knocked down a few larger chunks of plaster. Not more than a minute later, Davis came out of nowhere.

"Seymour, you're the man," he said, for no reason at all, as he patted me on the back. White clouds of dust exploded from my shoulder. I closed my watering eyes and hacked up more dust. Flakes fell like dandruff from my blue Sox cap.

Davis and a guy I didn't know, a tall guy, puffy and soft, in a blue suit, went into the manager's office. The girl and her red ball were gone. So were the voices.

2.

People you love die. It happens all the time, and not just to the old. You've still got to wake up and shower and demo plaster, because the world doesn't owe you a thing and the sun doesn't rise and set upon your sadness. You do what you've got to do so you can do the day. And then the next day. And then the next. Somewhere along the way you hope for a little happiness.

That's my mantra and I say it to myself every day and night. I'd said it out loud that night, and then the phone rang.

Ugly, white plastic thing, in our bedroom. I mean, in *my* bedroom. Large, upraised buttons. Red numbers atop smaller red letters. Mary had liked it. I kept it for that. It was *ours*, even if for just a short time. I kept the landline number for that reason, too. And for the wake-up calls at five in the morning, when Davis needed to get me off my ass because some inspector or bigwig was coming. My hearing was already shit at that time; I couldn't hear my cell most days.

Not that the landline rang often. Only Davis, telemarketers and wrong numbers. I usually ignored it and let my voicemail catch it all.

But that Saturday morning I was out-of-sorts, cranky and full-body sore, popping Percocet and thinking of Mary, so I picked it up.

"Hello," I said.

I waited a few moments. Nothing. No static. No breathing. Nothing.

"Hello," I said again, too exhausted and depressed to be annoyed.

After another moment of the same nothing, I hung up.

3.

Soon I'm back downstairs, in the hallway again, outside the manager's office, hacking away. Getting the job done. I dimly remember Chris being there that day. He was a tall, thin snowman. I was, too. Popping painkillers and not eating or sleeping much will do that to you. I was already coughing a lot, too, and not even out of my thirties. We were always covered in plaster snow.

In the distance, somewhere outside, maybe, kids were singing and playing. It was a warm December day for Rhode Island. Fifties. No wind. The kind of winter day I was thrown outside as a kid and told to come back by dinner. A man and a woman whispered loudly, somewhere. Like people do when they think they're being a lot quieter than they are. High, then low. It came and went. The man's voice got deeper, much deeper, then went silent.

I opened my eyes and Chris was gone. I wasn't in the upstairs hallway anymore, outside the manager's office. I didn't know where I was. I was looking at an original wooden joist from the 1850s, my crowbar poised, mid-swing. I couldn't breathe. I was suffocating in plaster-dust and tiny gritty motes of white flakes. My eyes watered. Everything blurred. I ran my arm across my eyes and looked down the hallway to my right. I saw the wall as it would've been then, years before a Civil War cannon was shot. Through the shimmer, I saw the old wood of that wall, part of the skeletal framework of the old mill. The empty spaces. The old rooms that had been walled up.

Behind me, in front of me, everywhere in the darkness, the voices started again. Whispers. Children. A few men. A woman or two. I couldn't make out what they said. The children sounded playful, the men serious. Very serious. Angry.

I heard myself mumbling in dread as the dust and darkness dissolved.

I was standing at a wall in the basement.

I didn't remember walking down there.

A deep voice moaned. The children's squeals and playing got louder. Happier. As if there were hundreds of them, all playing and laughing. But the moaning got even louder, thunderous, until all the sounds and voices melted into a single man's voice. He was clearing his throat and saying my name. It took a moment to realize I had not been dreaming any of it, that I was awake, that I was standing in the basement in front of that wall. That my crowbar was in my right hand, a bottle of water in my left.

I put my crowbar on the basement floor. The head sank a little in dirt free of fallen plaster-dust. I splashed water on my hands, my face. I touched some lightly to my eyes. I reminded myself again: I'm in the basement looking at the wall. The part Chris and I forgot about, to focus time on our living quarters, then to the rest of the upstairs. Prospective buyers of condo units don't care what the basement storage area looks like. We needed to fast-track upstairs. So half of the basement storage rooms and crevices were demoed. Half weren't.

Chris was beside me, still saying my name, clearing his throat and repeating it again and again. He was covered in sweat and chalky dust, his voice as emphysemic as mine. The plaster gets into your sinuses and lungs like coal dust in a mine. Like cotton or wood dust in a mill. A mill very much like Blackstone. The thunderous machines spat that shit all over the mill, blanketing the floor with it. You breathe it in and it gets into your lungs and the coughing never stops. Cotton tuberculosis, they called it. Mill TB. Some caught it and the real TB at the same time. Some got so sick they got careless. Many lost hands and fingers in the machines. A few lost entire arms. Sometimes the machines ate them whole. They got buried fast so the TB didn't spread. So the millworkers didn't panic and stop working. Made me wonder at the time what they did with the dead in the winter, when the ground was frozen.

Chris coughed and put a hand on my shoulder. He had a pitying frown, a touch of worry in his eyes.

"Hey, man," he said. "What the hell are you doing down here? You all right? I take a piss and you're gone." He attempted a smile. I didn't. I'd already looked down to where I'd placed my crowbar.

"I don't hear my cell," I managed to say.

A flickering smile, like from an old cartoon. "Davis said we need to pick up the pace. We're behind schedule. Way behind schedule."

"I don't hear my cell," I said again, for some reason.

Chris ran a hand through his hair, and plaster snow flurried to the floor. "What the hell are you doing down here?" he asked again, more in exhausted confusion than in anger or irritation. Before I could think of an answer, or remember, he shook his head, muttered, "He's losing his fucking mind," and walked away.

When I heard him climbing the stairs, I bent at the knees, ignored my screaming back, and picked up my crowbar. Beside it was an old, white-dusted ball. Red. Very faded. Chipped. It looked like it hadn't been touched in years.

But I knew it had.

4.

Later that night, after I'd showered and popped a few pills, the phone rang again. I ignored it and blew my nose. My sinuses were congested and infected. I sneezed fine, white powder, mixed with black specks and red blood. I stood and stared at nothing and the phone rang and rang. Finally I picked it up.

"Hello?"

Nothing. No wrong number. No hang-up. No one breathed. No music or sound. No children playing, or men and women whispering. Nothing like earlier that day. Nothing at all.

"Hello?" I said, unnerved.

Was there a sigh just then? A whisper?

"Hello?" my voice cracked. "Is someone there?"

And with a shock, I realized I wanted Mary to be on the other end. But she was dead. Not mill TB. Mill *cancer*. Diagnosis to death in six months. Not something you ever forgot. My mother died when I was twenty-nine. My father a few years later. Then Mary. The four of us were always together. Birthdays. Thanksgiving. Christmas. New Year's. She loved my family because hers had died from plaster TB. Lung cancer took both of mine. Now it's just me. I bought my plot and gravestone a few weeks before. It says *Neal Seymour. Husband. Son.* And nothing else, because I wasn't anything else.

I knew I was about to say her name, to ask if it was really her, so I hung up.

I dreamed of her instead. Sunny days at Newport. At Rhode Island's beaches. Smiles and laughs.

5.

I awoke, popped the pills, showered, picked up my favorite handheld crowbar, my buddy, and I did the day. The world doesn't owe you a thing, and it doesn't sacrifice itself to your sadness. I did the next day. And the next.

"What will soon be Blackstone Condominiums had once been the Smithfield Cotton and Woolen Manufactory, a textile mill," I said to Chris, in between blows to the wall, several months later. I held forth on local history to pass the time. You do what you've got to do, to do the day. "Kenneth Williams bought it in 1823 and expanded it. One thousand, two hundred spindles. Thirty-four looms."

Chris nodded and hacked into the wall and ceiling, feverish blows, really on a roll.

"For all that machinery," I told him, between swings of my crowbar, "guess how many men, women and children he hired."

"No idea," he said. He knew to just let me go. "A hundred." Chunks of the ceiling came down in front of him. His close-cropped brown hair was plaster-white, as was his thirty-year-old face. His mouth and eyes were clear. He usually wore a mask. I didn't. Not for COVID. Not for the job. Fuck it all. COVID could take me to Mary and her lantern in that tunnel of hers just as nicely as anything else.

"He hired just twelve men, thirty-seven women, and eleven children. Sixty people."

He stopped chopping at the ceiling as plaster-dust fell around him. "You're kidding. That's it?"

I nodded and pulled. A large chunk of wall came off. You could see the embedded asbestos. Light-green striations in the off-white plaster. Cancerous stuff. We've always been killing ourselves. "Yup. Williams bought four houses down the street for his workers. They were ex-farmers, so the money was better, but it was still servitude. Everybody worked twelve-hour days here, usually longer, like fourteen to sixteen."

"Like us!" he shouted. We laughed, then broke into coughing fits. When I finished gasping, he said, "The kids, too?"

I nodded. "That was normal for the time. Kids were half the workforce. Small fingers, small spaces in the machines. And their working careers were longer."

"Shit," he said, brushing an arm across his lips. "That ain't no life. How'd they get away?" He gasped and pulled on his crowbar. Ceiling fell. I noticed his voice had gotten quieter, as if he'd moved further away.

"They didn't. Guys like Williams didn't just own the mills. They owned the houses the workers rented from them. They owned the stores and markets the workers had to buy their food and necessaries from. And owners like Williams didn't pay in cash. They paid in credit that the workers had to redeem for everything. That kept the workers from ever having any money to save to move away *with*." I stopped and coughed.

"Shit, that ain't no life," Chris said again. His voice came from behind a white plaster cloud of dust and lazily floating motes. He stood just a few feet away and I couldn't see him. "So, what happened when they got old and couldn't work anymore?"

"Sometimes they stayed in the millhouses with their families, if the owners let them." I pulled on my crowbar. A huge chunk of wall collapsed around us. "Otherwise they went to homes for the poor, and for TB victims. They got buried at the local church, which sprung up near every mill. There were several churches in every mill town. They're still here."

"What'd they do with the bodies in the winter?" he asked. His voice came softly, as if from even further away. It was barely a whisper.

He denied afterward that he'd asked that. *Must've been someone else,* he said. *I didn't say anything else that day. Not after I said 'Shit, that ain't no life' the first time.* He's on an oxygen tank now, a tube in his nose. Plaster TB and long-COVID. Mostly he just sits up in his bed at home. He never married or had a family. I'm usually his only visitor, besides Davis and his family. Of course, Davis supervised and managed. Talked to the reps and bigwigs. Stayed far away from the plaster and asbestos.

They're all my family now.

I didn't answer the question, either way, because I didn't have the answers then that I have today. There are books on display now in that small museum room in Blackstone Condominiums. "A Look Back," it says. A bold admittance of the past, that room. Rather brazen.

If I had answered, I doubted I would've told him the truth. That I was putting it together. That I heard loud voices those last few months. That the dead were in my head. Loud, angry men. Sobbing women. There was that little girl and her ball. Children playing, and happy shrieks. Sometimes I just found myself in different rooms and hallways. Often, I awoke, as if from a trance, standing in front of the intact walls in the basement.

Later that day, maybe later that night, I trudged into the manager's office for a break. At some point, I'd slunk to a cot and slept. I hadn't been sleeping well, or often. The phone rang most nights and I had a fever and chill most days.

I felt my head hit the cot, no pillow, and I heard a deep, guttural snore. A second, maybe a third. The loud, angry voices came again. A man's deep voice I could almost make out. And sobbing. Women sobbing. Kids sobbing. Scratching sounds. A child's laughter, very faint, as if from a long distance.

I sat up in the cot and turned to the wall behind me. A tall painting of a man, in a thin wooden frame. I'd seen it before, standing behind a door with many others—all of them important, dead men. They were going up in the halls when we were done, all touched-up and ready for the recessed lighting and those tiny, illuminating lights aimed up at the paintings. A Hall of Fame of local, rich, white, dead guys.

I stood up in my dusty-white-caked jeans and suspenders. My Patriots' shirt was a torn, faded blue. My sneakers were permanently caked with off-white plaster and dust. Staring down at me—facing slightly to the right as was the custom of the day—was a determined, grim-faced Kenneth Williams. Circa 1823, when he bought the mill. In his late twenties but painted to look older. Less youthful, more dignified. Wearing a pitch-black coat and a white collar, fluffed to his bony, firmly set jaw. Long, thin nose. A recessed hairline, much deeper on his left than on his right, so his widow's peak didn't point correctly. His torso was amorphous in the black coat, from the waist up, without clearly defined arms. Uneven green matte, brighter after the touch-up. An oval surrounded him in the frame. The top of the oval touched the frame, but the bottom didn't. The left side of the oval touched the frame, too. The right side didn't.

The painting was Williams's coming-out. His entrance into the rich and successful business world. *Rhode Island's Who's Who* would use it for his headshot. And it was a bad job. A cheap job. And if he'd been cheap to himself, to his posterity, how cheap had he been to his workers? I wondered, with some dread, of the corners he must've cut with his mill. With his workers. His *people*.

What corners had he cut?

What happened to the dead bodies in the winter?

Children whispered again, louder and louder. They rose as if from his painting, until their murmurs almost formed words: *findoutfindoutfindout...*

Their giggles and whispers bled into an unintelligible chorus. From every wall I was battered by thunderous machinery—metallic screams, shrieks of mechanized belts, gratings and pulleys. I was smothered by smells of asbestos and dust, the pulling of my filled lungs. Penetrating all those sounds—coughing. A chorus of coughs. The pounding of machines became drumbeats of human coughs. The indistinct *findoutfindoutfindout* became "Find out where the hell he is now," and Davis, the boss-man, was right beside me.

"Never mind, I found him," Davis said to somebody I couldn't see. I could barely see Davis himself, a stocky man with muscle, and chest- and arm-hair to spare. He crossed his arms. "Jesus, man, you look like shit. Are you all right?"

6.

My last day on the job was a Sunday. I woke early. The phone was ringing.

I ignored its first few rings. Then the next few. But not the one after that.

I didn't say anything. I listened. I really listened. I listened for wind, for voices, for a television in the background. For whispers of children; for shouts of angry men. For women's sobs. For Mary, saying she loved me. *Can you see me? Can you see the light I'm holding?* But there was nothing.

And before I could help myself, I blurted, "Mary?"

Silence. Dead silence. I choked back a sob, but the dam broke and I finally let myself cry like a baby. I hadn't, really, since Mary died.

Very softly, a tremulous voice dripped from the receiver. A whisper.

"Neal," she breathed. "Oh, Neal."

I couldn't breathe. A scream froze in my throat. I white-knuckled the receiver to my ear. I stared at the wall in front of me. The walls all around me.

I cried out again and slowly placed the receiver upon its cradle. When it rang moments later, I picked it up. "Mary?"

A whisper: "Yes."

I choked on new sobs. Rapids of grief. A waterfall of grief. I unleashed grief again as if I hadn't before.

"I miss you," I said. I said I was alive but not living. I said I smiled but I wasn't really happy. I said a lot of things. Lots of "I love you." Lots of quiet sobbing and wordlessness.

My throat grew raw and tired, my eyes wet and burning. I sat, spent and silent. There was nothing more I could say to her. And she had nothing to say to me.

I'd been sitting in bed, sputtering and sobbing to my dead wife into a dead receiver. The mouthpiece was wet. My unit was dark. I was all alone.

And I was horrified. Had I lost my mind? I listened intently, the phone heavy in my hand. But there was nothing. No breathing. No static. Nothing.

I looked at the phone like I'd never seen it before.

"I'm so sorry," I heard myself say. I had a throbbing headache, a raw throat, body aches and chills, a fever, and I couldn't breathe. I was still all alone, and lonely. Some of the pounding in my head had also been Davis pounding on my door. He told me that, later, after he'd fired me.

"I'm sorry," I said again. "I wish I could be with you."

I placed the receiver gently upon its cradle. I sat there, my fingers caressing it, my head lowered, for a long time.

Then I bolted downstairs, past Davis and Chris and some guy I didn't know. They were shocked and said something I ignored. I ran into the basement, holding aloft my crowbar, yelling. I took the crowbar to Kenneth Williams's awful painting until it was shredded cheese, askance on the wall, its hanging wire very taut and soon to snap.

There was a lot of shouting, but nobody stopped me. The deep, angry voices, the whispers, the sobs and the children's laughter all bled into a crescendo in my head and I screamed louder than before.

I was still screaming when I ran into the basement. I dropped my crowbar when I grabbed a medium-sized sledgehammer leaning against the wall, near the door. I carried it with both hands through inch-thick plaster snow, like Jack Torrance carrying his ax through that snow-covered maze. I ran beside the demoed basement wall, seeing again its dark recesses and pockets of solid shadows and emptiness. I stopped, heaving and coughing, in front of the walled-up portion. The section Chris and I had left alone.

"What corners did you cut?" I yelled. "What did you do with the bodies in the winter?"

Twelve swings of the sledgehammer brought it down. By that time, two guys had grabbed me by my arms and I'd dropped the sledgehammer. Chris and a few others had crowded behind me and someone had turned on the fluorescents. Davis shined a flashlight into the aperture, the wall reaching just to our knees.

"Oh, shit," he said, breathless. "Oh, no."

In four neat rows were rotted wooden coffins, stacked two-high. Many others leaned against the far wall. Two had fallen, emptying their contents onto the dirt floor at their feet. Other skeletons laid in the dirt, without accompanying coffins.

One of these was very small.

I wrestled my arms free and grabbed Davis's flashlight.

I stepped over.

I trailed the yellow light in the dirt as I made my way, slowly. I saw a medium-height skeleton missing its thumb and index finger. Another was without its right hand. One didn't have a left foot.

I stopped. In the beam of yellow light, I saw what remained of a young child, maybe eight years old. At the feet were four strips of leather and some remnants of string that would've held them together. Filthy cloth, torn, with tiny holes from mice's teeth, that would've once been her socks. Wide burlap strips, laying among her bones, that had once been her shirts and pants.

And a small, still slightly inflated red ball.

– STEVEN E. BELANGER has been published in *We Are Providence: Tales of Horror from the Ocean State, Space and Time Magazine, Black Chaos II: More Tales of the Zombie*, and other places. His published stories vary, from horror, to mysteries, to literary fiction. He's currently finishing up a novel manuscript (or two). A former freelance reporter, he's been a high school English teacher for over twenty-three years and is a two-time Coach of the Year for the Rhode Island Academic Decathlon. He has too many books and lots of old, graded baseball cards. He's more interesting and exciting than this would lead you to believe. Trust me. He's on Meta, sometimes.

The Medians of Providence

Errick Nunnally

Moving homes was a special circle of hell that came with extraordinary stress and frustration related to both physical labor and money. But it was time; we couldn't sustain the rising rents. Our hunt ended in Rhode Island, several miles north of Providence. My wife, Lynn—bless her ingenuity and drive—had been searching in widening concentric circles for somewhere we could afford to land. She was looking right into and through Attleboro until…why not Rhode Island?

It was a lovely property, two and a half years vacant, and I was as surprised by it as my wife was enthusiastic about the find.

"Not a foreclosure?" I'd asked her.

"Nope, estate sale."

"Did the owner die here?"

"I have no idea. Does it matter?"

"You've read some of my writing. So, yeah, kind of."

She grinned and shrugged. "We've been renting for five years— most of Rose's lifetime. We need some permanence." Her hand traced the hollow of my back and slipped into the crook of my arm. I pulled her close.

A hard truth. The second-to-last property we rented got sucked underwater by the housing market. We were lucky to get out as fast as we did. My job producing marketing graphics only paid slightly more than my wife's fitness gigs, and the impermanence of home only exacerbated our anxiety over having children. We could handle a mortgage if things broke our way on my wife's ideas to use the property. The old land was lovely, if sprawling, and located on the other side of a brook feeding directly into a waterway that tied the mills of Rhode Island to Massachusetts.

"Money, money, money," I said.

"Money, money, money," my wife echoed and ended with a sigh.

The financial meltdown of 2008 still rippled through our lives. It affected our income and plans in unpredictable ways. Every necessity required money and the precariousness caused by that situation lurked, a beast we'd battled and merely held off for the time being.

To say it was a stress on our marriage would be the kind of understatement intended to brush off the pain and keep uncomfortable conversations at bay. We had to work hard at it to keep the family afloat. Maybe the original sheen could be buffed back into the relationship and soothe our shared uncertainty about the future. Neither of us indulged in our own personal interests very much. My sputtering attempts at being an author certainly suffered.

Our two daughters, Kelly and Rose, had no intention of crawling back into their mother anytime soon; they were here to stay. As ever, the priority of our children overrode common sense. Finding a school for bright kids who bucked public education standards had been as difficult around Providence as it had been in Massachusetts.

I chewed my lip, alternately scanning the acre of grass and watching Kelly as she ran, dragging her little sister forever in her wake. "You think they'll be happy here?"

"I hope so. They seem excited by the property. Not sure Rose understands this is going to be our home soon, though."

I nodded. Kelly spent her early years in a blue building and Rose, a white one. Now we were moving to a yellow house all our own. "I hope so too."

Three years later, they were settled into a private school and happy. Financial assistance and a two-child discount softened that monthly bill, but we'd pay anything to keep them there. Remember: common sense was out-of-pocket on the matter of our girls.

Besides the schools we researched, the only other things I knew about Providence were the old mills and the author, Lovecraft. And I hated Lovecraft. I disliked him for his writing rather than the color of his skin, the exact opposite of how he might have thought of me and my family. I certainly understood his contributions to the genre, but the only stories about cosmic mythos and madness that I enjoyed were from other, more modern authors who used superlatives sparingly and crafted coherent stories from beginning to end. They also didn't write letters declaring the inferiority of non-white ethnicities or compose racist poetry.

I pressed my phone tighter to my ear so I could hear Lynn over the train's rattle.

"I said 'are you coming home first or leaving from the train station?'"

"If I want to be on time, I need to leave from the station. What's up, worried about dinner?"

She took a deep breath and paused. "No, I got it, don't worry."

I wasn't worried, but I didn't believe she had it. Lynn hated cooking and preferred I did it. "Okay. Well, anyway, yeah, I'm driving right there from the station."

"Remember not to spend more than twenty-five."

"I know."

"Don't sound so down. We're just waiting for my group instruction check to clear, and I have money coming next week too from a couple private sessions."

"Next week. Right. Seems like the timing is never good."

"Seems like. Anyway, have fun, talk to you later, love you."

Twenty-five dollars of fun. "I love you too."

After I disconnected the line, I realized that I probably should have shared some optimism that she'd booked a couple of private sessions. I typed out a congratulatory text with supporting emojis and sent it.

151

Despite our personal gains, we were back in mounting debt, fighting for a future we invested in, but couldn't reap the returns. It's a tricky thing, starting and running a business. A lot had happened in the past three years to pile on unplanned debt or stall our plans. After a surreal reckoning with cancer in our youngest, and the kind of home repairs on an old house that drains bank accounts, creative desire came in a definitive last. It was something I'd ignored for too long and struggled to nourish as I commuted to Boston for my day job. The train ride could be good for a couple hours of enforced downtime, but little else while sitting shoulder to shoulder with other commuters. The unpredictability in my life didn't leave much room for finding writing opportunities or meeting their subsequent deadlines. My dream was on life support, something I could only watch in distracted disappointment.

Tonight, however, was going to be a departure from the rhythm of a simple meal, bedtime routines, and deciding which bills to pay. I was on my way to meet friends who were gathering because an author we all knew was making a stop in our tiny state of Rhode Island.

The first person came into view as soon as I pulled off the highway. The intersection was a nightmare during the week when delivering the kids to school, but at night, it was empty. In the sick yellow light of the streetlamp, I could just make out the placard that read: 'Need help, God bless.' He was tall and dark-skinned, with knotty locs clawing at his shoulders and sweat on his brow. I ignored him, much the same way I did most beggars. In this oppressive heat, it was easier because my windows were rolled up, and the AC roared.

It's not that I don't care about folks who've slid a few pegs below the poverty line, but these days I can't understand the concept of spare change. I rarely have loose cash on me. The next stoplight revealed more of the same: a man, tall, heavyweight, with sunburned skin, wearing a filthy gray ball cap. His cardboard sign read: 'Laid off, veteran, God bless.'

By the third one, they held my attention, and I saw others ahead, wandering the median. More than I'd ever noticed before.

Caught at another light, I could see that the next one was a woman: gaunt, morose, wearing a wide-brimmed sunhat, with bags laid at her feet. Her sign read: 'ANYTHINGS HELPS, GODS BLESS.' We locked eyes and her postured shifted to one of full attention. The woman had a long face and nose with sort of an elongated chin. She looked familiar, but the light changed before I could dig the memory out of my brain. In my rearview mirror, I could see she still watched me.

Parking was easy and in a rare feat, I was on time. The event itself and dinner afterward were fun, a recharge, a chance to embrace my individual self and pull away from the real world. For a little while anyway. The world that sent bills and heartache, made demands of time and effort. Even after a few beers, I felt invigorated on the drive home rather than sluggish from drinking more booze than I'd had in months.

Navigating out of the neighborhood, I could see dark figures seated on the corners just before the local expressway. Each one had a cardboard sign propped up next to them.

I got home around eleven and my wife was already in bed, waiting for me to arrive so she could go to sleep. She asked how it all went as I wound floss around my fingers in the bathroom.

"Great! We had a good time. It was nice to be out."

"You're pretty animated."

The observation hit me at an odd angle. After nearly twenty years of marriage, I still couldn't interpret all of her comments safely.

"Uh, yeah, we talked about writing, mostly. How were the girls?"

"They were fine. Kelly only picked at dinner and Rose was so out of whack by the time I got something put together that she barely ate her meal."

"She usually enjoys your chicken noodle soup."

"I can't improvise a meal the way you can. I made some chicken sausage and frozen vegetables. They wanted something fried, and I do not do big pans of hot grease." She yawned.

"I know," I said, and resumed brushing my teeth, unsure how to respond. I wondered what their lives would be like if I wasn't there to cook. It was such a trivial thing, in my view, but every now and then I was reminded how much it affected their lives too. The odd word 'sonder' crossed my mind. It meant knowing that other people's lives were as rich and complicated as one's own.

"Hey, Lynn? Do you know the word 'sonder'?"

She didn't answer. When I crossed the hallway into the bedroom, Lynn was already asleep, facing away from the center of the bed. I wondered what all those homeless people's lives were like.

The hum of the air-conditioning unit kept me awake even though I was spent from the night out. I'd spent too many years honing my paranoia while growing up in the redlined, urban delights of the inner-city. Looking over my shoulder was an involuntary and sometimes useful habit I couldn't shake. Not being able to hear the house triggered the feeling. On top of that, despite the cool air coming from the machines, the room felt stuffy and unnatural. My imagination insisted that I think of an intruder creeping up the tight stairs.

In my mind, it was the woman begging on the corner, somehow following me home. Her long face nagged at me as I slipped into that bizarre hallucinatory state between awake and asleep.

There was a time when one or both of the girls would bound into the room shortly after 5 a.m. Nowadays, we're lucky when both of them bother to say good morning. Our youngest, at seven years old, still clung to her glory days of a mere three years ago and the oldest, well, she was a tween now, and her verbal communication had devolved into a series of whispers and grunts. From under the covers, I heard Kelly's heavy footsteps going down the stairs as I unwound myself from hugging Lynn's back.

"Good morning, girls," my wife called as they tromped by our bedroom.

Kelly mumbled something—maybe—and continued downstairs. Later, she would insist that she'd responded, but now she was probably fixated on a bowl of cold cereal. Rose popped in and sat on the bed, her lovey, a blue elephant, slung over one shoulder.

"Hi, Mommy. Hi, Daddy." She hopped up and down on the bed.

"Hey, sweetheart." I smiled at my youngest daughter and reached out to touch her back.

These were the times I was guaranteed to smile. I wanted everything for them. As much as I regretted many of the decisions that I'd made to get where I was today, my girls would have better. I'd already made sure of that by marrying Lynn.

Lovecraft would probably have had a stroke worrying about someone like Lynn, the product of African-American bloodlines mixed with Native Americans and Okinawans. Fully human, in other words, but those sorts of facts escape racists—and why the hell was I thinking about Lovecraft anyway?

"Is Daddy taking us to school today?"

Rose had an odd habit of asking questions about either of us to the *other* parent when we were both in the room. A kind of verbal passive-aggressive martial art, I thought.

"Yup, so you've got to hurry up and get ready so he doesn't miss his train."

"Yay!"

"Why are you always so excited when I bring you to school?" Not that I'm above fishing for a compliment or anything, but I was genuinely curious.

"Because!" She hopped off the bed and thumped from the room.

"'Because'." I grinned at my wife.

She shrugged. "Can't fault that logic."

"No, I can't," I said and leaned in for a kiss before I hauled myself out of bed.

I'd agreed to take the kids to school twice a week to accommodate Lynn's teaching schedule and it hadn't taken long for the deal to morph into three times a week.

"They just like to be at school early."

"That's it? Why?"

She shrugged. "You know how Kelly likes to be at places before they get crowded. And Rose gets to play with some of her friends."

I acquiesced and got dressed. I loved that my girls were happy with their school.

Most days are a domino effect of sorts, one event cascading into the other. It made for a tight schedule and today was no different. Drop the kids off, head further into Providence for the commuter rail, walk to work, reverse. The perennial wrench was either the train schedule or the train itself. "Equipment failure," is what the conductors called it, or "switching problems." Delays. That evening, I got into Providence late. The sun was setting, casting a hazy, orange pall over everything.

"Can you spare any change to save the mills? Make a donation."

A little jolt ran through me as I recognized the woman with the sunhat. I never encountered any of the street folk in this part of the city. Probably because MBCR authorities ran them out, but here she stood.

I looked into her close-set eyes and said, "No, I can't help you, sorry." I always tried to treat the homeless with some honesty and maturity. Making eye contact, being polite. It tended to go a long way in these interactions, saving us both a little conflict.

"Can you spare anything else? What can you let go?"

That gave me pause. Then I remembered her odd sign and made the typical connection: she was probably mentally ill.

"I'm sorry, no, I can't help you."

"Can you help the anchors? Is it all safe?" She followed me.

I stopped walking and faced her. She was as unafraid as I hoped I looked. I wasn't sure what else to say, so I opted for brevity. "This is done. Okay? I'm leaving, you're staying."

"You'll stay. You'll see. You have to. We all do." She held her cardboard sign out to me.

I ignored it and moved along, getting into my car a little too quickly. My back, moist with sweat, felt gross against the seat, and I cranked up the air-conditioning.

When I got home, it was too late to even say goodnight to my girls. After dinner, Lynn and I watched a little television and went to bed. With the window unit roaring, we took advantage of the early night and each other, making love in relative comfort and privacy. A great end to a mediocre day.

Or so I thought.

After the usual hour or so of struggling to fall asleep, I was awoken by a light in the hallway. I heard one of the girls stumble into the bathroom and close the door. The minutes ticked by. It was after two in the morning. Several minutes passed. I rolled out of bed to check on my child. At this point, I was sure it was Rose; it wouldn't be the first time she dozed on the toilet in a half-asleep haze.

"What's up?" My wife mumbled.

"Rose has been in the bathroom a long time. I'm going to check on her."

"Okay." She rolled over.

I felt groggier than I would have expected after a few hours of sleep. Everything seemed muffled. I wanted to shut all the ACs off, but if I did, the bedrooms would be stifling within an hour.

First, I peered into their bedroom. Rose's bed was empty. That was no surprise. I pulled back the blanket Kelly tucked up for privacy, and her bunk was empty too. That was odd. She might be in the bathroom downstairs.

Upstairs, at the nearest bathroom, I tapped on the door and said, "Rosie? Sweetheart, are you okay?"

Then I opened the door. Our youngest hadn't developed the top-secret privacy needs Kelly had adopted over the last year. She was still young enough that she needed help or guidance in most matters. She sat slumped on the toilet with the light on, as expected. When I tapped her lightly on the shoulder and said her name again, she lolled to the side and caught herself as her weight shifted.

Rose looked me in the eye and said, "Daddy?"

Then she went rigid, her back bowing away from me. Her arms flew up and her eyes locked open wide enough that I could see red at the edges. Her teeth clenched and her lips parted, making her face a rictus of shock and agony that made my stomach feel as if it had fallen out. I stuttered and lunged for her, unsure what was happening or what to do. She felt hot and soft, like dough, and I could barely breathe.

My little girl's body flopped backward, rattling the tank, and her flesh smeared over the wall like molten wax and up to the pitched ceiling, defying gravity. Blood began pooling at the edges of her body and crawling over the walls and floor, flowing into the toilet. The blood was a too-familiar reminder of the terror I'd felt when cancer had consumed her kidney a few years before, flooding her bladder with blood clots.

Elongated, putty-like, her face stretched into a silent scream as she slipped through my fingers and—I couldn't contain myself anymore. I shouted for Lynn, screamed for her, raw and loud. I begged for my daughter's life, that she would be normal again, that she'd be safe.

I startled awake, thrusting myself out of bed, snapping the sheets off my wife. She jumped and rolled over to look at me. I was half in and out of the bed, crouched in a panic.

"What is it? What's wrong?" she asked, her voice bright with fear.

I ran from the room, slamming my toe on the corner of the bed. I barely felt it as I headed for the bathroom. It was dark, empty. My wife came out of the room, following.

"Hey! What's wrong? Answer me!"

My girls.

I plunged in and hit the light. Rose flinched, her eyes closed, deep in sleep. Her sister slept on the lower bunk. Lynn snapped the light off.

"What the hell are you doing?" My wife asked in a harsh whisper, clicking off the light.

I went and peeked behind the hanging blanket. Kelly slept soundly, both of them comforted by the white-noise hum of the air conditioner.

"Damn it!" My wife grabbed my elbow and pulled. "*Talk to me.*"

"I'm sorry...I'm sorry." I led her back to our bedroom and told her about the dream.

"Jesus," she whispered.

Lynn hugged me. She comforted me as long as she could stay awake, satisfied that it was just a nightmare, but I stared into the dark for hours, remembering the homeless woman at the parking garage, her words nagging at me. It left a tremble of fear that I couldn't ignore. Remembering, carping, humming in the background of my mind.

The next day was uneventful and hot. I was heading home when I saw the woman again. She held the same sign and pointed at me through the car's window. I rolled it down.

"Spare any change?"

"No," I answered immediately. Then, "Wait." I rummaged in the armrest tray. "Here." There were two quarters, a dime, and four pennies. "You remember me, don't you?"

"I remember you're not willing to do what's needed. The Colored Worsted is closed. Hunts might be next. Or Atlantic. Who the fuck knows?"

I felt a hot wash of anger. "What? Needed for what? Are those names?" I wasn't familiar with every neighborhood in Providence. Some of the names were informal. Maybe that's what she meant.

"To keep them safe."

"Who's 'them'?"

"You already know. Whos and whats." She spoke plainly, these immutable facts of the universe.

Cars started honking behind me, traffic needed to move.

"Bring some cardboard, next time."

"Next time?"

More honking.

Exasperated, I gave the car some gas. The woman watched me go—I could see her receding in the side mirror. Ahead, more panhandlers wandered the islands. I peered at each of them as I passed. Long faces and noses, close-set eyes, various colors of skin, age, and weight. Now that I was paying attention, their resemblance to the woman who'd rattled me was uncanny.

I couldn't get home fast enough, but I also couldn't put the homeless wanderers out of my mind. After a dinner of Mediterranean spiced chicken, and with the kids in bed, I told my wife what I'd observed. She laughed lightly at the bizarreness of it all.

I said, "Oh, *that's* a bridge too far?" When I licked my lips, I could tell that I'd used too much olive oil on the roasted chickpeas. "But your chakras, horoscopes, and crystals trump something that actually happened to me."

"Okay, fine." She rolled her eyes in a playful circle. "I can see that it's bothering you and I'm sure it's just a weird coincidence. It's a small city and those folks are always out there, they don't have anywhere else to go. We're safe."

"It's not…bothering…me." I crossed my arms and looked away.

Lynn put on her best skeptical face.

"Okay. Yes, it's bothering me. It's just…" I waved my hands, a little frustrated. "I don't know why."

"Honey." Lynn sidled up next to me and wrapped her arms around my waist. "We made it through cancer."

"And your sepsis," I said.

"And my sepsis," she agreed, "and bizarre strains of syphilis, and hernias, and creeping rashes, and—"

"I know, I know." I returned the hug, pushing our family's past medical horrors out of my mind. My actions belied my emotions; however, I couldn't shake the feeling of something I couldn't name. It clung to my brain like a creeping mold.

The next couple of nights were restless, hot affairs, and I didn't see the homeless woman, but I did see several other people who resembled her. They all had the look of being related despite the diversity of skin color and hair. The unease stayed with me, at the edges of my perception. At work too, it nagged.

She'd mentioned mills. New England was littered with mills. I clicked to open a web browser at work and brought up a map of Providence. The search for mills turned up apartments, restaurants, and historic sites. The locations were scattered around the edges of the city, near the waterways. Which made sense.

What didn't make sense was this woman's delusions. She called them anchors. One of the names was a weird one. I thought about it for a minute. The others were common words, but one—"Colored Worsted" popped into my head and I typed it in to search the map. It was an old mill, a historic site, and it was listed as temporarily closed. No other information was apparent. I scoffed and closed the browser, angry at myself for letting all of this strangeness fester inside me. Instead, I focused on layouts and edits in an attempt to ignore the steady vibration at the back of my skull.

It didn't work. Every night, I craved some kind of relief that was not forthcoming. Not in booze or sex or just plain fun and companionship with my family. I was getting clingy, worried that something was going to happen to my girls. The bizarre nightmare replayed in my memories when I least expected it.

A couple of days later, I was breaking down boxes in the garage for recycling when I paused. It felt stupid and confusing, but I tossed a bit of cardboard into the back of my car.

And I saw her the next night.

She pointed at my car, still holding her strange sign.

"I don't have any change today, sorry."

"Change. Change, change, change. We need change to stop change. Keep the anchors. You ready to help?"

"Help with what?"

"You got your cardboard?"

I narrowed my eyes at her. Where was this going, what was she driving at? And did it matter? I didn't *have* to do anything. Maybe she really needed help with something, maybe no one else was listening to her.

Car horns blared. I pulled forward and dialed down the AC before parking in an office lot. I grabbed the cardboard from the back of the car and jogged over to the woman. The sun was setting. It was that time of day when it got even hotter before cooling off in the slightest. Sweat trickled down the back of my neck even though I wore a loose, short-sleeve button-up with cotton pants. She wore a coat, knit hat, and sandals. Knotty, blond hair twisted down from the cap and she continued to hold her sign up with dirty fingers.

"Here." She handed me her sign. "No, hold it up, you've got to hold it up."

I humored her as she whittled my piece of cardboard down to a placard.

"Got a marker or somethin'?"

"I...no. Look, you keep saying 'help.' What is it you need help with? Medical...something else? I don't think standing out here with you is going to help."

She stood there, meeting my eyes. Her stare was unwavering; I detected not a hint of bullshit coming off of this woman. If she was deluded, it was complete, and her mind had taken her somewhere else. Her face still reminded me of someone—all of their faces did. The thin lips, almost a horizontal slash in the bottom of their faces.

It was an uncomfortable passing of seconds before she spoke again.

"It ain't for me," she chastised, "it's for *everyone*. Better if I show you. It's how I *learned* what needed to be done. Fix the anchors. Come on."

Without pause, she turned, scooped up her bags, and started off down the median. I followed. She crossed the street and marched up the hill, away from the highway entrances, then back down on the other side, through one of the many rundown industrial areas near the roads that transversed the state.

We'd gone far enough; I felt a sharp sense of an impending fear again, more acute than before. Just a straight unease. We were in a relatively open space, no one was behind me, and she was nonthreatening. Still, there was a chill inside me, a tremor of warning, and I couldn't pinpoint what was causing it.

It wasn't dark yet. I could see and hear everything. So, I stopped.

She went a few more steps before turning around. "It's right there. Just look in there."

She pointed at a manhole cover near the center of a wide throughway. It had been left ajar.

"Is someone down there?" I felt a small thrill of panic and heard the blood rushing through my head. I worried that someone might be hurt, that one of these people had been definitively discarded by society.

She issued a derisive blast of air. "No. Just look. See it for yourself. You'll know. You'll know."

"Okay, fine. Stand back."

"It ain't me you got to be nervous about. Gotta keep the mills in place, hold it all down." Her eyes twitched as she looked around.

A few other people wandered nearby. They were otherwise unassuming, but a closer inspection showed shoes with too many miles on them and clothes imprinted with the detritus of sidewalks. They carried their signs, looking as morose and stern as this woman.

I inched up to the manhole, trying to keep my eyes on everything. No one was close, the woman hadn't moved. She wanted me to see something down there and stood holding her sign a smart distance away. The sewer was dark, of course, but some light still bled onto the street from the setting sun.

With about half an arm's length between me and the underworld, I bent at the waist to peer in. I thought I saw something move as my eyes adjusted to the gloom underground. I could smell a disgusting wetness, like the stench of the ocean after it regurgitated rotting plants on the beach. Hot air boiled out of the hole in slow, rhythmic blasts. It felt smothering, as if something pressed against my face. What I saw had no form, no outline to latch on to. I fumbled for my phone to activate the LED flashlight and point it into the hole.

In a small circle of light, it writhed and slithered into itself, turning knots that undid themselves without reversing. Moist, it glistened, and gross mashing could be heard directly over the manhole. Somehow, the thing was both above and below me at once, stealing the air and gobbling sound.

My heart sank, replaced by a bright, hot fear. The threat was palpable, a wall of hate and disgust at humanity, loathing at the cellular level. I felt its malevolence stretched out in a miles-long pattern that met the edges of the city and ground against hot spots near the rivers. The mills, held by the mills, trapped and seething.

I pulled back from the hole, teeth grinding hard, and raised my hands to stop something that had no form, nothing to push back against. The geometry of it...

What I saw couldn't be life, not as we understood it. And so I tried to deny the evidence before me, tried to scrub the memory from my mind, the scent from my nostrils, the sound from my ears.

"It gets in your head, don't it? Can't look directly at it too long. Some people just know what's right under their feet, I can tell. You knew, you knew. We stay up here, all of us. We knew. We spread the word, *hold the words* that help, we *bind it* underground and keep the mills."

I looked at her, incredulous; I couldn't speak. She rummaged in her bags and said, "You can borrow my marker."

I scribbled 'PLEASE HELP, I HAVE A FAMILY' on the cardboard and held it against my chest. It felt secure, it was my shield against the creeping horror below. It would protect my family as long as I stood vigilant with the others, as long as I marched above.

And I would. To keep them safe, I would stand at the median. Forever.

– ERRICK NUNNALLY was born and raised in Boston, Massachusetts, and served one tour in the Marine Corps before deciding art school was a safer pursuit. He enjoys art, comics, and genre novels. A graphic designer by day, he has trained in Krav Maga and Muay Thai kickboxing. His work has appeared in several anthologies of speculative fiction. His work can be found in *Apex Magazine, Fiyah Magazine, Galaxy's Edge, Lamplight, Nightlight Podcast*, and the novels, *Lightning Wears a Red Cape, Blood for the Sun,* and *All the Dead Men*. His short novel *The Queen of Saturn and the Prince in Exile* is due out in 2025 with Clash Books. Visit erricknunnally.us to learn more about his work.

Cinched

Kristi Petersen Schoonover

There is a thing that roams the halls of my factory-turned-condos at night. Every stomp it takes jingles like a broken sleigh. When it reaches my metal door, it knocks in groups of four, with long, dreadful silences between each.

For hours, I am afraid to stir. Afraid to breathe.

But I know I cannot leave.

My condo is in the former American Buckle and Cartridge Company, and the place has been watching me my entire life.

I grew up in a three-family house within eyeshot of it. Founded in the 1880s, it made fortunes from belt buckles and ammunition until it closed in the mid-twentieth century. Then it marred Campbell Avenue, silent and dreary at Memorial Day parades, ominous and coal-black in the bright row of festooned stores at Christmastime. It was omnipresent, but unacknowledged—except for the occasional public notice of some proposal that would never come to fruition; the environmental clean-up was too expensive.

One of its brick and stucco wings, hugged by a cluster of decrepit metal drums, squatted beyond the chain link fence that hemmed our large garden. Its battleship gray wooded-over windows spied on my uncle and I harvesting vegetables twice the normal size. They were also uniquely colored: not indigo eggplants, but violet; not vermilion tomatoes, but scarlet; not leaf-green gooseberries, but emerald. We ate our produce at every meal, and it was in high demand in the extended family and neighborhood; nowhere else had vegetables as tasty. I thought, the way a kid does, that my uncle had Willy Wonka magic.

Now I know better.

As the seasons changed, the factory did, too. In spring, the smell of mud and Lysol tainted the breeze; in summer, moss tattooed walls that didn't get sun and weeds sprouted between its crumbling bricks; in winter, it seemed as forlorn as a shivering orphan.

In the fall, I'd sometimes see things. Once, I swore hot orange sparks shot through holes in the mortar. On one particularly snappish October afternoon, I was digging up the old crops and caught movement out of the corner of my eye.

Faces briefly hovered behind the wired glass of a chained door.

For a moment, I just stared, bewildered: reflections? Something inside like a sheet blowing in wind whistling through a fresh hole? I dug up an old root, then looked again.

Still there.

My uncle's back was turned. I crept to the fence; it was climb-worthy. I got halfway up when my uncle grabbed my shirt and wrestled me off.

"You stay here, on this side." He nodded in warning. "That ground over there's poison."

I apologized and promised. But I'd seen something in that window, and I was going to find out what, or who, it was.

When Mom died of an egg-sized brain tumor when I was eight, I suddenly had no one to ask girl things. No one to appear when I cried for help or to comfort me when I was scared. No one to step before me through this hallway called life and issue cautions about what hid in the dark. To forget my insides were on fire, I'd use a needle to start skin peels on the balls of my feet. I'd tear them off, wincing as they grabbed several layers and bled, relishing the smarting throb. There were days when I couldn't eat or drink because everything went down like lit matches. Days when the sight of a mother and daughter stabbed me through the heart. Days when *theholeinside* drove me to frantic pacing and hysterics, because it was so abyssal I couldn't possibly scale out of it.

I'd never get to know my mother intimately as a person, and there was no other person like her on earth. I didn't know if I was like her or not, who I was supposed to be, or if what happened to her would happen to me, because it was then I began to learn that the factory was more than our neighbor.

We were selling the house and packing to move three towns away. In an ignored under-stair closet, beneath boxes of newspapers pronouncing the assassination of JFK, the end of World War II and the Crash of '29, there was a trunk full of journals, photographs, and articles that told the whole story.

I was already aware Mom knew *theholeinside*, because before she died, she had her own: Gramma worked at the factory during World War II and died in a fire there when Mom was ten, and the factory shut down after that. What I didn't know was that Gramma had one too. My great grandmother, GiGi, worked at the factory during World War I and died on-site in an accident when Gramma was just twelve.

No one had ever spoken about what had happened to Gramma, let alone GiGi, but I wasn't the only one who had questions. Also in the trunk was Mom's diary; in it, she wrote about seeing faces in the window of the back door.

The memory of the faces was as fresh as the day it happened, but I never saw them again, and once we moved, I had no way to visit until I got my driver's license.

As an adult, I became obsessed with the place. I learned that it had produced shotgun shells when it first opened, then sold off that part of the business to focus on buckles for everything from belts to garters and hats. That the original owner had reestablished it after his other factory in Middletown had mysteriously burned to the ground.

That was about as far as I got. There were few records. Nothing about accidents, nothing about fires. No employee rosters, no plans of how the original factory had been laid out. I'd had great hopes for one librarian, who said she had some information, but when she pulled in to meet me, she merely stared with haunted eyes, claimed she'd been mistaken, and tore out of the Mister Donut parking lot onto Campbell Avenue without regard to traffic.

I took to sitting in my car in a vacant lot across the street from the old house most nights; it gave me a perfect sightline to that back door and the garden lot, which was barely recognizable under a chokehold of sumac and tall grass. I waited for the faces, but they never came.

I met my husband, Cain, and, for a while, *theholeinside* seemed to be easier to ascend, so I was distracted. Eventually, though, the factory beckoned, and as time wore on, he didn't understand why he wasn't enough.

"Pete told me he saw your car parked in the lot across the street from American Buckle again." He put a bite of lasagna in his mouth, wiped his chin with a napkin.

Cain was in real estate and heavily involved in the chamber of commerce. This wasn't the first time that Pete or Giovanni or Michael or whoever had spotted my car. It also wasn't the first time he'd brought it up at dinner.

"I don't understand your obsession with that place."

I pushed my pasta around. "I've told you this. It's…it's part of my family's history." If I'd told him about the faces in the window, he would've thought I was unhinged. "I feel—connected, I guess."

He swallowed his food. "Well, bad news. You're going to have to stop soon, because they finally got someone to spend money on cleaning it up." He twisted in his chair, reached into his folio on the marble counter, set a glossy brochure between us. "Luxury condos."

The cover was white with gold stamped lettering: *Silver Chape Residences*.

"You keep sittin' out there, they're gonna think you're a stalker." He cracked a nervous smile.

"That's ridiculous."

He forked a piece of lettuce. "Is it?"

I doubled down on my watch as the garden plot was cleared and building equipment trundled in. There was still no appearance of the faces, and then one day the chained door had been removed and bricked over.

Shortly after that, Cain asked for a divorce; he said I could stay in the house until I figured out what I wanted to do.

People have convinced themselves that alleviating despair is no more complicated than wiping out bronchitis—a doctor's visit and a magic pill. But there's no real panacea for chronic hopelessness; no salve for the first thought of the day being *I'm still in hell*. I had been left behind again.

There were still boxes of our paperwork I had to cull. One morning, the first box I pulled had the Silver Chape Residences presale kit he'd shown me in what seemed like someone else's life.

That's right. The factory. *Luxury condos*, Cain had said.

I opened the brochure. *Buckle up for your new lifestyle!* it read in script over an artist's rendering of the American Buckle and Cartridge Company, reborn: the bricks clean, new white-framed windows, a sparkling indoor pool, cozy café, and upscale convenience shop. On the inside of the back cover, it heralded the completion and opening date was still a year away, a note that one could *Purchase before build and customize to your taste!* and a business card.

I knew exactly what to do.

Sliver Chape Residences' official sales rep swanned through my front door, her paisa hat fashionably cocked to one side and her ivory poncho fluttering behind her. "Well, hello…Amalea, right? I'm Tori!" she cooed.

She reminded me of Mom's Avon Lady.

"Come on in." It hadn't occurred to me to be embarrassed by

the mess until just after I'd called her, so I'd done what I could in the kitchen: whisked away dirty dishes and mail, then hostessed with musty teabags, expired Girl Scout cookies, and yard-plucked dandelions in a rocks glass. It was presentable compared to the rest of the house.

"I was thrilled that you called. We're looking for residents who would be stewards of the building's storied past, so we're selective about prospective tenants. You said you grew up next door?"

"Yeah. I lived at eighty-nine Atwater until I was about ten. We sold it after my mother passed away."

"I'm sorry to hear that." She pulled out a chair and sat down, opened a folio not dissimilar to the ones Cain always used. "I mean, I'm sorry about your mother. I'm very happy that the old place is once again going to be part of the community. Would you like me to—"

"No need for a hard sell." I picked up a cookie and bit into it. It was so stale it snapped and crumbed, and I could barely taste the mint. "I'll take it."

She froze and considered me curiously. "So…um…"

"Is there paperwork?"

"There is, yes, and of course we'd have to check your credit—"

"I'm not worried."

"—and I think there's still time to customize."

An uncomfortable silence fell between us; she broke into a wide smile of surprised joy and held up her index finger. "You know what? I'll be right back."

I'd be lying to insist I wasn't stunned by the commitment I'd just made, but it was true: I had great credit, my home with Cain had too many painful memories, and the faces had never reappeared. Perhaps the only way to see them again was to be in there with them.

Tori returned with an enormous silver-cellophaned basket. "I decided to be bold and bring your official welcome basket since you seemed so confident." She hefted it onto the table, accidentally knocking over the dandelions; water made a beeline for the edge and peed on the floor, but she didn't seem to notice. "Go ahead, open it! There's a signing surprise and nothing wrong with before the ink is dry because it's just good vibes, you know!"

I untied the oversized navy ribbon and jockeyed down the silver wrap to reveal an elegant arrangement of bread, olive oil, mozzarella...and something else.

Enormous scarlet tomatoes, color completely even with no blotching, blossom scars tight. The envy of the extended family and in demand in the neighborhood, because nowhere else had vegetables as tasty.

"Aren't they so gorgeously unusual? This is from what's going to be your *very own patch* of garden, right behind—"

"I know."

She blinked.

I moved to the kitchen sink, grabbed a towel, sopped up the water from the spilled dandelions. "That garden...the whole thing used to be ours. I used to tend it myself, with my uncle."

She processed for a moment. "Well, when you let things go, if it comes back, it's yours, right?"

"Indeed."

Squeamish regret stung me. What I hadn't known growing up was that the earth that had provided us with such beautiful eggplant and tomatoes and gooseberries sat abreast of where the factory's waste had been dumped. It was a different time, a world shrouded in ignorance and fraught with immediacy to solve current problems because lives were short. No one, back then, thought of things like long-term environmental impact, that toxins could cause cancers—and that those toxins could seep into the ground and had no respect for fences.

In the end, the factory had gotten my mother, and there was every possibility it was going to get me, too.

Now I own unit 4D. It was a bit of a budgetary and divorce-related nightmare, but, at last, I no longer have to stare at this place from my car across the street, and there is something about knowing *home*. Sitting in this space and haunted by what might've happened in it all those years ago, I can't imagine how I ever lived anywhere else. This is where I belong.

My unit is tucked at the back, in the very wing that had once called to a younger me. My great room windows face trees that have grown up beside the chain link fence that borders my old house.

I think of GiGi and Gramma. Standing, perhaps, where I am now. Shirtwaist sleeves rolled and pinch-tucked to thwart dangerous flirting with voracious metal beasts, primitive versions of rotary barrel tumblers and strapping machines with all manner of hungry orifices. Sparks branding bare wrists and hands with petal-shaped burns. Sweat trickling into burning eyes. Bronze or brass or stainless-steel buckles raining to the floor in volcanic cacophony, clubbing toes crammed into inappropriate shoes. The smell of something like exhaust and turpentine, burnt oil and aging wood, air thick as miasma.

Did they peer out these windows, wishing they could touch the gold dappling of the leaves, kick at the first snow of winter, deeply inhale the first hint of spring's petrichor and forsythia on the air? Mill hours were long and grueling; twelve hours a day, seven days a week—at least until the forty-hour workweek was mandated in 1940. That didn't make the work less jeopardous. How much would that one precious second of distraction risk?

For a moment, I can feel it, and I wonder if the past can be carried in our DNA.

Yet standing here is akin to standing before the door to heaven: every answer I've ever wanted, I'm certain, is here. In these bricks, in these boards, in these halls. The present and the past move in sync. It is contemporary polished silver and bamboo and marble, but some of the floorboards are grooved with the imprints of what they originally supported—like the feet of a large machine—or stained with grease and chemicals. Near my ultra-modern metal front door, there are three curious marks that look as though someone branded the boards with a Y-shaped iron.

There is a smell beneath everything, something old, like sawdust and charcoal. I tell myself that some smells can never truly be removed, because everything is energy, and it never disappears; it simply changes form. Still, it's unsettling, because it makes me wonder what lingers. My family's house had its share of harmless-looking decay that was actually rot underneath—like the tiny stains in the ceiling that betrayed the larger structural problem of leaking pipes and an aged roof.

Another smell drifts into the room—lilies. Not lilies like in the bouquets Cain used to bring me in lieu of *I'm sorry*, but powdery lilies. Like Avon's Lily of the Valley eau de toilette.

Like Mom. That was what she wore.

Comforted, I turn out the lights. But once the television and lamps are off, the dark is thick as ink and echoes with unfamiliar sounds.

The first time I hear the bells, I think it must be another condo resident hanging a Christmas decoration on his door.

Then I remember it's July.

It's distant at first. Like sleigh bells, but much slower. Almost like something heavy is walking with shackles on its ankles. As it gets closer, I feel it in the bed frame, which vibrates with each step.

I grope for the bedside lamp's switch, turn it on.

It immediately fritzes out.

The noise stops.

I hear only my own breath, loud in my ears.

Bang.

I scream.

Bang. Bang. Bang.

Whatever that thing is, it's at my door. The strike of the hollow metal reverberates in my chest. I shriek into my quilt.

I hear a familiar voice, a hushed whisper in my ear. "Leabug."

Only one person called me that. Terror, excitement, and shock battle inside me.

"Mom?"

The thing bangs on the door.

Terror wins. "*Mom!*"

Three purple translucent figures shimmer in the midnight. And two of them are wearing the faces I've been seeking for nearly two decades, only now they're clear, and I recognize them from the photographs in the trunk: it's Gramma. And GiGi.

I gasp.

The third one is…I ride a tide of joy. I can barely speak. "Mom."

She smiles and glides over to alight next to me. She touches my cheek. "You're all grown up."

I just keep thinking *God, I've missed you* and suddenly realize that my eyes have been physically hurting for years from *not* seeing her, because now they don't. "I have so much to tell you, Mom. So much. All the things you missed. And I need answers! All the questions I have—"

She looks sad. "Gramma…"

…the plum-colored wisp with the round face and kind eyes nods…

"…and GiGi…"

…the orchid-colored revenant holds up a thin hand in silent greeting…

"…and I, we…we can't answer anything, honey."

I frown. "Why not?"

The thing bangs on the door. Fear biles up my throat. "What *is* that?"

"Our keeper." Mom pulls aside her lavallière to reveal the tender flesh of her neck. There is a Y-shaped scorch mark there; it mirrors the three carved into the wood at the threshold of my door.

I gasp and touch it. It feels puffy, like a scab.

"We can't tell you until you're one of us." A tear trickles down Mom's cheek. "You need to give yourself to him. Which means you'll never leave."

What is out there for me? The *holeinside*. Eternal wondering. Despair.

I pat Mom's leg and muster every ounce of courage I have. I rise and go to the door.

Bang.

Bang.

I slip off the chain.

Bang.

I wrest the door open.

The thing towers above me. It is a human-shaped molten constellation of belt buckles. Flaming orange, glowing white hot. Its steaming gaze bores through me, and it breathes a low, sinister growl, and I know instantly it is not a ghost. It is something else. Something evil. Something that has come from man's greed, man's waste. Something that wants me, just like it wanted the women who came before me.

I'm shaking. I want nothing more than to run, but my body won't move. I glance back at GiGi and Gramma and Mom.

They smile like a trio of Mona Lisas.

I face the thing. Its smoky breath clouds my face. It smells of charcoal and burnt fuse box, and I choke as the thickness forces its way into my throat. The thing extends something that looks like a finger, but I recognize it as the prong of a belt buckle. It pokes against my forehead, and it's like the press of an electric coil, and all goes dark.

When I wake in Mom's lap, she says that I am with them, now. She helps me sit up.

Outside, summer has gone, and it is winter; the trees are coated with ice, and gray light casts the room in a salty hue. The condo is furnished differently: no more contemporary polished silver and bamboo and marble; there are gold fixtures and rustic dark wood and tile. The ultra-modern metal door is now painted goldenrod, and at its threshold, the three Y-shaped marks have befriended a fourth.

It's been said it's not wise to seek, because something might actually be found. I know all the answers now: about Gramma, and GiGi, who my mother is, and who I am.

The line may have ended with me, but we still look out the windows at the garden. There are many women who harvest their violet eggplant and scarlet tomatoes and leaf-green gooseberries, and one, in particular, with a young daughter, whom I'm sure has seen us at least once.

– KRISTI PETERSEN SCHOONOVER's grandmother lived within eyeshot of the abandoned American Buckle & Cartridge Company on Campbell Avenue in West Haven, Connecticut, and spent plenty of afternoons eating gooseberries in her uncle's garden while its boarded-up windows watched. Her short stories have appeared in almost one hundred and fifty publications. She holds an MFA from Goddard College and is founding editor of the dark literary journal *34 Orchard*. She adores ghost stories and dinosaurs and lives in the Connecticut woods with her husband, Nathan, where she still sleeps with the lights on. Follow her adventures at www. kristipetersenschoonover.com.

We Created a God Monster

Gage Greenwood & Kylee Jones

Justin read the texts again:

James is awake

WE R FUCKED NOW

Justin sat in his car and as always after a band practice, he struggled to quell his adrenaline, but the texts mixed with his punk-rock high and had pushed his heart rate to match the beat of the windshield wipers.

Clunk. Clunk. Clunk.

Fat raindrops slapped against the Volvo.

The rest of the band had already packed up and headed home but the lights were still on in Gains, the local gym. Gains was the only business in the mill, outside of the tiny square basement rooms rented out to local bands for practicing.

Justin didn't see anyone inside the gym, but when the lights dimmed, the parking lot turned tar black.

He looped the car around, heading onto Park Ave.

"Shit, my notebook!" He spun the wheel and drove up to the side entrance. Graffiti covered large swathes of this side of the building, most of it the product of the same bands who rented spaces within.

His key slid into the lock, and the metal door creaked open.

When he clicked the inside switch, it turned one section of lights on at a time, until the whole hallway lit up—*dunk, dunk, dunk*—as each area emerged from the darkness. He walked the hallway toward his band's practice space, noting the crudely made signs of band names on each door. *Chuckle. Rhode SkaLand. Against the Grain. We're Wolves. Kevin Bacon and the Colorful Blobs of Everything. Bunker Dongs.*

He reached his space, where Angie had posted a sign for their band: *We Created a God Monster.*

The lock was loose and needed some finagling to make the latch unhook. When he finally wiggled the door open, a chilly breeze slapped his face.

That strike of air brought him back to the night James fell into a coma. Was pushed, rather. His head had hit the hard winter earth. An oak root snaked out of the ground under James' temple. Justin remembered the frosty breeze on his cheeks as he stared down. A warm hand curled around his own.

Escaping the memory, he found his way to the couch, picked up his palm-sized notebook off the arm, and pocketed it.

On the way down the hall, he reread the texts. Maybe if he stared at them long enough, the letters would wriggle off the screen and rearrange themselves into new words, something less concerning.

Justin glanced up to the door.

"What?" he said aloud.

The security bar was missing. It was as if the bar had never existed. There wasn't even a key lock.

He pushed on the door where he knew the bar had been. No give. The red light of the EXIT sign overhead flickered as Justin pushed again, but no luck.

"What the fuck?" He pushed harder, then banged his fists on the door, his hands scraping against the flaky metal. Justin turned back toward the hall. There had to be another exit.

Buzz. Another missed message:

Hello???? WE R FUCKED DUDE

Justin swiped the message away, and continued down the hall, past the practice rooms. The hall forked at the end, but he'd never needed to go that far and always assumed it was just unused practice rooms.

Choosing left at the fork, he turned the corner. This passage was shorter than the main hall, with a lone, thick wooden door at the end. Probably not an exit but worth a try.

He pulled the handle. Locked.

Justin noted the lack of a keyhole in the knob. In the quiet, the raindrops pinged off the building, but Justin heard something else behind the door. He leaned in, hoping to hear a person. Maybe this door led to the gym. With his ear flush to the wood, he heard muffled noises.

He nearly knocked, asked for help, but something about those noises emanating from the other side of the door haunted him. It was animalistic, like an unfed dog finding a live catch.

He turned back the way he came and was met with a concrete wall.

Justin stared, heart pummeling his rib cage. Sweat beaded on his neck. They'd been practicing here for months with no issue, minus thieves and dirty bathrooms. The sound continued behind him, and he tried to ignore it, more pressing issues at hand. There was maybe six feet of space between the locked door and the impossibly erected wall in front of him.

DUNK.

The overhead lights cut out. Justin swiped at the flashlight app on his phone. Shining it around the small space, he searched for a light switch and found none. His shoes squelched on a substance pooling from underneath the locked door. Leaning down, he was met with a coppery scent. Shining the paltry light at his feet, he knew it was blood.

He froze, afraid to make a sound. He suddenly became aware of his own breathing, the loud huff it made when air passed his lips, the whistle that came from his nose. When he shifted, even a centimeter, his pants made a swoosh.

He stepped slowly away from the door as far as he could. The crimson pool reminded him of that night with James.

Another text appeared on his phone. He jerked when it vibrated in his hand. Another sound to give him away.

They'll know. We need to figure something out.

He turned the flashlight off. The chewing had stopped and there was a slow shuffling sound behind the door. The blood puddle hadn't grown any further, but Justin's Vans were drenched, dark red staining the white canvas.

He turned his phone to focus mode, hoping to avoid any further noises. He wondered if the dim light of his phone screen could spill through the cracks, so he clicked it off and stood in a small square space of galaxy black.

More shuffling on the other side of the door.

How does a wall appear out of nowhere?

Something scraped against the wood, streaming from top to bottom. He sensed whoever lingered there knew Justin stood on the opposite side, but he needed to find a way out, undetected by whoever sent a pool of blood his way.

Maybe some kind of drug deal gone bad had occurred, or maybe a serial killer had found the benefits of a weird ass mill used only by kids in bands. Eventually someone would gut this place, renovate, and turn the entire building into high-end apartments. Justin imagined if that happened the band would cease practicing, move on with their lives. They wouldn't need much of a push.

Bang!

It sounded like a fist slammed against the wood. Justin, already back against the wall, pushed back further, shoulders pressing into the uneven cement, legs straightening. He squeezed back until he was flush with the wall.

He felt like he couldn't breathe, like this new enclosure vacuumed all the air out. In the thick black room, Justin couldn't make out anything, but he *felt* the walls spin around him, the floor wobble under his weak feet.

Bang.

He closed his eyes, a panic attack pressing heavy on his ribs.

Bang.

And the wooden door swung open, spilling light into Justin's makeshift cage. The thing was naked, with brick-red skin, as if it had coated itself in blood. It had no hair, not on top of its head or anywhere on its body. It was humanoid, but the shape, the way its limbs pulsed like critters crawled beneath the surfaces of its flesh showed Justin it was something other.

The creature stood at the doorway, facing away, with its hands by its chest. It mumbled something, but Justin couldn't make it out.

Justin wanted to take a photo, to have some kind of proof of tonight's insanity, but his fingers trembled too much for him to type in his password. His teeth chattered, and his body quaked.

He hadn't been this terrified since James.

Not since James.

The thing turned toward him. Justin winced. Its face was thin. Its eyes, demonic. The sclera inflamed with large black pupils in sunken eye sockets. Its nose was missing, a mass of scarred flesh around brittle bones. Its mouth was gaping open, almost as though it felt just as surprised about an unexpected visitor as Justin did. It had no lips but many small, triangular teeth. Blood coated its teeth and trickled from the edges of its mouth, dripping down its naked front. The thing had dagger-sharp nails on each gore-stained hand. It stared in his direction, as if staring through him and past the stupid wall.

Justin wasn't convinced it could see him. Maybe this whole thing was brought on by the stress of James. *James is awake.* The text repeated over and over in his brain.

The thing moved toward him. Nowhere to go, Justin stood helpless. He realized he couldn't hear the rain anymore. He couldn't hear anything anymore, except *James is awake*, ping-ponging across the corners of his mind. The creature walked with a strange gait, half-dragging its right leg, the skin pulsing like something underneath was trying to break free.

It reached out a clawed hand to Justin, touching his face, a sticky smear of blood coating his cheek. The creature was surprisingly gentle but somehow that felt more violent.

He wanted to scream, but before he could, the thing let out a loud, shrill shriek. Thick saliva, blood spraying from its mouth, dark flecks staining his favorite Verse shirt. Justin's phone fell from his shaky hand; he had forgotten he was still holding it. The screen lit up upon impact with the cement floor, spiderwebs snaking through the glass.

The thing still hadn't really met Justin's eyes. Justin tried to peer into the room behind, hoping to glimpse the red glow of an EXIT sign in the distance. Dark liquid coated the floor, littered with viscera of unknown origin.

James is awake.

James was awake, and did it really matter? Had it ever mattered?

James had circled Justin's group of friends for years, a friend of a friend, a cousin to another, and a short-lived boyfriend to Angie. James, with those blank eyes, emotionless as he scanned a room, unblinking. When he stopped and focused on someone long enough, it became obvious he wasn't seeing another person, but a target. Someone to unleash on; someone to hurt. James wounded. It's what he did by nature. Justin didn't even think it was malicious, just the natural function of James' existence. A tidal wave didn't topple a city because it was evil. Yet, still, if a person could stop a tidal wave, they were obligated to do so, right?

And if nature could be controlled, no one would have to live in terror ever again. Or so Justin had thought.

Nothing mattered anymore.

Locks disappear. Walls bred from the ether. Beasts lived behind doors. And James, dead or alive, asleep or awake, wiggled his fingers and made his marionette's limbs rattle.

The monster tilted its head, now examining Justin closely. And then it spoke.

He couldn't make out the words, because the thing spoke during inhales, like someone begging for help while choking. It gasped.

"GIVE."

Gasp.

"ME."

"What?" He understood the creature but didn't know what it meant.

The monster put its hand out. Its fingers trembled. No. Pulsed.

Justin cried. It all made sense now. He reached into his pocket and retrieved the item he'd come back into this mill for in the first place. What would the monster do with it? Kill him or save him? He didn't know. But as he thought before, it didn't matter.

No more fear.

His hand landed on top of the creature's, their skin touching. Justin unfurled his fingers. Time to let go. He closed his eyes, so terrified to lose it all. Time to let go.

As he pressed the notebook into the creature's hand, the pulsing in its fingers intensified. Goodbye to the songs he'd written after the incident with James. Justin had never planned on sharing these; it was just a catharsis of guilt and fear. It would all come out now— monster or not, he was as good as dead.

The monster wrapped its bloody claws around the notebook, pulling it away from Justin.

It melted, absorbing into the thing's hand, disappearing into its body as if it was never there at all.

The creature pressed its hands against Justin's ears. Justin screamed. He could hear music. The lyrics from the notebook playing in his head as fully formed songs performed by his own shitty band, a soundtrack of his wrongdoing and guilty conscience. The rage. The fear. The blood. Checking for a pulse. Leaving the scene. Relief. Coma. Paranoia.

James is awake.

Through the searing pain in his brain, Justin noticed through blurry vision that *his* skin had started pulsing, the movements in time with the beat of the music in his ears.

All the pressure, the physical pressing of fingers on the side of his head, the emotional tightening in his chest, and the lyrical screams in his brain, pressed tighter and tighter until Justin felt himself explode. His body turned to ash, blackening the world. He felt that sensation before, the explosion from within, the loss of vision, the ending of it all. He'd lived it with James. Boom, one Justin died and another...

Just like that, the creature disappeared. Justin slid backward, the wall behind him no longer there.

Dunk, dunk, dunk. All the lights clicked back on.

On shaky legs, he stood up and turned. Seeing the newly opened hallway freed the oxygen stuck in his lungs. If it weren't for the caked blood and the slithering movements under his flesh, he'd have wondered if the whole thing were a dream.

His feet left crimson prints as he slowly walked back toward the band spaces. Red strikes spread across his flesh as he dug into the itch. The pulsing was deep within him now. Whatever it was had burrowed into his bloodstream.

When he reached the door, the security bar was where it always had been. He pressed it, and the door flung open, revealing a crisp autumn morning. He winced at the sunlight.

His phone vibrated. With a shaky hand, he checked the message. Words appeared under the spiderwebs.

We should meet up and figure this out.

The text came from Angie. While everyone knew Justin had something to do with what happened to James, and the rumors had grown wilder and wilder, only Angie knew the real story. Because she'd been there. Because she'd helped.

He hopped in his car and turned it on. Music came from the stereo as the Bluetooth connected to his phone. He immediately turned it off. A song already played in his head. The volume had softened, but the melody lived with him, and the lyrics swam through his veins.

As he pulled away from the building, he noticed a tag on the mill's brick wall. The crudely spraypainted words matched the lines playing in his head as the song reached its crescendo. *I am the God of my own hate. I create. I create. I create.*

He wondered if Angie would feel the song inside her too.

Over time. One monster creates another.

Isn't that always the way?

– GAGE GREENWOOD is the best-selling author of the *Winter's Myths* saga and *Bunker Dogs*. He's been an actor, comedian, podcaster, and even the vice president of an escape room company. Since childhood, he's been a big fan of comic books, horror movies, and depressing music that fills him with existential dread. He lives in New England with his girlfriend and son, and he spends his time writing, hiking, and decorating for various holidays. For details, see gagegreenwood.com

– KYLEE JONES is an avid horror writer and reader, and she also enjoys music, running, and hanging out with her dogs. She is currently pursuing her MLIS at the University of Oklahoma. This is her first published horror story.

Kiss of Death

Ricardo D. Rebelo

Unwanted and ancient, the Temperance Mill stood along the Blackstone River, resembling a rotting tooth. In its day, it was the very model of Victorian-era manufacturing, but now it just looked hollow.

Mills like Temperance made the textiles that clothed Americans for decades at an enormous human cost. Children were used as cheap labor and worked to death, many never living past their twenties. If they survived the crush and rip of the machines, the cotton fibers they inhaled eventually caused their lungs to seize.

When child labor could no longer be used, manufacturers sought greater profit and less restriction overseas, leaving the giants on the coast of the Blackstone empty. For a time, the Temperance was lauded for the jobs and wealth it produced, but it had a darker history, and those who had worked in it remembered.

Misfortune is how Mack and Wanda Hughes came about renting storage space within it. After losing their jobs during the COVID pandemic, the Hughes' turned to reselling household items from people who had died, abandoned their homes, or were evicted from properties. It wasn't glamorous, but it was steady and kept the banks from taking the car.

It was a gray day when Mack and Wanda pulled up to the loading dock of the Temperance. Decay had settled into the building. The red bricks were pockmarked by age and abuse. Most of the walls on the first level were covered in graffiti. Murals revealed who had been there, who they had loved, and a dictionary of profanity. Weeds and vines wrapped themselves around any pole, pipe, or wire and hung on like jilted lovers trying to take the building back to nature. The stench of wet trash fermenting in the sun was created by mingling all the world's refuse.

As Wanda took in all the urban art, she came upon a mural of a woman in anguish. A cord was wrapped around her mouth, gagging her. Painted above the subject's face: Ties That Bind.

"That is some disturbing shit," Wanda said.

Mack sighed and said, "It doesn't matter what it looks like. It's just a place to store stuff. You gonna be OK bringing this stuff in without me?"

"Yeah," Wanda said, shifting a box in her arms, "just help me throw it on the pallets, then you can head out."

This wasn't the life she and Mack had hoped for, but they were making the most of it.

"Hey!" came a voice from behind them and Wanda turned.

A boy on the cusp of adolescence rode a cheap Wal-Mart bike to a stop.

"Hey!" replied Mack.

"What you all doing here?" the boy asked, skidding his feet along the ground.

"We are loading stuff up in our storage unit." Wanda placed her box on the pallet.

"You mean that junk?" He pointed at the items unpacked on the pallets. Lamps, old VCRs, assorted threadbare clothing, and mountains of ephemera.

"You gonna run a flea market out of there?" the boy said.

"Kind of," said Mack. "We get this stuff out of people's houses and resell it on the internet."

The boy's eyes widened. "You steal this shit?"

Wanda laughed and shook her head. "No, when people lose their houses or apartments, sometimes they leave things behind. The owner or landlord asks us to come clean the place up and we get to keep and sell anything we find."

"That sounds sad as hell," the boy said.

Mack and Wanda laughed. "I suppose so," Mack said.

The boy looked toward the mill. "My mom told me never to go in that place."

"Why did she say that?" Wanda paused, holding a box of antique lamps.

"Said, when it was a mill, a lot of kids died there." The boy leaned forward on the bike's handlebars. "Kids my age, some younger, some grown people. My mémère said it was cursed and the kids who died there are still around. She called them fantôme—that's French for ghost."

The boy's story fired a chill through Wanda, and she shivered. Mack's hand lighted on her shoulder.

He spoke to the boy. "That was a long, long time ago. There is nothing here anymore."

The boy shrugged. "Okay, mister. Whatever, I'm just telling you what I heard."

Mack's hand tightened on Wanda's shoulder. He replied, "Well, thanks for the info, little man. Hey, you got a PlayStation?"

The boy's face lit up. "Yeah, I do, but it is a PS3. I can't afford a 4 or a 5 yet."

Mack smiled. "Well, we've got a box of PS3 games over there and you can have it."

The boy's eyes lit up. He examined the box and filled the milk crate on the back of his bike with as many games as it could take. Mounting his bike, he said, "Thanks, people! And if you wanna know more spooky shit about that place, I'll be around!"

When he was out of earshot, Wanda turned to Mack and said, "What do you think of that?"

Mack shook his head. "It was a long time ago. If every person who died in a mill haunted it, we would be shoulder to shoulder with ghosts in this town. Let's finish up. I gotta go to South County today."

With a crash, the freight elevator descended. Wanda Hughes could never grow accustomed to it or the disdain she felt the elevator harbored toward her. Everything at the Temperance Mill gave her chills. The rust and rot of the old gears gave a shrill cry of pain as the elevator traveled up toward the sixth floor.

"Don't yell at me, you old bitch," Wanda said, as the machinery continued to grind. "I'm just doing my job."

Lifting the gate, Wanda looked into the massive void on the sixth floor. With the lights off, it was cavernous. She felt her way along the wall to where the circuit breakers stood and threw the switches one by one, illuminating the room.

Wanda dragged the wheeled pallet jack from the elevator to the storage area. After about twenty feet, the pallet stopped abruptly. Wanda figured something was stuck in the wheels—maybe a chunk of debris made its way into the works. Stooping, she saw something, so Wanda reached in to grab it and pulled it with a tug. In her hand, she held a piece of wood in the shape of a small canoe. The center was bored out and inside the cavity was a ball of yarn. She wondered if it was a piece of textile equipment used in the mill a hundred years ago, but what was it doing here now?

An intrepid reseller, she immediately considered whether it might be valuable. Some Bostonians would probably pay a handsome sum for an old Yankee artifact like this. The buyers would probably put it on their fireplace mantel and bore the shit out of party guests with stories about it. Wanda stuffed it in her pocket and repeated the trip up and down the elevator two more times. After stowing her last pallet, she took a break.

Sitting beside a wall-mounted fire extinguisher on an old futon that they had scavenged from a previous trip, Wanda inspected the piece of wood. She pulled out her cell phone and the Google search bar. But what to search for? She tried *mill wood canoe shape*, and all that came back were pictures of gorgeous wooden canoes. The next search was for *mill spindle thing*, which offered a few hundred pictures of metal lathes. Perhaps adding the word *antique to mill spindle thing* would do the trick? It took a few seconds for the pictures to load, but this search called it a bobbin.

Wanda was disappointed to find out that the bobbin was only worth $59.95 for a buy-it-now price. Other listings on the page had it for as low as fifteen dollars. This meant that her new antique wouldn't provide a retirement nest egg.

Wanda clicked back to the original search and looked further down at the results. One was titled 'The Kiss of Death' from a website called *Historic Ipswich*. At the top of the page was a picture of a woman holding the bobbin up to her lips. The wooden canoe was from a spinning loom used to make thread in the mills.

Below the picture was a link, 'The Kiss of Death Story by Horatio Rogers, M.D.' Rogers recounted how the spindles like these spread tuberculosis and killed many mill workers. This could be why her find was not worth a fortune. The chances of it still carrying the life-ending virus were minimal, but who wants a cursed stick on their mantel?

Wanda thought of the boy. The story added credibility to what he told them earlier.

She gazed at the bobbin and became drawn to the hole that was used to thread the line. Could the disease still be there? All of those women who sucked the line through this hole to get the machines working were ignorant of what the bobbin held. Wanda brought the bobbin closer to her mouth but stopped just short of her lips.

Just then, the line shot out and hit Wanda's mouth. It stung like a hornet. She pulled the bobbin away and felt the line tearing her lip. Now something tightened around her wrist. She raised the hand holding the bobbin and saw the thread inside, emerging and slithering around her skin and cinching itself down.

She screamed. The echoes of her terror bounced around the walls of the mill. Coarse thread wound its way up her arm. It had grown thicker and longer as it slipped from the bobbin like a snake made of hemp. The fibers chafed her skin, and the pressure increased, until it was on the verge of breaking her forearm.

Wanda reached for a box cutter. She extended the blade a good two inches and jabbed it into the rope at her wrist, cutting the threads in two and crying out in pain as the blade scored her flesh. She pulled at the thread and struggled as it fought to stay attached to her. Thick as a rope now, it was trying to burrow into her arm and sent out threads like needles trying to get under her skin.

When she had a good grip on the bobbin, Wanda threw it across the room. She grabbed her arm as the pain increased and blood flowed into her sleeve. Wanda pulled her sleeve tight around her wound. The cut was not deep but needed medical attention. She wrapped her arm with duct tape, and it looked like a half-assed silver superhero bracelet, but it would do for now.

Wanda's attention returned to where she threw the bobbin.

"Where the fuck are you?"

She glanced around the giant space to no avail.

A crash shot through her like a bullet. The elevator. That old miserable bitch had come screeching back to life. Her heart was pounding, causing the wound in her arm to throb. She turned to pull the fire extinguisher from the wall, a decent defense from whatever was coming next.

The elevator strained its way up to the sixth floor, then locked into place. Wanda grabbed the hose of the fire extinguisher and aimed the cone at the large gate, waiting to pull the trigger. The gate began to open. Without hesitation, she let out a stream of ice-cold foam chemicals into its belly.

"What the hell!" It was Mack.

Wanda ceased the stream of spray as a foam-covered figure emerged.

"Mack?" Wanda asked in fear of the response.

"Damn woman!"

"I'm so sorry," she said. "I thought you were...?"

Mack coughed but cut her off. "What? A fire?"

Mack paused, then reached for Wanda's bloodied sleeve. "What happened?"

Wanda dropped to her knees as Mack reached for her. "We need to get you to the hospital."

Overwhelmed, Wanda couldn't find the words as Mack enveloped her in his arms and led her to the elevator. She listened as it creaked its way back down to the loading dock.

At the hospital, the doctor gave Wanda a mild sedative to deal with the shock and Mack held her hand as she dove into a deep sleep.

Dr. Gupta came in and asked, "Can I talk to you in the hallway, Mr. Hughes?"

Mack nodded without turning his head. He leaned over her and put a kiss on Wanda's forehead before walking out with the doctor.

"Mr. Hughes, has your wife shown any signs of suicidal thoughts?"

"No, absolutely not!" cried Mack as a tear rolled down his cheek.

"Then how do you explain those wounds?" Dr. Gupta touched his own forearm.

Mack raised his head, looking like a man trying to worry a hole through the ceiling. "I don't know. I've got nothing."

"We are going to keep her overnight and do a psych evaluation tomorrow." Dr. Gupta touched his shoulder. "Perhaps you can go home and collect some things to make her more comfortable."

Mack wiped away a tear as he drove away from the hospital, wondering why Wanda would do this. What the hell happened in the mill? He went back to Temperance to see if he could figure out what happened. It needed to make some sort of sense, and he could not rest until it did.

Standing outside the mill, the giant mural of the tortured woman stopped him. Staring at the mural, Mack swore he saw movement— the ropes across the woman's mouth tightened.

He knew he needed to go in. He needed answers.

Mack headed back up the rattling, noisy elevator to the sixth floor. Every rattle and squeak beat a tattoo in his mind. With one last clunk, he reached the sixth floor.

Wanda woke in the hospital room, completely disoriented. Pain shot through her arm and she saw it was heavily bandaged.

"Ahh, you're awake," said Dr. Gupta.

She focused on the doctor standing in the doorway but had a hard time processing his words.

"I am Dr. Gupta, and I have been treating you today."

Wanda touched her bandages hoping they could jog her memory. "Treating me for what?"

Dr. Gupta crossed his arms. "It looks like you tried to cut yourself. Can you explain why?"

Wanda pushed the question aside. "Mack, my husband?"

"He was here," Dr. Gupta responded. "He left to get you some personal items for you to stay overnight."

A chill passed over Wanda like a breeze in February. "Where did he go?"

The space was in complete darkness and Mack opened the gate to an abyss. He was sure they didn't leave it this way.

Mack felt his way to the circuit breakers, tracing his hands over the grime of the stone walls. They were cold, dimpled and dirty. When he reached the steel box, he threw the large switches, breaking the silence in the room like thunderclaps.

But the room did not light.

Not right away, at least.

Mack turned to see into the space.

First, a flicker of light illuminated everything—all the junk they had accumulated. Then the space fell into darkness. Again, the lights flickered, and the entire room was empty before darkness enveloped the space.

Upon the third flicker, the overhead fluorescent work lights stayed on and a small girl stood alone in the cavernous space. She didn't look over twelve. She wore tattered clothes, so threadbare that the fabric streamed from her to the ground, the shade of burlap. Her face appeared to be made of the same cloth, her eyes mere indentations below her forehead.

Adrenaline pumped to Mack's heart and muscles. The speed of it hit him so fast that it left him dizzy.

"Little girl, what are you doing here?" Mack asked. In the light, the little girl's appearance became more distinct. It was familiar, but something was off. Her dress and skin all shared a similar texture.

"Little girl?" Mack's voice wobbled, pleading for an answer.

The cloth on the child's face tore open to reveal two eyes, ebon as the night. She raised her hands and said one word, softly as falling snow, "Eternal."

At that, ropes shot from her palms toward Mack.

He spun and raced for the elevator.

In a blink, a thick rope wrapped itself around Mack's neck. He tried to scream, but the tension yanked so tightly it choked any sound coming from within him.

Another line shot out and wrapped around his leg. With a tug, it took Mack to the floor. Flailing, Mack reached for the one thing he could grab: the handle of the pallet jack. A third line shot out and grabbed his other leg. A fourth took his right arm, then his left, which held a grip on the pallet jack so tight that the skin sloughed away from his hands.

Pain shot down from his fingertips to the nails on his toes. Mack let go.

Wanda was in an Uber in the pouring rain. She had told Dr. Gupta everything he wanted to hear and, satisfied, he went home for the night.

It was late, and the hospital was down to minimal staff. She dressed and headed out.

In the Uber, it all came back to Wanda: the bobbin, the thread, the knife, the blood—all of it. When the doctor told her Mack was getting her things, she knew he'd go back to that damned mill.

When they reached the mill, she leaped from the car before the driver could finish thanking her. It was raining harder now—a warning perhaps that she should stay away.

Wanda slipped as she ran toward the building and tumbled. Soaking wet in a puddle, she thought about giving up. But she could not.

Mack might be in there. Mack might be… the thought trailed off and as she looked up, the mural now looked different. The woman's face had collapsed from the pressure of the rope and her eyes had gone black. Trickles of blood appeared to flow from the corners of the victim's eye socket.

Undaunted, Wanda ran into the freight elevator and slammed the gate. Inside, she heard voices.

"We never left," a voice said from nowhere.

"Who's here?" called out Wanda.

"Our blood is woven into the thread," another voice whispered behind Wanda, causing her to snap around and see…nothing.

"He's with us now."

The words burned into Wanda. It could only mean one thing…

Mack, they have Mack. But who were they?

When she reached the sixth floor, she pulled open the gate and ran out into a shimmering, brightly lit space. All of their merchandise had been replaced by giant looms—and the ancient mill machines wove back and forth, back and forth. The motion stunned her, leaving her catatonic until a hand touched her shoulder: a hand so cold that her muscles froze. Wanda pivoted on one foot and turned.

The thing before her looked like Mack but was more of a husk than the man she knew. His eyes were sunken and dark as ink. The mechanical looms shed their threads in long strands and the lines jumped off the machinery and hit Mack on his back. Dozens of threads penetrated him and moved beneath his skin like worms turning the earth.

The sutures broke through his skin and dove back in, weaving stitches along his body, creating a burlap texture. Mack's eyes were woven shut.

Wanda was about to swoon when the golem that was once her husband spoke. "It's okay, Wanda. They're just so lonely here. All we need from you is just one more kiss."

Lightning crashed outside the mill. The eight-foot windows, illuminated by nature, revealed hundreds of children standing behind Mack, each one with eyes of deep obsidian. Their mouths dripped with threads of blood. They were a legion whose trade had damned them to an eternity of toiling in this limestone hell.

Turning again on her heel, Wanda ran with haste toward the elevator.

Mack extended his arms toward her. The threads beneath his skin broke free and shot toward her.

But Wanda's feet moved so quickly that they hardly touched the ground.

Ropes shot all around her. Slicing through the air.

When Wanda came within a few feet of the elevator, she leaped the rest of the way.

But there had been no elevator in the shaft. She had jumped into an empty abyss. She was plummeting.

Wanda could see the base of the elevator shaft racing toward her and could smell oil, wax, and blood. In the pit was a huge piston and four coils that caught a free-falling elevator.

But Wanda was not made of forged steel.

When she hit the piston at terminal velocity, it impaled her.

Despite her trauma, Wanda lived for a few more moments. Long enough to feel the threads wrapping around her body, lifting her from the bottom of the shaft, taking her back to the workrooms where they had lived, worked, and died.

The threads bound inside of her, combining with her. One stitch at a time, they wove together a new Wanda, a doll of cotton and hemp. One that would never die.

Wanda was part of the Temperance Mill now. She was part of the machinery, like so many before her.

The following morning, the little boy came back hoping to get a few more games, but the couple was nowhere to be found.

When he looked up at the mural, he noticed something. The woman was no longer bound, and across her face had spread a smile.

– RICARDO D. REBELO has published several horror shorts for magazines and anthologies such as *Halloweenthology* by Wicked Shadow Press, *Monster Mag, The Chamber*, and *Scars*. He also co-wrote the films *Beyond the Dunwich Horror, Frankenstein in a Women's Prison*, and *Lizbeth: A Victorian Nightmare*. Ricardo has also directed the award-winning PBS Documentaries *Island of My Dreams, Dark New England*, and *Lizbeth: A Victorian Nightmare*.

The Devolution of Doyle

Aron Beauregard

Ronan Nunley gazed out the foggy window, his face as rigid as the rolling hills of darkness illuminated by the moonlight.

"We have no choice, my dear."

His wife rocked her chair by the fire. She stared into the flames like she was facing doomsday. "He may still blossom," she said, her words tinged by the same Irish accent he possessed. "He's able to find his way around the village without help; he's able to do some things—"

"Orla," he interrupted, "the boy hasn't spoken a word in five years." He turned to her. "He speaks in grunts—like an animal. His head is the size of a cheese wheel. If we sign him over now, we can turn a profit and have another try at one that's not broken. We had the boy so he could one day look after us, but if we stay on with him, we'll be looking after him until God calls upon us."

Her eyes glossed, face lit by the fire. "And what would God say of your proposition?"

Ronan didn't flinch. "He'd want a better life for Doyle. Overseas, he'll at least have a chance. He'll have a place of housing and a purpose."

Orla pushed her fingernails into the arm of the chair. Ronan could see she was struggling with the idea.

"And what would we tell the village?" she asked.

"Let me worry about that." He gazed back out into the darkness. "That man will be at the docks tomorrow. I shall take Doyle before daylight."

Orla bit her lip and nodded. "Understood."

Doyle held his ear against the hollow knot in the attic floor, listening intently. As his parents concluded their conversation, a lone teardrop beaded in the corner of his eye.

SEVEN YEARS LATER

The heat inside Weaver Mill was unbearable. Every day, for twelve hours, Doyle felt like he was roasting inside a giant oven. Black droplets slid down his cheeks as sweat coasted over his filthy pores. The cotton dust caused a roaring cough to escape him.

As he lifted the dustpan and brush, he blinked several times over, doing his best to moisten his enflamed eyes. The contaminated air not only attacked his lungs but his entire body. Doyle's oversized head hung forward as he stared at the bane of his existence.

Over the last seven years, the spinning mule machine had given so much to people—cotton, clothing, warmth. And while it had given to others, in the same stroke, it had taken from Doyle. Its earsplitting hiss had destroyed his hearing. The positioning of the device's architecture had warped his spine. The hazardous dust hampered his breathing and sight.

Still, as much as it had taken from Doyle, it had taken even more from others. He looked over at Savina Wyatt.

The eight-year-old girl worked the bay beside him and was one of the only workers who bothered to interact with Doyle. Savina didn't judge him for the few words in his vocabulary. And while Doyle's oversized head and hunchback made him look strange, that didn't bother the girl.

She noticed his gaze, lifted her left hand, and waved. Doyle recalled when she used to perform the gesture with the other limb before the accident.

Savina was a mule scavenger—just like Doyle. When the lengthy row of spindles attached to the spinning mule danced forward, they crawled under the lines of cotton and scrounged up scraps. Because of how low they needed to drop, the job, laborious but crucial, was carried out exclusively by children. With the boiling temperature required to run the mill, should an excess amount of the fiber fragments be allowed to accumulate, the entire building could catch ablaze.

Doyle stared at Savina's nub. The day her forearm had become entangled in the spinning mule was one he'd rather not remember. When the limb was torn from her elbow socket, Doyle had sprung into action. At the time, Savina was new—they hadn't even spoken a word to each other. When the machine stopped, he'd removed the spindle and used a row of string to tie off the end of her limb. He'd seen enough injuries inside Weaver Mill to understand a tourniquet's purpose.

After the incident, he understood it more intimately.

There was no way to be sure if Savina had befriended him because he'd saved her. Doyle liked to think that wasn't the case and imagined that she enjoyed his company since no one else— including his own parents—ever had.

"Hey, wake up!" a voice yelled.

Doyle turned to see the bulbous nose and grimace of the overseer, Horace Brooks.

Horace banged his baton on the machine's frame and pointed out the window toward the water wheel affixed to the mill. "When you're here, you're like the wheel! Never stop moving!"

The fear Doyle had for the overseer sent him crawling under the spinning mule. But for Doyle to collect the scraps, the machine needed to be moving away from him, not toward him. Doyle pulled himself back out, maneuvering his oversized head just fast enough to avoid being crushed.

Horace scoffed and shook his head before disappearing through a doorway.

As the machine shifted directions, Doyle carefully resumed his scavenging. Picking up the scraps, he thought back to the overseer's reaction when he'd stopped Savina's bleeding.

He'd brought Doyle into his office and held up the bloody spindle. Horace wasn't impressed with his heroics; instead, he'd belittled him for being stupid enough to remove the spindle and get blood all over the cotton.

"You could've used your belt!" he'd screamed. "I told you, never stop the machines without my say so!"

He expected Horace to be upset—he was always upset about something. But he hadn't expected to see Milton and Effie Weaver—the owners of Weaver Mill—appear in the office moments into the berating. They somehow seemed angrier than Horace. Effie ground her teeth beside her husband as he set a rusted nail and hammer on the overseer's desk.

"You're supposed to stop my mill from burning down, not stop production," Milton had said. He'd turned to Horace. "Hold that boulder of a head on the desk!"

While Horace held him down, Doyle had yipped out one of the few words he knew. "Sorry! Sorry! Sorry!"

Milton paid him no mind, placing the tip of the eroded nail against the cartilage of Doyle's ear. "Since this mongoloid doesn't like to listen, let's make sure he remembers."

Effie watched the fear on Doyle's face and bit her bottom lip. She wasn't wincing; she was excited.

"Yes, sir," Horace said.

The hammer slammed against the steel causing blood to erupt in all directions. Doyle squealed like a pig caught in a pork grinder. The three of them watched on, scolding him while he stood with his ear nailed to the desk.

Doyle lifted himself off the floor and dropped the scraps of cotton into the trash. He shuddered as Milton Weaver's final words from that day echoed in his head. *And if you muck it up again, it'll be the other ear next!*

He reached for the V-shaped split at the top of his ear, feeling the ruthless void they'd left in him.

Ding! Dong! Ding! Dong!

The sound of the lunch bell rang out. Living on the grounds offered few perks. Many days, Doyle wasn't provided a lunch, and, even on the days when he was, often there wasn't enough time to eat it.

Doyle looked to Savina, who dug into her satchel with her hand while signaling him over with her nub. As he approached her, she held out a wedge of bread, forcing him to grin. There was little for Doyle to be happy about in life, but eating somehow made things seem less horrible.

But, as quickly as his smile arose, it melted away. Horace appeared and snatched the bread out of Savina's hand, then grabbed Doyle by his torn ear. He dragged Doyle back to the site of his scarring. When the office door closed, Horace pushed the boy onto the ground.

"You and that ridiculous head of yours almost caused another accident!" he yelled. "All you've done today is stand around! You're more trouble than you're worth!" He held up the wad of bread and glared at Doyle. "You don't deserve this." Horace pointed into the small door at the back of his office. "Get inside!"

Inside the lavatory sat a wooden box with a hole inside that contained a bucket. Several days' worth of urine and feces were piled high inside.

Doyle watched in disgust as Horace dropped his only opportunity for nourishment that day into the hole. He then stepped back from the latrine and pointed at it.

"If you work like shit," he growled, "you'll eat like shit."

Doyle's heart started to race.

"Eat it!" Horace bellowed, his oversized nose twitching.

Doyle stepped forward, his nostrils flaring from the pungent smell of the overseer's excrement. Arm trembling, he reached into the hole. As the dark piss and muddy feces touched his fingers, he retched. Just the idea of putting anything from the foul pit into his mouth was torturous.

When his fingers finally connected with the mushy bread, Doyle pinched the slice and lifted. The smell of amplified ammonia wafted up his nasal cavity.

"Eat it, you dummy, or else!" Horace screamed.

Doyle gagged as he opened his mouth. His dry tongue quivered as it felt the weight of the soggy morsel. A bitter liquid bled out from the spongy bread, ravaging his tastebuds. The clumps of shit smeared against the dough felt grainy against his teeth. A sour taste dominated his palate, as if he'd licked a laborer's armpit after a full day's work.

"Swallow it, you freak."

Doyle's eyes watered as the vile portion slid down his gullet. And while the dreadful bread had disappeared, he knew the sickening flavor and memory of the abuse would linger indefinitely.

The door to Horace's office opened. Effie stood with several papers in hand. "Horace, here's the upcoming order—" She stopped when she saw Doyle. "Why, I know that face. I couldn't forget it if I tried."

Horace led Doyle out of the bathroom and back into the office. A drizzle of urine and excrement still oozed off his chin.

"He's mucking about out there again," Horace said. "Thinks he can just stand around all day—"

"Oh, don't be so hard on him," Effie interrupted. "He's a retard."

Horace sneered at the boy.

"I'll...give him a talking to," Effie said, dropping the papers on Horace's desk.

Horace nodded.

"Follow me," Effie said.

Doyle trailed behind Effie out of the office and down to the far end of the mill. The broom closet was in an area mostly used for storage. When he finally confirmed where they were going, it felt like someone had poked his belly with a knife and twisted.

He was all too familiar with the closet.

When they stepped inside, Effie closed and locked the door behind them.

Doyle took his seat on the chair that seemed oddly out of place stationed in the center of the storage room.

"Had a tough day, big head?" Effie asked.

She slipped off her panties and lifted her dress. Hocking up some phlegm, she greased her fingers and rubbed her pussy.

Usually, when Effie brought him into the closet it began like a psychotherapy session. She typically started by complaining of Milton's impotence and lack of interest in her. How even when they got into bed together, he couldn't help but constantly look out their window and down the hill—obsessing about what was going on inside the mill. She claimed the money the mill generated was wonderful—more than they could ever hope to spend—but secretly, she wished he'd eliminate the night shift. And how maybe if her husband did that, he'd finally take some kind of interest in her physically.

But there was nothing like that today. She'd cut right to depravity.

"Nothing to say?" Effie took a step toward him.

Doyle's limbs felt heavy. Sickness stirred as the vile woman descended upon him.

Effie smirked. "That's exactly why I like you. You've never got a thing to say."

Doyle stared blankly at the spinning mule as it reactivated. The hours of monotonous machine work did nothing to distract him from the horrors that loomed. They were becoming more than his mind could handle.

Savina looked at him, using a series of hand gestures to ask if he was okay. His subtle nod was a lie, but he'd rather not worry her. There was no sense in both of them feeling more terrible than they already did.

As he watched the scraps of cotton accumulate, he slid under the lines of yarn.

This is your life, he thought.

There's no way out.

His thoughts were cut short by the unforgiving stride of the machine. Doyle had been so lost in his head, that he hadn't realized he was directly in the path of the spinning mule's frame. It was just like earlier when Horace had scolded him, except this time, Doyle was too defeated to dodge.

The bar pressed his head against the steel backing as Doyle cried out. His howls of suffering paired with the sound of his oversized head cracking. As the blood rained over his face and filled his mouth, Doyle lost consciousness.

Horace used a cart to wheel Doyle's body past the mill. His head looked like a cracked egg. While he still had a faint pulse, the gaping wound in his skull wouldn't allot him much longer.

He's almost lost, Horace thought.

Milton appeared on the other side of the stone bridge. "Quickly, come this way. We don't have much time."

Horace furrowed his brow. It wasn't often that Milton requested he leave the mill. Whatever was in the works must've been important to put Effie solely in charge of things. This was more than the standard burial.

As the sunlight dried up, Horace followed Milton into the woods, until they reached the old carriage house. Milton used it as a storage facility for landscaping equipment, but it was the land close to the dark structure that was of most value.

Horace had helped dig many graves for the countless children the Weavers had purchased. Some accidents were irreversible. When they had to cut ties with a slave, the old carriage house was where it happened.

But Horace was surprised when he noticed that the window of

the house was illuminated. Usually, the disposing of the children was a solo activity for him.

"Bring the boy inside," Milton said.

Horace wasn't sure if he'd heard him right. "Inside?"

"Yes, quickly!" Milton replied. As he opened the door, he declared, "We've got a live one."

As Horace wheeled Doyle's limp body through the large doors, he was shocked by what he saw. The body of a dead little girl hung naked and upside down. He recognized her face; it wasn't long ago he was hurling tyrannical requests at her on the mill floor. But she looked much different than she had while she was still breathing.

The girl's unfortunate demise occurred after her hair had gotten ensnared in a machine—tearing the scalp from her skull. But the ghastly baldness wasn't what made Horace's stomach turn. The skin on each side of her ribcage had been cut open, and inserted into the torso were four additional arms. The duplication of limbs looked demonic—the skin tones clearly from other children who had been buried on the grounds.

Beside the girl stood a man with long, white hair, black glasses, and an overgrown beard. He glanced up from a table riddled with surgical tools, beakers, liquids, and needles, grinning madly.

Milton looked at Horace. "This is Dr. Emil Vogel. I have put him here in an effort to try and salvage some of my investments."

"Wh—what is this?" Horace asked, taken aback by the ghoulish child.

"The future," Dr. Vogel interrupted.

Horace couldn't quite place his foreign accent.

Dr. Vogel looked down at Doyle with adoration, caressing his mashed skull with his fingers. Then he turned back to his monstrosity. "Imagine a child that can do the job of three. Or better yet, a child that even the grisliest accident cannot claim."

"Focus on the boy, Doctor," Milton said. "I'll fill him in."

Dr. Vogel grinned. "As you wish."

Horace turned to Milton, shaken by the thought of such reanimations. "But where would they even go? They—they couldn't possibly work with the rest of the laborers. There would be outrage."

"You think I haven't thought about that already?" Milton sneered.

They watched Dr. Vogel position Doyle on another table. He inserted a needle into the gore hole in the boy's head and put his fingers over the subject's neck.

"We still have a chance," Dr. Vogel whispered.

Milton turned back to Horace. "The basement inside the mill has plenty of space. If we can actually bring one of them back, we'll keep them locked down there. Think of the profits! With Dr. Vogel's help, paying for one of these children off the boat could mean getting a worker for life!"

Horace watched Milton's eyes twinkle. He nodded, trying not to let the fear ravage his body. While Horace had participated in his share of awful deeds, even for him Milton's proposal went too far. The abominations would serve as new nightmares. He stared at the pieces of the dead repackaged for profit but bit his tongue. It wasn't as if there was anything he could say that was going to make Milton Weaver reconsider.

Despite hanging on, Doyle wasn't showing any signs of life. But that didn't mean he wasn't aware. Even though the machines had damaged his hearing, in the quiet of the carriage house, Doyle heard everything the men had discussed before Milton and Horace left him in the perverted care of Dr. Vogel.

The doctor had run various tubes into his veins, loading him up with fluid of an unknown origin. His vascular system felt like it had been pumped full of lava. But the weakness Doyle felt when he lay on death's doorstep after his skull had been squashed was gone.

The crater in his head had somehow mended. The indentation felt like it was no longer glistening with gore. Doyle sensed the soft touch of bandages, but even beyond the dressings, the flesh had somehow closed. It seemed there was some validity to the doctor's ravings. Even in Doyle's dimmer perspective, he knew such a trajectory was miraculous.

"No! No! No!" Dr. Vogel screamed. "Don't stop breathing!"

The doctor was right. Doyle was yet to notice, but he hadn't taken a breath since he'd regained consciousness. While he felt a strange sensation of reinvigoration stirring inside, his body remained unable to move.

"Damn you!" Dr. Vogel slammed his fist onto Doyle's sternum. "You worthless pile of skin!"

From the corner of his blurry eye, Doyle watched the doctor pick up the bone saw. The frustration of failure curled his lips. He hadn't even met the man and already he'd become his whipping boy. How he yearned for a new role. The fiery fluid surging in his system made him feel different—as if he was suddenly somehow capable of halting the atrocities the world continuously lobbed at him.

"Maybe I can still make use of his limbs," Dr. Vogel grumbled, adjusting his glasses.

As Doyle watched the deranged doctor align the bone saw with his shoulder, the thought entered his mind: *You're not dead.*

When the teeth of the steel nestled against his shirt, his mind screamed louder.

Don't just lie there!

The intensity in his veins exploded into action. Doyle's arm shot upward, knocking the old doctor on his backside. The saw screeched across the stone floor to the other side of the room as Doyle hopped off the table and turned his gaze upon the six-armed girl. The miscreation was strung up like a cow in a slaughterhouse.

Doyle's mind raged as he staggered toward the doctor. *He's just like the rest of them.*

Dr. Vogel bore a grin of astonishment—more amazed than fazed by his subject's outburst. "It's a miracle!"

But when Doyle bent over and lifted him by his coat, his sentiment shifted. "Wait, you fool! You mustn't overexert yourself! You've just—"

Doyle slammed his hand between Dr. Vogel's jaws, clamping down on his slimy tongue. As his dirty fingernails dug into the back of the muscle, he felt it wiggle.

He thinks you're a dummy too.

When the clump of throbbing pink ripped away from his mouth, the ruby cascade commenced. Dr. Vogel tried to scream but choked on his blood.

Doyle felt the power he'd lacked fueling him as he collected the tubing still attached to his veins. Carefully, he wrapped it around Dr. Vogel's throat, heightening the tension until more crimson erupted from his orifice. As air hissed from the doctor, he watched his face turn blue. And, for the first time since Doyle had awoken, he felt alive again.

Horace attempted to rest in his chambers but couldn't. He tossed and turned in his bed. The abomination in the carriage house haunted his dreams. He pictured the arms starting to move. He saw himself inside the gloomy basement of Weaver Mill trying to manage a floor overrun with monstrosities. He wondered how God would view such perversions, or worse, the men responsible for incubating them.

The question of ethics wasn't one that often crossed Horace's mind, but tonight he began to question everything. From the beatings he'd given the peasants, to the verbal abuse and humiliation. He gazed out the window up the hill where moonlight illuminated Milton and Effie Weaver's mansion.

He wasn't sure how he'd grown so callous and unforgiving with the workers. Certainly, he enjoyed the perks of his position—extra food, his private quarters, the admiration of the ladies. But had he traded that for his humanity? Was he afraid that if he didn't separate himself from the common folk he might one day be lumped in with them? Did displaying such vitriol make him feel closer to the Weavers? Was he a sad, selfish man?

The bread covered in his feces flashed in his mind.

He felt sick.

Like most big changes, his devolution hadn't happen overnight, it had been continuous. Gradual, until the man Horace had become was unrecognizable.

He shook his head, looking away from the mansion. The night shift had finished just a short time ago. The grounds were stuck in those strange hours of darkness before the morning shift, when the demanding building that controlled him was eerily quiet. It was in those hours that Horace heard nothing so much as the repetitive sound of the water wheel.

His brow furrowed.

The sound of the wheel was absent.

Horace's eyes darted to the patch of forest near the outskirts of the property. In the darkness, he saw an outline.

The oversized, misshapen head.

The array of off-white bandages.

The small frame suffering from severe hunchback.

He scrambled for his clothing. Suddenly, the questions of ethics and the comparisons to his own moral compass fled him. Fear was now the only factor on his mind. If the water wheel was out of commission, then Weaver Mill was at a standstill. If he could somehow resolve the issue himself, such an amendment would be lucrative. Maybe one of the other men or children had noticed the issue already. He wouldn't be wise to let them take credit.

As Horace slipped on his shoes, he glanced back out the window. The outline in the darkness was no more.

Doyle waited by the control panel patiently, holding the oversized wrench in his hand. Such a weight would've been a struggle before Dr. Vogel had set his veins ablaze. The tubing in his body burned almost as violently as the rage in his chest.

They all thought he was a retard. But inside his head was a dissection table. A treasure trove of information, and a deep knowledge of his environment and the people within it. It was the same as it'd always been. Whether he was a young boy in Ireland memorizing the land in their village or, more recently, understanding the intricacies of the hordes of workers at Weaver Mill, he absorbed his surroundings. But he'd never considered that being unable to verbalize such things could be an advantage.

He brandished his bloodstained teeth in delight.

The wheel never stops, he thought.

As the door to the control room creaked open, Doyle raised the wrench. When the overseer stepped inside, Doyle brought the heavy steel down onto Horace's kneecap, collapsing it in on itself.

The overseer wailed.

Doyle raised the wrench above his head, realizing the man who'd been his monster wasn't anything to be afraid of. He brought the wrench down on his cranium and watched his body go limp.

Milton slowly approached the old carriage house. The glowing light from the small windows made his heart race. As his wrinkled fingers wrapped around the door handle, he held his breath. Dr. Vogel's lab was revealed—Milton's dream had come true, but not in the way he'd imagined.

Dr. Vogel was slumped on the floor, his body broken into several pieces. Doyle stood over the doctor, his face oozing through his bandages like an oversized, crushed cranberry, pulling Dr. Vogel's hip out of his socket.

As Milton's jaw dropped, his dread-filled eyes fell upon the little girl with six arms. She mounted the doctor's mutilated torso, each of her hands holding a separate surgical instrument. They moved at an impossible speed, powered by the hatred in her eyes. The pointed tools continued to puncture the doctor's lifeless body, each stab sending a surge of blood up from the cavernous holes.

Red painted each of the children's faces as they turned their attention to Milton.

"No, I—I just wanted to bring you back!" Milton yelled. "I wanted to make you live forever!"

Before Milton could escape, the six-armed girl's freakish pace caught up to him. She latched onto his back like a spider would its prey and sank the points of steel into his flesh. The rhythmic slaughter pushed through Milton's flesh into his organs. As his lungs filled up with blood, Doyle squatted in front of him. The red oozing from his mouth was the last thing Milton saw before the boy's cold thumbs pushed deep into his eye sockets.

"Nooooo!" Milton screamed.

When he awoke in bed, his body was covered in sweat. Milton stood and made his way to the bathroom. He grabbed hold of a cloth and used it to wipe off his face.

"Is everything all right, darling?" Effie asked.

"I'm fine," he replied. "Just a rotten dream is all."

Effie grinned fiendishly. "I had a dream too, but it was a naughty one." She bit her lip. "Why don't you come back to bed, and I'll tell you more—"

"What on earth?!" Milton interrupted.

Effie exhaled in annoyance.

Milton dropped the rag onto the floor and gazed out the window. Through each pane on the backside of his mill, he saw several lit oil lamps hanging. The lights ran throughout all the building's frames.

"What is it?" Effie asked.

Milton checked the clock again, his blood at a boil. "The late shift has ended, but some idiot left the lamps on! It's a damned fire hazard! We've got to get in there right away before everything we've built goes up in flames!"

"Oh, dear, that sounds like something you can handle yourself."

Milton turned to his wife and brandished his discolored teeth. Spittle exploded as he spoke through his clenched jaw. "Get out of bed *now*, before I wring your neck!"

When they entered the mill, the Weavers scrambled up the stairs to the floor where they'd seen the lights glowing.

"What the hell is wrong with the water wheel?" Milton yelled. "I pay that bastard Horace to keep an eye on such matters, and of all nights, he's not in his quarters! When I find him, he's going to regret this!"

Effie scrambled up the stairs behind him. "That fool! This building might've burned down already had you not awoken!"

They started at the far side of the factory floor passing the bloodstains that Doyle's earlier accident left on the floorboards. They extinguished each lamp, one by one, until a faint glow at the end of the floor was all that remained.

"That's the storage area," Effie said. "Why would there be a lamp lit in there?"

"Strange," Milton mumbled.

As they moved closer, they noticed there was more than one light source inside. A closet door had been left open. On the shelves rested dozens of lit lamps. In addition to the army of flames, a lone chair sat in the center of the space with a lamp glowing on the seating.

Effie's eyes glossed over as she put her hand over her mouth.

"This is no accident!" Milton yelled. "This is sabotage!"

He raced into the closet and terminated each flame as quickly as possible.

The thud of the heavy wrench shattering Effie's knee resounded. As she hit the floor screaming, Milton whipped around. But by the time he saw Doyle's ghoulish face, the door had already slammed shut.

The blood-soaked bandages hung off Doyle's face like strips of peeling flesh. He removed another kerosene lamp from the area behind the crates where he'd been hiding. While he lit the lamp, he listened to his abuser's pleas but didn't entertain them.

Milton pounded on the door, screaming and cursing.

Doyle grinned.

Inside his misshapen head, he replayed the words Milton had said to him before nailing his ear to the desk: *You're supposed to stop my mill from burning down, not stop production.*

As Doyle raised the lamp above his head, he knew production would be stopping indefinitely. When the glass shattered against Effie's face and the flames engulfed her flesh, he knew there was no stopping the mill from burning to the ground.

Effie shrieked. The fire quickly expanded as her hair blazed and her skin bubbled. But before it spread too far, Doyle knew there was one more thing he had to do.

From a distance, hidden by the cover of bushes and trees, Doyle looked down the hill. As the sun rose over the horizon, the flames danced on the roof of Weaver Mill. Workers filed out of their housing and gazed upon the nightmarish inferno. Doyle read the emotions in their faces.

Some were aghast.

Some were confused.

Some were relieved.

Despite the building providing consistent work and prompt payment that few other professions could, Doyle knew he was doing them a favor.

As the diabolical sound of the water wheel churning reached his ears, a smile crossed Doyle's crumpled face. The gasps of suffering and dread continued as the massive circle completed another cycle.

Rising from the water, tied in innumerable ropes of cotton, was Horace. His body was malformed in a manner that saw each of his limbs wrapped around the sides of the wheel and hogtied around his back.

With each agonizing rotation, Horace was submerged for a short period of time. After the water rushed into his lungs, his thighs, chest, shoulders, and face scraped against the harsh stone. The base of the wheel had grated much flesh off his skeleton, leaving several areas of red, exposed bone. And while Horace rose with each rotation, he continued to bleed and cough. Once he was elevated from the water, his ruined body ascended to the top of the factory. The intense flames were not enough to break the soaked cotton ropes but scorched his wounds. The torture continued until it looked like a red blob of butchered meat was attached to the wheel.

As Horace's coughs and bellows played on, Doyle knew he'd done right. None of the dismayed laborers looking on stopped it but allowed the former overseer's anguish to supersede itself with each additional revolution.

Doyle thought back to what Horace used to say to him. When you're here, you're like the wheel! Never stop moving!

Within the crowd, Doyle's gaze keyed in on Savina. Wide-eyed, she watched in horror. He looked at her nub, and with the factory in flames, he knew that dismemberment would be her last.

A bittersweet feeling bubbled inside Doyle. To his only friend in the world, he was dead, and in his mind, it was better she believed that. He still hadn't taken a breath since he'd awoken and wasn't sure how long Dr. Vogel's unethical experiment would propel him. There was no need for her to mourn him twice.

An emptiness grew inside him now that he'd done what he needed to. A feeling of sickness hibernating. He longed for a purpose.

But when Doyle's eyes drifted from his friend and back to the water, a flash of imagery from years ago sparked his brain.

The road that brought him to Weaver Mill.

The port he'd arrived at.

The dock he'd arrived on.

The vessel he'd traveled aboard.

The man who'd owned him.

Another barrage of memories invaded his warped head.

The port in Ireland.

The roads in the village.

The house he grew up in.

The parents who'd forgotten him.

The words he'd heard with his ear pressed against the floor of the attic resounded in his head. The woman who'd birthed him. The woman who was supposed to protect him.

"He may still blossom. He's able to find his way around the village without help; he's able to do some things—"

Doyle balled his fist and squeezed until the bones in his hand cracked.

Even though Doyle was dead, that much hadn't changed. He might not have been able to verbalize it, but he knew his way around. And while it might not have been the metamorphosis his mother had envisioned, he'd blossomed.

What kind of a son would he be not to show her?

– ARON BEAUREGARD was born and raised in Central Falls, Rhode Island. He's been writing horror since the 6th grade and has now released over twenty-five books. An avid supporter of horror art and illustration, Aron has made it his standard to hire cover and interior illustrators for every book that he puts out himself under his brand AB Horror. His style of writing is dark and without boundaries, and has been translated into multiple languages. He's won the Splatterpunk Award twice after garnering four total nominations. He has achieved #1 Bestseller status in horror on both Amazon and Barnes & Noble. To get the latest updates about upcoming releases, signed books and merchandise, film news, and so much more, visit his website: ABHorror.com. To subscribe to his free newsletter, join the AB Horror Maggot Mailing List at: https://aronbeauregard.substack.com/

www.ingramcontent.com/pod-product-compliance
Lightning Source LLC
Chambersburg PA
CBHW030035030726
47500CB00001B/110